COMING INTO CHRISTMAS

A NOVEL

JEANNE C. ANDEREGG

ISBN 0-7414-4085-7

Cover photograph: "Almost Winter" by Doyle Anderegg.

Published by:

INFI∞ITY
PUBLISHING.COM

*1094 New DeHaven Street, Suite 100
West Conshohocken, PA 19428-2713
Info@buybooksontheweb.com
www.buybooksontheweb.com
Toll-free (877) BUY BOOK
Local Phone (610) 941-9999
Fax (610) 941-9959*

Printed in the United States of America

Printed on Recycled Paper

Published October 2007

A gentle note of caution: This is a work of fiction. The little community of Campbell's Point exists only in the author's imagination. However, the hills, streams, and glorious wild forest places of western Pennsylvania are very real and very special.

Sara Harvey Cameron, her friends, her enemies and her adventures are also imaginary though they seemed to come to life as the story unfolded.

ACKNOWLEDGMENTS

My thanks go to both my harshest critics and my kindest friends. Each comment was taken to heart.

Heartfelt thanks also to my several diligent readers who kept me believing in my characters, their lives and their adventures.

Other books in the Sara Harvey series

Summer of the Doves

Idaho Interlude

In the shadowy world of espionage,

names are everything and names are nothing

COMING INTO CHRISTMAS

CHAPTER ONE

Another round of sleet hurtled across the ridge, pelting my face and hands with shards of ice as painful as shattered glass. Soon, I would have to admit that my promised task couldn't be finished. One long row of carrots remained to be lifted and the growing darkness was coming to put an end to my efforts.

I turned toward the main building of the convent and whispered a plea for a last bit of strength and stamina. What came to me instead was real help, my beloved husband, Cade. I could tell that he was angry as he came down the row to meet me.

He scowled from the twists of muffler wrapped around his neck. "Sara, I had no idea you'd gone back out this afternoon. I thought you were curled up in front of the fire, napping. Why do I always seem to find you tangled with the forces of nature in some gigantic battle of wills? What can I do to help you finish?"

At least he'd brought some common sense back into my world, and I was thankful once again for his steadying influence in my life. I shrugged my shoulders in defeat.

"We can't finish. In fact, what we should do is just hill up the last row with soil and mark it with sturdy stakes. Then, we'll pray that some dear little novice from the Middle West will come out here into the garden next spring and have something to do, while she weeps with homesickness for her family and the life she left behind."

1

We were loading the last carrots, when I realized how close I was to hypothermia. "I need to get inside, Cade. I'm freezing cold and have no reserves left."

He didn't wait to discuss it. He walked with me down the hill to the back door of the kitchen and then returned for the wheelbarrow of carrots. There was only one entrance he was allowed to use, so I made some scalding hot tea and went there to wait for him. My hands were beginning to swell in the warmth of the room as he slipped in the door and accepted his mug in silence.

We'd come to Willow Run seeking respite from the constant roar and thundering of the huge planes from Mountain Home air base in south Idaho. They flew twenty-four hours a day now since September 11th. Cade's plumbing skills had come in handy again, as he traded our board and room for some needed repair work in the convent bathrooms. It was already late October and we planned to head east to Pennsylvania and the tiny town of Campbell's Point soon, before the weather turned too bad to travel.

I asked him, "Are you about done with the work that you promised Mother Alice Marie?"

"I finished this morning. I've been doing paper work this afternoon getting ready for our next move."

I took his hands in mine. "Could we leave tomorrow morning? This weather has really spooked me. I'm worried about the traveling we have ahead."

He took a little longer to answer than I expected, as though he were measuring his words with care. "I had a phone call from Johnson early this morning. He asked if we would be willing to come back for a while to help out with the dogs so he can go to get Anna. Tim wants to be home by Thanksgiving and it should be possible to work it out."

"Yes, of course. I've had my respite and I'm ready to go back into the world again. I'll go start packing."

"You won't need to. I've already done it. Let's say some very short good-byes and head out within the hour. We need to get to the ranch by tonight."

I had a feeling that there was more to this quick trip back to Mountain Home than he was telling me. I was filled with increasing dread, the closer we got to the ranch. At least it was a little warmer in the valley and I was finally warm after my dangerous day of outdoor work.

The dog-raising business was going well and I could see there'd been several new litters of pups born since we left. I was Johnson's silent financial partner as well as his sometime helper, but thanks to Tim Campbell's coming from Pennsylvania, I was able to leave with a clear conscience. Tim was out doing the last of the chores. He looked up and waved as we went by. Johnson met Cade at the back door and they went off to the office together.

I stopped in the kitchen to see about supper. The men would be glad to have me back doing that chore, as well as the others in the pens. The soup was ready to dish up when everyone, including my dear German shepherd, Violet, gathered in the kitchen. Tim's smile was as sunny and sweet as ever. His brilliant "Campbell red" hair was a little shaggy but he looked contented and happy.

"Ma'am, it's great to see you. We sure missed you and the Commander. It's not as much fun with just two guys. I can't wait to get Tricia out here and show her what the West is like. People are really different, more independent and a little less trusting. You get used to it."

Tim's chatter continued, as I stopped in my tracks. How could I have been so foolish as to believe that my new husband, Cade, was only a plumber and only guarding me for his brother's sake? Of course he would have been in it up to his ears all these years, just like his brother, Michael. What a perfect cover he had forged, and now I'd found out from the mouth of a babe.

I dished up supper and sat down. Cade's touch was gentle as he reached out to take my hand.

"Sweetheart, we'll deal with it later. Right now, let's be family and find out what's been going on here."

It was the "Ice Queen" who presided over the supper hour as I made appropriate comments to keep the conversation going. Inside, my heart was breaking, as I realized the full extent of what I had just learned. By the time I'd cleaned up from supper and joined Cade in the office to take care of our paperwork, I was frantic.

I whispered in misery, "Why didn't you tell me?"

Cade's answer was a complete surprise. "That day last June when Mike called me to come and help, I made him promise he'd tell you. I assumed he had."

I froze, then pulled away from him, as he reached for me.

"Does it make so much difference to you, Sara?"

Our chairs were pulled up close together at the desk. Suddenly I felt like a wounded animal caught in a trap. From far away, I heard tiny whimpering sounds, as if that little animal were struggling without hope of survival.

Finally, I realized it was my own voice. I rose from my chair, toppling it to the floor with a screeching crash. My whole body trembled in panic as I turned away from him. Just when I thought I'd begun a happy and safe life and believed that I was finished with the world of espionage; the chute of blind terror had opened to swallow me again.

We were facing the first real crisis in our new marriage and I would have to decide right now what I was willing to do or thought I could do. Cade and I always seemed to be too busy to share the most important things from our earlier lives. Now it was past time to do so and time was running out.

Another plane took off over the ranch. The windows chattered and the floor trembled with the force of the noise. He didn't reach out or speak, but waited. I felt the growing desert darkness pressing in at the windows, clawing and crawling to slip in and trap me with my fear.

"Cade," I whispered, "I'm terrified for your safety. Can't they find someone else for this job?" I turned away and stepped toward the yawning darkness of the window.

His fingers grasped my shoulder. I tried to twist away from him as he asked, "How did you know? Who told you where we were going?"

He turned me loose and I fell away, gasping with the pain. "It was my nightmare last night. In it I saw that you would be going away and would be in great danger. That's all. No one told me anything."

I wept as I closed my eyes and prayed for strength. Then, the whole horrible incident was over as quickly as it had begun. Cade took me in his arms and cradled my head to his chest.

"What am I going to do with you, Sweetheart? Your powers continue to amaze me. You could be the most devastating secret weapon in any man's Navy. Please forgive me."

I could feel my heart beat slowing as his did and we were close enough to share the special intimacy that had become so precious to me.

Then his body shifted to another message and he began to explain in businesslike terms what lay ahead. "Johnson and I leave tomorrow night. General Ryan has ordered us to fly to Lisbon to pick up Anna at the Embassy. At least she's on her way home. Johnson is to bring her back.

"I'll be gone longer, because of the job I must do. The general has convinced me that I'm the only one suitable to try it. Actually, he gave me a choice of two assignments; the other one was infinitely more dangerous.

"He would line me up in front of the firing squad if he knew I'd said even this much, so you've got to do the best acting job of your life, to protect us from his wrath."

I sighed as we sat down together to begin the paperwork. "In which languages should I pray for you, Cade?"

He whispered his answer. "Italian, Finnish and if God so chooses, Russian."

I knew he'd told me more than he should have. It would not be spoken of again. A wall went up around it, closing it off from my everyday life and yet, I knew it would haunt each living moment until he was safe in my arms again.

He was so like his brother Michael in the way he went about solving a problem; trying to be fair but not taking the human element into the equation. I thought about my beloved Michael, who had died in my arms such a short time ago in love time.

I wondered now if I'd made a terrible mistake, accepting his brother as my husband so soon. We had not been lovers, only two desperate, grieving souls in need of solace. There hadn't been time for proper grieving for Michael.

We returned to the work at hand. "Please forgive me for not getting these chores done before now, Sara. I guess I hoped we could pretend we wouldn't need to know such things. I must make sure that you understand our business and personal finances and can manage our affairs in my absence."

I think he was surprised and pleased with my understanding of the things he wanted to explain. My first husband, Henri Lambert, was a wealthy man, with business dealings in addition to his salaries and then retirement from his position as a college president. We kept our financial dealings separate from the first day of our marriage. He gave me a generous allowance for the household and my upkeep. As long as he approved of my work and appearance, I was allowed to keep the rest of the money.

Over the twenty-three years of our marriage, it was invested well. I had become independently wealthy. Then, as the inheritances began to accumulate with the death of my first husband, Lambert, and several close friends, I had acquired valuable property in several countries. I needed to inform Cade about my finances. I didn't hesitate to do so, as I had when talking with Michael.

Cade and I made a promise that we'd visit the properties in the spring. We finished the rough drafts of our wills and durable powers of attorney. I was relieved that I still had copies of all the papers prepared by the financial planner, Kostyan Skorski, before he left the mountain ranch.

Everything was in neat stacks on the desk as Cade brought the evening's work to a close.

"I called Sam Sawyer at the base for an appointment in the morning, even though it's Saturday. He can write these up, notarize, and get things ready for your lawyer. Let's take a break and get cleaned up while there's still some hot water. I know you'd rather be somewhere else, Sara, but General Ryan feels that for now, this is the safest. Besides, he plans to ask you to be his Russian translator."

I was glad someone else was giving me orders right now. I needed a schedule and job responsibilities to keep my mind off the situation. What had brought me to southern Idaho after Michael's death would keep me going now.

As we rose from our places, I whispered to him, "I need to love you now, Cade. I want to be so close I can feel your heart beat with mine. I need to fill up your heart with my love, to protect you until you return to me."

Our loving was filled with gentleness and desire, weeping and laughter, coming full circle to our private good-bye.

When we returned next morning from the appointment at the base, I put out dinner. It was wintertime hot soup and sandwich weather, and the kitchen smelled of simmering beef soup and fresh bread. Then, Tim and Johnson went out to finish up the last minute instructions for the dogs' training. Cade and I returned to the office to make lists of things to be done in the next few months.

First, I answered his concerns about the upcoming professional meetings in Helsinki in late January. "I've already sent all the material for the presentation to Caroline Myers, along with her plane ticket and registration money. She's the most logical person to do it since she worked most recently on the project with Dave Finch."

I had been surprised at my ability to write such an even-handed obituary tribute for my former mentor and professional collaborator, Dave Finch, after what he had done to me, including several attempts on my life.

"Caroline will give the tribute first. There's a time allotted for her to present the finished data of two decades of research. It should be a professional coup for her."

My sigh had a sense of finality. For the time being, my professional scientific career was on hold. What would happen later remained to be seen.

Cade continued to explain the liquidation of his business interests and what he'd chosen to retain. His cover as a plumbing contractor was important to maintain. Besides, he was very good at his work and enjoyed the salary.

Our time was short now and I began my good-bye time.

"Do you remember Michael's lockets? I've replaced the pictures in them. Would you carry mine with you while you're away? I'm already wearing yours." I opened my shirt to expose the silver locket with the doves on the front.

"I'll guard it with my life and bring it home to you."

We shared one last private kiss before we left the ranch to return to the base. The note for Anna Skorski, my dearest friend since college days in Paris, was tucked into Johnson's pocket. The chocolate chip cookies I'd made were in a box for the men to take on the plane.

In my nightmare, I'd seen the pale, frightened faces of the raw recruits, along with the hardened faces of men who'd done this many times in other places and other wars. Perhaps my gift would let them know that someone cared.

I was surprised to see General Ryan on the tarmac, as the men were loading into the plane. When he saluted them, I saw, with their returned salutes, their backs a little straighter, heads carried a little higher, and faces, for the moment, filled with pride and resolve.

As the plane taxied away, General Ryan stepped to my side. "Begin praying, Sara. We're going to need it this time."

It was deep dusk when Tim and I headed back to the ranch. Low clouds scudded across the moon and most of the creatures were already bedded down for the night.

I turned to Tim with a smile. "Well, my friend, what's on the docket first? Do you want some supper? Remember, you're in charge and I'm only a helper and the keeper of the kitchen. Since we're done outside for tonight, how about a game of Scrabble after we eat? It's already cold enough to light a fire in the living room. Let's play in there."

Tim was working on his GED and was about ready to take his exams. A bit of word play should be good for him. The evening was a pleasant combination of games, and visiting about our mutual friends in Campbell's Point.

Tim's hometown sweetheart, Tricia, was getting more and more impatient for him to come home and I'm sure he was anxious to get back too. He was making good money working for Johnson, but JW Campbell, the local contractor he worked for in Campbell's Point, needed him to finish up some jobs before winter came in earnest. Tim would put the Idaho money into his marriage savings account.

I dreaded the first night alone without Cade. By now the men were headed out over the Atlantic into their dangerous unknown and I must wait at home for their return.

After our evening, we tidied up the living room and put the fire to bed. I asked Tim, "How do you want to arrange the work schedule? I promised General Ryan I'd be there as soon as I could after my chores are done in the morning."

Tim smiled. "I know you're a lark. Let's start at six o'clock. If you do the morning cleanup I can do the rest. Would you like to keep Violet inside with you tonight?"

"Thanks. I'd like that a lot. How's her training coming? I was thinking about asking Jacques if he would like to have her but I want to keep her here until Cade gets back." I sighed. "There are a lot of things we don't know about yet. I guess we'll have to live one day at a time. It shouldn't be too long before we can head out for the East though. I know how much you want to get home."

Violet bounded down the hall when she figured out she'd be allowed to stay in with me. When I got to my bedroom, I found the Mason jar full of late autumn wildflowers on my dresser and Cade's favorite shirt draped across my pillow. I gathered it into my arms and buried my face in its softness.

The male presence of him clung to the fabric and was both a solace and a reminder of how much I loved him. I prayed for his safety and for the strength to be brave in my waiting. My sleep was restless but Violet knew something was different and climbed onto the bed to share my night.

CHAPTER TWO

Our work routine at the ranch settled into a simple pattern and most days I got to the base by nine o'clock. My specific job as a Russian translator was a no-brainer after all the years working with the language and with codes. I was looking for imbedded code, or unusual forms or phrases. These could suggest where the text originated because of the colloquialisms or idioms they used. I enjoyed the process as much as the finished product.

I spent my lunch hours visiting the airmen in sickbay. After the time I'd spent there helping my work partner Jacques Grayson recover from his jungle ordeal, I recognized many of the men who had come to help with prayers and songs and simple acts of kindness.

We were a close-knit family since 9/11 and security was very tight. Somehow, they trusted a woman to write letters for them, and to take care of small problems in their lives, like buying birthday presents for their kids.

Into the second week of waiting for the men to return, I decided one evening to start going through the box of Michael's possessions that he'd asked Cade to pack for me. Tim was studying in the kitchen where it was warmer, and I carried the large box to the kitchen table. I took the garden scrapbook out and began to go through the pages. There were articles cut from magazines as well as sketches he'd drawn of ideas he wanted to try. We were going to make a French kitchen garden in the back yard of his home in St. Louis as soon as we were married.

I was beginning to realize that it was too soon to be remembering, when I came to an envelope tucked into one of the divider pockets. It was lovely, cream-colored parchment and the handwriting was exquisite. It was addressed to Michael Cameron, postmarked in early June, a short time before his death. Since the return address was in Finland, I assumed it was from his artist friend, Wilhelmina

Porter. The letter had been opened. I slipped it out and began to read the Finnish text.

> *My dearest Alex,*
> *I cannot tell you how much I enjoyed your last precious visit. Time does drag on as we grow older, but I have my painting and my remembrances of our loving time together to carry me through the lonely times. It has meant much to me that you have been so faithful over these long years.*
> *When we met, twenty-five years ago, I could not have imagined the heights your sexual skills would reach. There were many joys, and for that I thank you.*
> *You have been a special model for some of my most celebrated paintings. They are, of course, only in my private collection for now. Thank you for your contributions to my skill and pleasure.*
> *As always, my best wishes to your lovely wife and daughters*
> *Wilhelmina*

I was shocked, as the possible significance of this note became clearer. Questions went racing through my mind. Why would Michael have received a letter addressed to him, but an enclosed love note obviously meant for someone else? Did that someone receive Michael's note? Could she have made a mistake and put the letter in the wrong envelope, or was it done on purpose by her or by someone else? This was bad enough, but I was appalled by the hint of longstanding blackmail of the person named Alex.

I tried to recall the story Michael had told me about his relationship with Wilhelmina Porter. Many years ago, she was injured in a fall while hiking, and in concern and guilt, he had paid all her bills and supported her for the twenty-five years after. In a sense, was he blackmailed too? Did he know about the lover named Alex before this letter arrived?

I wondered if Michael's name in their relationship might have been Alex. Could he have been married with two daughters? At this point anything was possible.

I glanced up and saw Tim's concerned look. "What's up, Mrs. Cameron? You look like you've just seen a ghost."

"I may have seen two of them. I think I might have a clue about why Michael chose not to have his operation."

I got up from the table to make some hot cocoa. As the milk heated, my mind tried to piece the information together. Perhaps Michael was so dismayed and felt so guilty about what was done to him that he couldn't bear to tell me the real truth, and merely made up a clean, tidy lie. If he were not Alex, I wondered whether he might have been another one of her lovers.

In my heart, I suspected so. It would explain some of the puzzling things I'd learned during our courtship. He said he returned to Finland every year even after he retired from active duty in the SEALs. As a doctor in the Reserves, his place would have been at Coronado Island or elsewhere in the States. Oh, my dear, naïve Michael. I could see him drawn to her for many reasons. I wondered how many others might have been in her stable.

"I have some interesting things to think about tonight. I think I'll turn in a little early."

Violet and I went around and locked up for the night. The wind howled around the corners of the house. I stopped back in the kitchen to say good night.

"Tim, we have to get out of here soon or put in some baseboard heating. I don't care if it is a rental, maybe we could go look for something this weekend. I wish I knew when we could leave, but we made a promise to stay until Johnson gets back, no matter what. Sleep well, my friend."

The Wilhelmina story went to the back burner while I puzzled over some text I'd been working on. Several odd idioms used in the material simply didn't fit and I was sure they would be the clue to the information we were seeking.

Morning came too early. Violet and I went out in the dark to do morning chores before we left for work. The wind was slinging pellets of sleet into windrows along the fence. The smarter dogs were hunkered down inside their kennels waiting out the weather and we finished in record time.

I said to Violet, "Let's go, even people have sense enough to get out of this wind."

I got to work almost an hour early. The general had a meeting at seven-thirty in another building, but the lights were still on in the office. I was surprised to find the door ajar, since he usually locked things up, even when he just took off to the john.

11

An instant of happy hell broke loose as Violet slipped through the open crack of the door and bounded across the room. Just as she reached him, I realized it was Johnson there by the window. He was clutching two small metal boxes to his chest while he tried to fend off Violet's exuberance with his other hand.

I rushed to his side. "When did you get back? Why didn't you come home to the ranch?" I grabbed his jacket and shook him. "Johnson, where's Anna Skorski?"

He stood, shaking his head. After several moments he reached out to me. His voice trembled as he whispered, "He shot her in cold blood before I could kill him."

"Who shot her, Johnson? Tell me!"

"Kostyan Skorski."

I released him and stepped back. "What happened?"

"Cade and I took Anna back to Andretti's town in Italy. We were there several days reading police files, trying to find clues about Skorski's disappearance. The military and the CIA needed to know where he was and what happened.

"We found no clues and decided to go out to the estate. The place seemed deserted, no lights or signs of anyone around. When we went to the front door, he opened fire on us. I was the only one with a weapon and wasn't expecting to need it. He got them both before I could shoot him."

"Both?" I whispered, "Is Cade gone too?"

He handed me one of the metal boxes. The identification tag read: Commander Cade Cameron U.S. Navy SEALs ret.

I dropped it into my cloak pocket just as the general returned to the office. My heart had turned to stone.

In my grief, I said, "May the hounds of hell pursue you forever, Ryan, for what happened to Anna and Cade."

Slipping past him out the door and down the hall, I ran from headquarters, dodging around corners and cutting across the compound of buildings to the one open entrance at the edge of the airfield.

I stumbled on the gravel path, skinning my hands and bringing blood. Violet was running alongside as I reached the narrow entry. I put my scarf down in the opening and told her to stay. This would give me several extra moments if anyone followed me. She could not go with me.

The landing lights of the incoming planes were strung out in the early morning sky like a necklace of jewels, cascading down in measured order to the runway below. I checked my watch and figured the next touchdown would be in one minute. I could just make it to the appointed place in time. The next one after would be for me.

I ran parallel to the landing strip on the taxiway, gauging the place to cut across to meet the first plane. I needed to know just where touchdown was, to place myself enough farther down the strip so he wouldn't miss me. My breath was coming in great rasping gasps, as I stepped to the edge of 280-W and knelt in the grass; to watch and wait.

I never heard him coming. He threw his body over me, pinning me to the ground, just as the first plane landed within feet of us.

A big, tremendously strong man, breathing hard yet in complete control, a viselike grip held me as he yelled above the roar of the plane, "Dammit lady! Couldn't you have tried a little cleaner way to commit suicide? Think of the bad PR."

I struggled in vain to break loose as the next plane touched down. Somewhere far off, a frenzied screaming noise pierced through the roar of the engine. I didn't realize what it was until he put his hand over my mouth. "Hush, little sparrow. Things probably aren't going to be all right, and you'll probably hate me for what I did; but it's my job."

Then, gut-wrenching sobs came, until I was gasping for breath. His hold never loosened, as he waited for the jeep to arrive with two MPs. I had no fight left and collapsed into his arms as he lifted me in.

My nose itched but my hand wouldn't or couldn't move when I reached to scratch it. Another tug brought me to full alert. My hands were restrained to the sides of the bedrails and tubing went in and out of my body in casual confusion. I went ballistic. Bloodcurdling screams of frantic fear and anger brought Father Patrick and Doctor Spanne rushing in to my bedside.

Dr. Spanne reached for my hand and held it tight. "You're going to be all right now, Sara. They brought you in two days ago and when we couldn't get through to you we put you out."

The doctor made no move to untie my hands so I figured I'd put on quite a fit. At least I knew where I was and that I was among friends.

"Would one of you be kind enough to scratch my nose? Then we might talk about why I'm trussed up like a chicken going to slaughter."

The room came into better focus. Someone was sitting

hunched over in the far corner, his face white as an alkali flat. It was General Ryan. My voice came out somewhere between a growl and a hiss. "Get out, Murderer."

He rose from his chair and left the room without speaking, his grief-stricken face and utter exhaustion lost on me. Father Patrick watched this melodrama without comment. His eyes were filled with such sadness and compassion, that I wondered what had happened.

Perhaps things I couldn't or wouldn't remember, now separated me from my waking world. I closed my eyes in infinite weariness and whispered, "My God, You have forsaken your weakest and most humble servant. What am I to do now?"

Father Patrick touched my hand. "He hasn't abandoned you, Sara. He's waiting for you to ask for His comfort."

"If He loved me He wouldn't have allowed Anna and Cade to die. I can't bear it. I want to die too." I closed my eyes and turned my head to the wall. "There is no God; only emptiness, misery and grief."

I heard faintly, the keening of my ancestors, the Scottish women, grieving the losses of their kin in battle. I sang the lament to the fallen warriors; choking on tears I couldn't hold back and couldn't wipe away.

Father Patrick turned to Dr. Spanne and pleaded, "Do something. We'll lose her if you let her go on like this."

The doctor sighed in resignation. "Well, we've tried everything else. Go see if the guard is still out by the door. We could turn her loose if he's willing to sit with her."

Father Patrick went to find him while the doctor did his rounds assessment, and removed the IVs. Finally, when the guard entered the room, Dr. Spanne untied me from the rails, gave him a few terse instructions and left the room.

It was the man who'd snared me on the tarmac. I didn't trust anyone now. I turned away toward the wall, pulled the blanket tight around me and curled into as small a form of misery as I could. In the quiet room, I felt a small, growing sense of sanity, a glimmer of safety, as the medication they'd given me allowed my body to relax into sleep.

CHAPTER THREE   GENERAL RYAN'S LAMENT

It's been two days since Sara Cameron learned about the deaths of Anna Skorski and her husband Cade Cameron. I feel responsible for her breakdown. I'd argued for hours with my superiors when the operation in Italy and Finland was being planned; that they shouldn't send Cameron and Johnson and Anna Skorski.

I was overruled. We had no other operatives with the balance of language and disarmament skills, except Anna and Cade. They were leftovers from the Russian spy days, just as I am, and there aren't many people left who speak Italian, Finnish and Russian.

Johnson thought that he was going to pick up Anna in Lisbon. Instead, his orders were to go on with them as far as Italy to help investigate what had happened to Kostyan Skorski, and then to come home alone.

Now, Anna, Cade and Skorski are dead. It is more like some spy novel than reality and I am devastated by their deaths. I'd worked with them on various missions, and despite Skorski's apparent straying from the fold, they were well-trained agents and I respected their work.

What a damnable, tangled web Wilhelmina Porter wove for us; working both sides and selling military information to whichever side would pay the most.

Yes, she was a marvelous painter, well-known for her watercolors of the Finnish lake country, but her portraits are of strategic interest now. We should know soon how many were involved in her scheme. We must retrieve those portraits before they fall into the wrong hands.

For several years, we'd found increasing evidence that information was being leaked from Mountain Home air base. An insider with Russian connections was stealing secrets even in this day when people on the outside thought we no longer needed to fear the Russian military.

It is our theory now, that he was part of Wilhelmina's

15

group of men; perhaps one of several Russians who went at first to visit her, to spend time in her home and her bed, and who gave away secrets perhaps without knowing or suspecting that she was the enemy.

Then she blackmailed them with their portraits. She required them to infiltrate into the United States military or onto the base, and then to gather information from the inside. They are most likely long-timers, from before the breakup of Russia.

The recent strange mix-up of Wilhelmina's letters was our first breakthrough. Until then, I had no clue she was doing anything except some tawdry blackmail against me.

It broke Michael Cameron's heart when he learned what she'd been doing and that I was involved too. Only he knew that my code name from earlier spy days was Alex. He'd received my letter from Wilhelmina and I'd received his.

Skorski was working on Michael's final death papers when he learned of Michael's involvement. I'll give Skorski credit for confessing that he knew her and had been dealing with her off and on too. The size of the plot mushroomed as we wondered who'd received Skorski's letter and whose letter he'd received. He refused to tell us and was the reason he was given three days to leave the country.

Now that Wilhelmina is dead, it could become a deadly race, if the men involved decide to head for her place to retrieve the portraits she was using for the blackmail. We need to know whose pictures are in the art studio, and then, to retrieve or destroy them. I expect that the Russians have portraits there too; pictures we can use to identify them as the traitors in our midst.

The question is whether Wilhelmina's house in Finland still holds the portraits. Now that Anna and Cade are dead, we will have to send two young, inexperienced operatives to Kotka where Wilhelmina Porter lived.

My skin crawls when I think about all the different ways a house can be wired with booby traps and explosives set to blow when simple tasks like flipping light switches and opening windows are done. It could take weeks to disarm the house enough to make it safe to enter. It was one of Anna's specialties. And now, Anna is gone.

CHAPTER FOUR SARA CONTINUES THE STORY

I had no idea what time it was. The clock said two, but it could have been day or night. I felt like I'd fallen down a flight of stairs, and there was a big bruise on my belly. I suppose it was from the rough treatment I'd brought on myself as I struggled with the guard. Cade's metal box had been in my front pocket and could have gouged into my stomach as we wrestled on the ground.

The guard, where was he now? I moved to turn toward the door and saw him sitting in his chair by the bed, watching me. It didn't look like he'd moved at all while I slept, however long that was.

I had to get out of this place right now. There were no windows and I had an increasing feeling of claustrophobia. It was a relief to realize my first inclination was not to scream. Not only would it cause a great flap, but also might keep me here longer or cause me to be sent to an even worse place.

I needed to hear his voice before I could decide how to proceed, so I asked him, "What is your name, sir?"

I was surprised at the gentleness of his voice. "Zachary, ma'am, and I see that yours is Sara Harvey Cameron."

He was holding a file in his lap, perhaps something General Ryan had given him. He was not a simple soldier, but someone in the deeper recesses of the intelligence community. No one else would have been given access to my personnel files.

I'd have to work on that puzzle later. Right now, my stomach said it was way past feeding time and I was ravenous. I also realized how thankful I was to be alive.

I managed a small smile. "I may not have another private time to thank you for saving my life. I'm going to be all right now and I have work to do. What time is it? I'm starving and you must be too. Any chance we might be able to weasel some food out of the nursing station?"

His grin was infectious. "It's about two in the morning. Why don't you call the nursing station and tell them you'd like to get up and walk for a bit. They should have time to do it for you and while you're up I'll make a run to get some junk food. What sounds good?"

I didn't have to think very hard. "How about a chocolate milk shake, a big greasy hamburger with lots of onions and fries? I can smell them already. If my cloak is here, I think there's some money in the pocket."

"Don't worry; you can pick up the tab next time. Besides, I think they locked up your clothes to keep you from running away again."

"Zach, did I do anything embarrassing?"

He chuckled, "Nothing they weren't expecting. Man! You're a pretty good fighter for a girl. 'Course you had the element of surprise on your side until someone filled me in on who you were. I think they were enjoying the show.

"Call the nurse so I can take off. Someone will have to come and stay with you until I get back. Maybe I'll ask if they want something too. The hospital food isn't too great."

He left his chair with unexpected grace and control for someone so large. He was well over six-feet tall. The military haircut couldn't disguise his black curls and his eyes were the deepest, darkest, metallic black I'd ever seen.

He returned with three pizzas for the night staff and my milk shake, hamburger and fries. The smells wafting into the room almost brought me to my knees. It was the milkshake I reached for first. I closed my eyes as the first swallows slipped down my throat. My tiny moan was pure animal delight.

Zach whispered, "Good for you, Sara. Welcome back."

He sat outside my room and finished his pizza while I cleaned up and washed my hair. A clean gown, and two extra blankets later, I was ready to sleep again. Zach closed the door and returned to his post by my bed. The railing was down as he reached for my hand.

"Sleep well, Mrs. Cameron."

As he turned away I saw tears glistening in his lashes.

"Zach, what's the matter? Can I do something to help?"

He shook his head in mute misery. "No, Sara, nothing; except to trust me."

My intuition guided my answer. "I trust you Zachary, whatever that may come to mean. Rest now too, my friend."

He was gone in the morning when I wakened. My door was ajar and I could hear the scurrying feet of the nurse aides doing their various morning chores. A nurse came bustling in, her arms full of my clothing and cloak. She cranked the bed and helped me up.

"General's orders. You're to be in his office by eight o'clock. He wants to see you before you leave."

"What?" I shook my head. "Where am I going?"

"I don't know ma'am, but we follow the general's orders around here so you'd better get moving."

I had no belongings to pack, and only the clothes I was wearing when they brought me in. Cade's metal box was still in my cloak pocket and I slipped it out and opened the lid. His watch, his military ID and his wedding ring were inside. I shook them out on the bed. Something was missing. Where was the locket I had given him on the night he left to begin his mission?

It was almost eight when I passed the nurses' station and hurried over to the general's office. The men were waiting for me. Johnson stood by General Ryan at the desk. Tim Campbell and Zach were across the room by the window.

"Gentlemen?"

"Good morning, Mrs. Cameron. I hope that you slept well." General Ryan's voice was hollow and filled with exhaustion. He seemed to be struggling to stay in control.

"Thank you for your concern. I did indeed sleep well."

There was some kind of play going on. I was in it but hadn't been given the script. I glanced at Zach and was stunned by the expression on his face and something in his body language, warned me to be careful about what I said.

My voice was controlled and without emotion. "Sir, I'm ready to go back to work if you wish for me to. What did you need to have done today?"

The general sighed with obvious relief. "I think your work here is finished. The men have loaded all of your belongings as well as Tim's things from the ranch into your truck. I'm putting you on temporary leave for now and Zach has been assigned to go with you to help drive. The meteorologist says you have about two and a half days to get home before the big storm everyone's been watching will catch up with you. With both of them driving nonstop, you will make it, if all goes well. You need to get to Campbell's Point. Margot and Thad Penard are expecting you."

He stopped. An infinite sadness came into his voice. "Dear Sara, I pray that one day you will find it in your heart to forgive me." He turned and left the office.

Zach reached for my hand. "Come on. We need to leave right away."

"I know, let me have a moment with Johnson and then I'll be ready to go."

I put my arms around Johnson and hugged him. "I'm so sorry about your loss. Anna was my best friend and an honorable work partner. Thank you for making her life a little better and happier. I'm going to miss her and I'm going to miss working with you. Keep in touch. I'll try to send for Violet when I get settled somewhere. I don't know whether Campbell's Point is ready to forgive me or not, I guess I'm going to find out. Take care, friend."

Tim shook Johnson's hand. "Thanks for the job and the training you gave me. I hope we'll meet again."

We hurried out to the truck and headed east toward Rock Springs. The ugly black line of the front on the western horizon dogged us as we turned onto Interstate 84. The men had made their own schedule and the maps were laid out on the dash. I was only a passenger and I was glad.

The first surprise came at noon break when the men pulled off into a truck stop. We scattered to take care of our personal needs and when we returned, Tim took out a box with the lunch Johnson had packed for us. Tucked into the top, I found a bunch of yellow sweetheart roses with a big wide ribbon tied around the bottom.

Tim grinned. "He asked me to give these to you at lunch. He said you'd understand. Pretty nice of him to remember you like that, in the midst of all the goings on."

I took the flowers from the box and propped them up on the dash. The wind was so penetrating that we gave up trying to eat beside the truck. I was thinking with fondness of a nap but it was Zach who needed sleep. He crawled into the back, wooled around the blankets and pillows and collapsed into deep sleep, punctuated with tidy snores, even before we were up to speed on the next leg of the trip.

While Tim was searching for something besides a country-and-western music station on the radio, I reached for the bouquet and found a pencil and note pad in my purse. I untied the bow and unrolled the bills in the order they were stacked. After a few minutes I slipped the note I'd decoded into a hidden pocket in my cloak.

I smiled as I remembered the evening Cade and I, in fun, had figured out the coding, using paper money for a message, including two one hundred dollar bills for C.C., my husband's initials. Surely neither of us thought we might need to use it so soon. My eyes were closed when Tim reached over to touch my hand. "Are you OK, ma'am? What's with the money?"

My smile was serene. "Just a little personal note from someone I love very much."

The message to Johnson would have described the sequence of the bills he was to wrap around the roses. My translated message said that Cade was still alive, he asked for prayers to keep him safe and promised to be home as soon as he could manage it. Backed up by the missing locket, I could believe Cade was all right.

Johnson took some real risk to do this but I think he knew how much I needed the reassurance. I'd have to compliment him later on his acting skills. The note hadn't mentioned Anna. I didn't know if she still lived.

I had no idea what kind of game General Ryan was playing or what part I played in it. I glanced into the big side mirror to see the storm still coming behind us and knew first things must come first. We needed to get to Pennsylvania as fast as we could.

By the end of the second day, the truck smelled like a hippy hovel and I insisted that we stop long enough to air it out and get ourselves cleaned up. I took off for the shower at the truck stop. On such a bad weather night, the ladies' shower was nearly empty and I enjoyed a luxurious hot shower and washed my hair.

I learned a lot about my mysterious guard by the personal things he'd packed in my bag. He knew more about women than the usual man and must have lived with one at some time in his life.

What interested me most was what he had packed; the shampoo without scent, no makeup, and he packed only black clothing. The message was obvious. I still had work to do. I thought about him going through my dresser drawers and packing for me. I wondered what he thought when he came upon the Cameron necklaces.

I put on the black outfit and looked in the mirror. My face was so pale, my hair so silvery white that my head seemed to float above my body. There was a black beret in the bag and I put it on.

21

We arrived back at the truck about the same time and headed on the last leg of the trip. The trucker road condition board had no good news. The storm was only an hour behind us, moving fast.

I looked at the two men. They were dog-tired. I whispered, "We'll make it guys. We have to. We're almost there and I haven't run out of prayers yet."

The driving conditions after we left Indianapolis deteriorated until we could drive only thirty miles an hour in some places. Even the big truckers were pulling off to wait out the storm.

The snow had started in earnest and it was pitch black, with low scudding clouds, when we pulled into Campbell's Point the next day. Margot's gentle, lilting French was the final sign of homecoming as we blew in the door with the wind. She took me off to her sitting room while Thad took the men to his office. As we went by the living room, I caught sight of a wonderful fireplace and hoped we could enjoy it later after their business was over. Thad and Zach wouldn't talk business until they got Tim on his way home.

I turned to hold Margot in my arms. She was even more beautiful since she'd become pregnant. She and Thad married in July and I knew how much they wanted to begin their family. I slipped into the more familiar French of our friendship. "Marriage appears to be good for you, My Dear. You are lovelier than ever, if that's possible."

"Madam, you are too kind. It is good to see you again though I am so sorry about the circumstances. We will do our best for you. I think you will be feeling better after you get some rest and enjoy some pampering by your friends. All of us are anxious to return you to our hearts.

"The fires and riots have left scars but we are struggling to mend the rifts as quickly as we can. In some ways, things are better among us because of our trials. We have grown in our neighborliness and kindness towards one another."

I sighed with relief. "Give me a chance at one full night's sleep horizontal in bed and I'll be ready. I'll go out to the truck and retrieve my duffle bag and perhaps we could join the men in front of the fire. You have such a wonderful, comfortable home; I'm looking forward to spending some time here with you."

When we stepped to the door, I found my duffle and small suitcase already delivered. Zach continued to be efficient and thoughtful. I wondered how long he would be staying.

The front door blew open and a gust of wind threw swirling snow into the hallway. Zach came in grinning, carrying his own duffle, my heavy cloak, and some boxes.

"I got Tim delivered to Gary's Grill. Tricia Forester knew he'd be coming in tonight so she stayed in town. Do you suppose she could spend the night here, Mrs. Penard? The driving is treacherous and I'd hate to send anyone out in it." He smiled. "I think Tim hopes he can stay here with her for a while before he has to go home."

Margot smiled. "Yes, of course, I'd enjoy having them. There may be many stranded travelers in need of food the next few days and she'll be needed at Gary's. I'll call Kylie Lou and let her know. Will you be staying too, sir?"

He looked over at me as he answered. "Yes, ma'am, I'll be staying a while. Perhaps you can put me to work in trade for my board and room."

"That won't be necessary, sir. It's an honor to have you in our home."

As she turned to go into the kitchen, I joined the gentle flow of small town life. I felt safer than I had in a long time.

Tim and Tricia arrived in a flurry of snow and settled by the fire. Zach took off for the guest room. My nest was upstairs opposite the landing and my first night of uninterrupted sleep was pure bliss.

CHAPTER FIVE ZACH CONTINUES THE STORY

With the strange schedule we'd lived through getting to Pennsylvania, I was up early and ready to check things out. Tricia was in the kitchen, dressed in her uniform and ready to take off for work when I came down about five o'clock the next morning.

I smiled and asked, "Would you like some company on your way to work? I'd like to get out for some exercise before everyone else is up. How soon will you be leaving? If there's time, I'll shovel the walk before we go."

"Yvette gets there early, about four o'clock, to start the morning rolls. I don't have to be there until six but I like to go a little early to catch up on the town news and to visit with her while she works. She's been good to me and I like her a lot. I call her my second mom.

"I have a feeling that her life was quite different when she lived in France. Sometimes she gets a look on her face, a faraway look of sadness. I wonder what or whom she left behind. She's a good friend of Margot and Thad's since they speak French together and I think they might be from the same part of France.

"There's time for you to do the shoveling. Thad will thank you, because he leaves early to get to the store and Margot will have you extra people to take care of."

I stepped to the back porch and found the snow shovel leaning against the wall. While I shoveled, Tricia kept up the chatter. She'd be a prime source of information about Campbell's Point, since she worked at the only restaurant. Gary's Grill was the hub of the downtown, and I expect it was the place to learn news and pass it on. I finished my chore and fell in step beside Tricia as she headed off down the street.

She pointed out the houses and told me who lived in each one. We came to the bigger, fancier Victorian places and she pointed out one with a lovely rose garden. The well-trimmed and mounded plants were covered with snow, but the outline of the formal garden, the empty fountain and stone planters said that a true gardener lived there.

Tricia whispered, "That's where Millie Greer lives. The Crazy Lady shot Millie's husband, Hank. It took him weeks to die. We're worried about Millie. When it first happened, she had a lot of visitors and she went to church and things in town. Then one day about three weeks ago, we didn't see her any more. When we called, the servant, Lars, said she was napping or busy.

"Margot and the other ladies left messages for her to call and we haven't heard from her. We took food to the door and he would take the dishes but not let us in. I'm scared for her. I think something bad is going on in her house and we women are trying to decide what to do. Look, she hasn't even filled the bird feeders for her beloved cardinals."

We walked in silence while I thought about what to say. I didn't want to frighten her but it sounded bad. If Millie were ill, she needed a doctor's care. If something worse were going on, the women shouldn't try to get in to see her.

"Tricia, has Margot said anything to Thad about her concerns? Or have any of the men been told? Let me check around and we'll take care of it for you. Maybe Dr. Campbell knows something that could help us know what to do. I don't like the sound of it and I want you to promise me that you ladies won't take things into your own hands."

"Yes, sir. At least I feel better because I told you. Let's go in the back way so we don't track snow into the dining room. Yvette always makes cinnamon buns for the morning and a double batch when the weather's like this. We have a lot of regulars who have no family and they practically live at Gary's. We don't mind. Some of them are very lonely and sweet." She smiled as she added, "And they tip well."

She stomped the snow off her boots and went inside. I reached for the snow shovel leaning up against the wall, and began to take care of the walks. It felt good to work up a sweat and I dropped my jacket onto the steps.

I wished this thing about Millie Greer had waited a few days. I needed some time to get a better feeling about the habits and minds of the people in town. I knew Millie was one of Sara's friends and had looked after her when she came to town looking for a farm to buy. I knew Sara would want to see Millie as soon as possible. I needed to warn her not to go right now.

Gary's was on a corner and with the alley there were three sides to clean up. As I finished, Tricia came to unlock the front and I handed her the shovel.

"I need to get back to Thad's place before he leaves for work. See you later, Tricia. Maybe I'll be down in a bit to meet your special friend."

I took off at a fast walk and got there just as he was leaving on foot for his hardware store.

I called out to him, "'Morning, Thad. Mind if I walk downtown with you?"

"No, 'course not. By the way, thanks for the shoveling job. Want to do the one at the store too?" He chuckled. "I'm just kidding. I have a nice kid who does it. He's saving up for college and I try to help him out."

The youngster was already at work. He couldn't have been an inch taller than the shovel but he was working away at it. He looked about twelve.

Thad grinned at him. "Good job, Tommy. This is Dr. Zach. He's going to be around for a while. He's a friend of Sara Cameron's and he's staying with us. Now you get finished and I'll bet the car wash could use some help too." The kid turned back to his work as we went in.

The smell of fresh coffee filled the store office and I was thinking about those cinnamon buns down at Gary's. "Let me go down and pick us up a couple of buns to go with the coffee. We need to talk."

Thad looked at me with a puzzled frown. "What's up?"

"I walked Tricia to work this morning and she was telling me about Millie. Has Margot said anything to you about it? It sounds like a bad scene to me, but I don't know any of the characters."

When I got back from Gary's, his office was full of men. Tim Campbell was there with a guy he introduced as Dr. Campbell. A man wearing a very visible gun was introduced as Sam Saunders, the town's marshal. The other two men were Casey Borders, Hank Greer's replacement as lawyer in town, and an older man, Doc Pete Hamilton, who said he was the town's doctor. We got right down to what they each knew and the marshal figured it was time to take action.

I was surprised when he asked what kind of weapons people were carrying. Each man carried a knife big enough to gut an elk and handguns in several different places. From what Sara had told me on our trip, Campbell's Point was under martial law for a while during the riots and I figured the truce might be a bit more tenuous than the ladies thought. I showed just enough of my hardware to know I'd be acceptable for whatever they were going to do.

The cop was good. He told us what he planned to do and then asked for comments or suggestions. We made only one minor change in the tactics and headed out to surround the Greer place. Tim knew the inside of the house because he'd done a carpentry job a year ago for them. His job was to get into the back of the house and then to go to the places Millie might be and get her out.

The marshal, Thad and I were to go after the servant and disable and disarm him if need be. Border's job was to go into the garage, disable the car and then stand guard there. While JW covered Tim at the back of the house, Doc Pete was to cover the front. He was carrying a real beauty of a Colt revolver and I figured he wouldn't hesitate to use it. As the stranger in the group, I got the job of going to the front door to gain entry and to distract the servant while Tim got in the back way.

It was eight o'clock when everyone was in place. I rang the bell on the front door. A large, unwieldy package blocked most of the view of me as Lars came to answer.

I yelled at him, "Package for Mrs. Hank Greer. I need her to sign for it."

He swung the door open just wide enough to see me as he growled that she was not available. I shoved the box ahead of me and the door knocked him down onto the hall floor. He let go a string of Norwegian swearing as he rolled away, scrambled up and headed off down the hall with all of us in hot pursuit. He was just far enough ahead to get to the kitchen and slam the door shut. We heard the key turn in the lock.

Thad and Sam headed back outside to get into the back of the house. I heard the glass shatter as they broke in. Tim yelled that he'd found Millie. She was wrapped in his coat as he carried her down the stairs and out the front door to safety.

I smelled it and heard it at the same time. My skin crawled as I realized what it meant. Gasoline fumes gagged me as I struggled to open the kitchen door. I heard the eerie whooshing sound as air began to rise with the heat and then there were explosions.

Thad and Sam broke out of the kitchen into the front hallway. We headed outside as the lovely old house erupted in flames that towered thirty feet above the trees. There was no way anyone could have saved it. The old lath and plaster walls, the hardwood floors and beautiful wood frame of the house were helpless against the ferocious inferno.

As we huddled together in the yard, Thad told us that he reached the top of the basement stairs just as Lars was pouring gasoline on a huge pile of papers and curtains and furniture. Lars ran for the stairs and turned back to toss a lighted propane torch onto the pile. As he hurried up the stairs, he tripped and fell back screaming onto the now blazing pile. Thad said he closed and locked the door and walked away. It was over in minutes.

Tim carried Millie to Doc Pete's house a block down the street and we didn't see her right away. I was sorry Tim was the one to see what had happened to her. The marshal took over and the backup volunteer help directed traffic to keep the curious crowd away from the burning rubble. The fire crew stood by, helpless, as the house collapsed into the basement.

Sara and Margot were sitting hand in hand on the porch steps, huddled under a blanket. They were watching the dying flames, when I came down the street.

Sara flew into my arms. "Is she all right, Zach? Are all the men safe?"

"Yes to both questions. The only person who died was Lars, who burned to death by his own hand. We won't know the rest for a while, but for now I hope the worst is over."

Sara sighed with relief. "Thank you. The town has literally given you a 'baptism in fire' this morning. I hope the rest of your visit is more gentle and relaxing. Come in and we'll fix breakfast. Or better yet, let's go down to Gary's and have cinnamon buns. It's a morning tradition in Campbell's Point and I expect you'll get a hero's welcome."

The women went in to put on walking clothes and we went down to town to be with the other townspeople who'd gathered to hear about the rescue. Casey Borders was doing a good job of the tale, so we slipped into a back booth and waited for Tricia to come take our orders.

When she found us, her first move was to give me a big hug and a sweet kiss, as she whispered her thanks to me. "Thank you, sir. My Dad wants to meet you. Mom has invited you and Sara to come up to the farm for dinner tonight. I'm off at three so Tim and I'll be there too. Now, what would you like for breakfast, you three?"

"Cinnamon buns of course, unless they're all gone."

We shared the simple breakfast and I asked not to talk about the fire just yet. I took Sara's hand, as I said, "I want to ask you to wait to see Millie until I've spoken to Doc Pete about her condition. He'll let us know when she's ready to have someone sit with her."

After what I'd read in Sara Cameron's files, the last thing she needed right now was to see Millie and what had been done to her.

It was crowded at Gary's and people were waiting for our places. We went to the cash register to pay and Tricia took care of it. As we turned to go, she touched my arm.

"Thanks again, sir. Yvette says you're to come to the kitchen when you walk me to work. She'd like to meet you."

"Tell Yvette I'll look forward to it."

The women did a few errands at the store and when we got home there was a message for Margot and Sara on the answering machine. Millie was going to stay with Doc Pete and his wife Laura for a while and would they scout up some clothes and essentials for Millie, since everything was destroyed in the fire.

I went off to work on some reports while the ladies began to put together a suitcase full of women's things. I heard them call to find out if Millie wanted mourning clothes or just simple things that fit. Laura would have to decide, Millie was unconscious.

The weather report was good. No more snow for a few days, and the snow on the dark roads was melting fast. We shouldn't have any trouble getting out to the Foresters in the big truck. I was looking forward to meeting Abe Forester and Kylie Lou and their passel of kids. Sara loved them and I knew I would too. I finished one report and went off to my bedroom for a nap. It was four o'clock when Sara came to waken me for the evening.

First thing I noticed was that Sara wasn't wearing black. The soft gray slacks and apricot sweater with her white fur boots looked much more cheerful than mourning clothes.

She answered my unspoken thoughts with a smile. "I didn't want to frighten my dear little friends, especially baby Susan. Besides, Millie needed my black clothes."

When we pulled into the farmyard, the famous dogs she'd told me about were on their best behavior. Sara didn't even need to tell them to stay or be quiet. Children of all shapes and sizes tumbled out the door to meet us. Baby

Susan was in Sara's arms, hugging and kissing as though she would never stop. When the little one came up for air, Sara put her down and whispered in her ear. Little Susan giggled and wiggled, but she stood as Sara did a ceremony.

She pronounced, "I dub you My Lady Susan. May you live in joy and happiness, for ever and ever."

Sara looked around the group of watching children. "My Lady Susan, you have some friends here tonight that I haven't met. Would you introduce us please?"

Susan was very solemn as she reached out to a young boy about seven-years old. "This is Steven Crosswick, his sister Lane is over by the tractor, she's four, and baby sister Pam is two, she's sitting on the porch. They're staying with us a while 'cause their mama's sick."

We all went in together in a swirl of little legs and arms and I had my first look at Kylie Lou Forester. What a lovely woman; matronly and probably exhausted with her load but her face radiated love and welcome. She was in the late stage of pregnancy. I guessed another month or so and there would be another babe in the family. She was tall, with long chestnut braids wrapped around her head like a crown. Abe Forester stepped to her side and put his arm around her shoulders.

He said to me, "Welcome to our home, sir. Thanks for your part in helping to save Millie this morning. We are eternally grateful to you."

I could feel his goodwill and sincerity as he reached out to shake my hand. Tim and Tricia were standing by the kitchen door and I saw the striking resemblance between Tricia and her mother. I wondered if Tim realized how lucky he was to be joining this loving family.

Since it was Saturday, the children were allowed to stay up later and we had a wonderful evening playing games. Then Abe settled everyone down while he did his nightly Bible reading. He was reading a children's Bible and I saw Sara smile. She'd told me about her disappointment at not being there to help the Foresters with their reading. Tim and Tricia had done a fine substitute job. When he finished, the women went off to get the children ready for bed while Abe, Tim and I sat by the fire to visit.

Tim looked vulnerable and sad as he whispered, "I can't believe one human being could do such things to another. I don't think I'll ever forget the sight of her or the look in her eyes." He shuddered and closed his eyes.

I let Abe answer, since he was going to be Tim's father-in-law. He spoke softly. "The world's not a perfect place, Tim. Ugly, evil things happen even to good people."

Tim looked at him. "I don't want to go home tonight. May I stay here with you? I need you and Kylie Lou and Tricia and the little ones to help me trust in the wisdom of God."

"Yes, of course. Give Doctor Campbell a call so he won't wait up for you."

He turned to me and explained, "We're still pretty concerned about where people are these days. The veneer of peace is mighty thin and it's easy to jump at every shadow. Come on, Zach, I'll give you a short tour around while the kids get settled. We're a little tight for space but you and Mrs. Cameron are welcome to stay too, if you'd like."

When we returned, the women were sitting by the fire. Sara rose from the rocker. "It's been such a nice evening and I hope we may come back again very soon Kylie Lou, but I'm still weary from traveling and I need to get to bed. It's been a long, difficult day."

I didn't mention Abe's offer to stay the night to her. I knew that Sara would need help to get through the next few days. I didn't know Millie's full condition yet, but Sara was suffering for her in a deep personal way. I could see her slipping into a desperate and frantic struggle to stay in control. We thanked them for dinner and headed home.

About half way back, Sara lost it. I pulled over to the side of the road at a turnout. In my professional work, I wasn't allowed to touch my patients. But this time, I reached out and she came into my arms. I unfastened her cloak and laid her trembling body as close as she could get to mine. Her sobs slowed as she buried her face in my chest. In a few minutes she looked up at me with a wan smile. Then, she really surprised me.

"Is there something you could do to help Millie and me get through this? Could you work with us together?"

"How did you know?"

"I put two and two together. General Ryan isn't very subtle when he tries to help someone. I suspected from the first night that you were assigned to do more than just keep me from committing suicide. I assume you're either a counselor of some kind, or a psychiatrist."

She moved a gentle distance away, still touching but regaining her reserve and control. It was a good sign.

"I plead guilty to the charges but ask for the mercy of the

31

court. I need to get in touch with Doc Pete first thing tomorrow to see if I may be allowed to help Millie. Then we can decide how to proceed. Of course I'll help you both.

"Sara, we need to clear up something right now. We don't have time to play games, considering the other issues at hand. Do you believe that Cade wasn't killed in Italy?"

She hesitated for several long moments. I figured she was in prime-spook-mode while she formulated her answer and I wouldn't learn a thing. Instead, her answer was so open and loving that I had trouble taking it in. What an amazing person Cade Cameron had married.

She settled into her warm cloak as she began, "Three things fit together so well that I have no doubt in my heart that Cade is still alive. The first came on the morning we were getting ready to leave the Mountain Home air base. I was given my clothes and cloak and told to be ready to leave by eight. I sat down and opened the metal box with Cade's things, to look through it. Something was missing and I was sure Johnson would not have left it behind when he removed Cade's ID tags and ring from his body to bring home. He knew most of my life story and understood how important Michael's locket was to me. I gave it to Cade on the evening they left for Lisbon, and it was not among the things in the box. I assume Cade kept it because he promised me that he would bring it home.

"The next thing happened when we opened Johnson's lunch box at noon of our first day of travel. The yellow roses were not just sentiment. There was a message coded into the money folded around the stems. Just in fun, Cade and I had thought up a code one evening before this all started. We had no idea it would ever be used. Johnson knew only the sequence of the bills and not the message."

It was my turn to smile now. I quoted the message I'd found on a piece of paper in the secret hiding place in her cloak. "I am safe. Keep praying. I'll be home as soon as I can. I love you more than life itself. C.C."

She answered me with mock displeasure. "It wasn't very nice of you to search my cloak. Besides, the hiding place was beautiful; only a true professional would have found it.

"Oh, by the way, I haven't thanked you for your packing job at the ranch. You probably learned a lot about me by doing it, but I also learned a great deal about you because of what you chose to put in my duffle bag and suitcase. A woman was an intimate part of your life at one time."

She reached out to take my hands in hers. "My dear Zachary, the most telling message came from you, during the time you sat at my bedside watching over me.

"I'm sure that you thought I was sleeping, but I was not. I turned away from you and curled up into as tiny a ball as I could. I was hoping that I would die before morning. You were praying softly, and you sounded so wretched and upset. Somewhere along the way I heard you begin to say the Ten Commandments. First you said them all, but then, Zach, you singled out three and said them over and over. Do you remember what they were?"

I whispered my answer. "Yes, Sara, I remember. Thou shalt not steal. Thou shalt not covet thy brother's wife and thou shalt not commit adultery." I looked into her eyes and saw only compassion and love.

Then she said in a puzzled tone, "Neither Michael nor Cade spoke of you and you were not present at Michael's service. What happened to your place in the family?"

"It's a long story for another time, but I haven't had any contact with my family since I left home on high school graduation night. I made my way alone. It was when I was reading your files after your rescue that I realized you were connected with my brothers; first to Michael, as his fiancé, and then to Cade as his wife. When General Ryan asked me to take care of you, I didn't know who you were, and I don't think he has made the connection even now.

"Sara, I hope you'll allow me to continue to watch over you. You have become very precious to me and I'll do my best to protect you. You'll be in danger until the mission in Finland is complete and it could be as long as Christmas.

Her voice was gentle. "Do you believe Cade is alive?"

My answer was honest. "I don't know. The mission he was sent on was extremely dangerous and he hadn't even gotten to Finland. Finding the portraits of the Russian spies, taking pictures of them and then destroying the originals was going to be a hellish job.

"In the meantime, there are some very specific things I think you need to do to progress in your healing, and we have until then to work on them. If you're feeling better, let's get back to Penards' and a reasonable night's sleep. It's getting late and I'm exhausted."

Sara's smile was serene. "Lead on, McDuff."

My heart was filled with admiration for my brother's wife.

My body schedule was still screwy and I wakened long before normal getting up time, especially for a Sunday. I was restless from lack of exercise and needed to ask Thad where he worked out. I couldn't afford to get soft during these weeks away from my regular job. My safety depended upon my own skill and strength. I decided to go for a walk downtown to get loosened up.

The lights were on in the kitchen at Gary's. I wasn't walking Tricia to work, but I decided to drop in to meet Yvette anyway. As I knocked on the back door, I could hear her singing in French. The song stopped as she called out, "It's open. Come on in. My hands are all sticky."

I couldn't help smiling. She had flour on her nose and her hands were indeed busy, kneading the famous buns for Sunday brunch. Her hair was tied up with a bright red, flowered scarf and her blue jeans and shirt were covered with the famous white jacket of a real chef.

"Ah, Mr. Zach, I'm glad to see you. Sam just called to say you were on your way down here. He keeps an eye out for my safety since all the bad things happened last summer. He works strange hours, especially now with the Lars thing.

"You men got there in the nick of time. Sam says Lars was probably going to leave her tied up in the house after he started the fire and took off. You know, the investigators couldn't find any sign of possessions in the ruble. They think he must have moved out every stick of furniture, all the beautiful family antiques, and they had an original Picasso and a Matisse.

"Casey Borders found suitcases and boxes in the garage loaded with silver and stuff ready to haul away. Sam hopes Lars put the rest in storage somewhere, maybe in Pittsburgh. He's called in the big guns to help. They'll be here tomorrow.

"It's a while before we'll be open for brunch. Would you like some breakfast; how about steak and eggs or a mushroom omelet?"

She cocked her head to one side like a robin searching for worms. "Zach?" And then she began to sing a merry song in French as she went back to her work. I was acting like a blasted teenage boy, so smitten with her beauty and innocence that I was almost speechless.

"Ma'am?"

Her pixie grin preceded her merry laugh. "Zach? I asked if you wanted to share some breakfast with us. Sam is at the back door."

I was dismayed by my rush of jealousy as the big man stepped into the kitchen, his holster slung low on his hip and his hat tilted at a rakish angle. He sank into a chair pulled up to the table as if the place belonged to him, and put his head down on his arms.

He was talking low, like he was talking to someone who wasn't there. "I hate this job when people get hurt like Millie did and we didn't know. I haven't been home yet 'cause I can't bear to see Peg's face when she asks how Millie is and I don't dare tell her the truth. She knows when I'm lying.

"Maybe I'll quit this damn job and shovel coal like an honest man, just making enough money to feed the kids and keep them in clothes and keep a roof over our heads."

He lifted his head and looked at me. "I don't know what you do for a living, Zach, just be glad you're not a cop."

Yvette was crying. "Sam, you need some breakfast and then you have to go home and get some rest. You need your wife right now and she's waiting for you. She can get the kids ready for church and you all need to go. The whole town will be there this morning and we need to pray together to get through this."

She stepped away, put two steaks in a pan and made toast and eggs. She served the platters, poured coffee and then turned to go outside. We ate in silence, buried in our own thoughts. After we put our platters in the sink, Sam went back out the door and down the street, walking like he was on his way to a funeral.

Yvette was still outside, sitting on the back step, her eyes all puffy and red. "Sam's a good man and a good cop. He's been through hell since the riots. Peg and the kids are bearing the brunt of his exhaustion. It's a good thing Peg and I are close, at least she trusts me. I feed him when he comes in to crash and burn, and I listen when he says stuff like he did just now. He knows how much it frightens Peg when he talks like that and he needs to say it to someone."

She stood up and stretched. "Come on back in. I have more work to do before I can leave."

She scrubbed her hands and then put cold water on her face. A big sigh escaped as she got back to work. "We'll be extra busy today since everyone will want to talk about the latest disaster. People need to talk about what happened and work through their guilt, even if they don't know that's what they're doing."

"You're a wise woman, Yvette. It's an honor to meet you. Will you get time off to go to church?"

"I make time. I need it too. Sara's Catholic, are you?"

"No, but I'll be sure she gets to Mass this morning. If you promise I may come back again, I think I'll get on home."

"Zachary, you're always welcome. By the way, do you have a last name?"

"Did you know Sara's husband Cade?"

She shook her head. "No, I knew his brother Michael though, he was a real peach. I loved him dearly."

I smiled and relished the words as I said, "My name's Zachary Cameron. I'm the third Cameron brother."

I had to get out of there while I still could. I wanted to take her in my arms and make love to her right there in the kitchen. God she was beautiful, even with flour on her nose and red splotches on her cheeks. I didn't quite get away without touching her. On my way out the back door, I stepped past her and drew my fingers across her cheek. "Thanks for breakfast. See you later."

I felt an irresistible urge to run to exhaustion. I swung around the corner onto Main Street and high-tailed it for Thad's. By the time I got there I knew I'd already started on the downhill slope to sloth-hood.

Thad was standing on the front porch with his hands on his hips, grinning. "I know what you're going to ask. Jamie has the place we all use. We have keys and go when we have time. I'm sure you'll be welcome. Now, come on in and we'll make plans for the day."

CHAPTER SIX SARA CONTINUES

It was going to be another nice, fall day, but you had to take it on faith. It was too dark and too early to tell, except that the sky was clear and the late night stars were starting to fade in the growing light. I was bone tired. Those gentle, lazy days seemed to continue to elude me. What day of the week was it, and how long was it until Thanksgiving?

I thought about growing up in our small Illinois town where celebrations like Thanksgiving were communal and most of the churches got together to serve the people who had no home or family. I wondered if Campbell's Point had recovered from the riots enough to reach out to one another this holiday. I rolled over and went back to sleep.

Next time awake, Margot was tapping on my door. "Sara, we're going to early Mass this morning. Would you like to join us? I haven't allowed you much time to get ready, but I remember you're a whiz at getting ready on short notice."

I was already up by the time she finished the invitation.

"Give me five minutes and I'll be ready. Thanks for asking."

It was warm enough that we didn't need coats. I was glad to put off winter a little while longer. Mass in the little church was a healing experience. The Foresters were there, and several other people spoke to me with kindness. The prayers were very personal and I felt the people relieving some of their fear and guilt.

My response to Millie's ordeal continued to puzzle me. I was horrified and sad for her, but somehow I couldn't equate it with my own terror and my own experience of violation. I didn't know whether this meant I was healing somehow, or that my experience was barricaded into a place where no one, not even I, could enter.

I needed to talk to Zach. I noticed he hadn't joined us. I guessed he was protestant and in Campbell's Point that meant Presbyterian. I hoped he would make the effort to go to church too. Somehow, the whole incident seemed to call for a time of public mourning and the town hadn't fully recovered from the one before.

We were walking home in thoughtful silence when Zach went by, going in the other direction. He was dressed up and there was a cheerful jauntiness in his stride.

"Nice day. See you in a bit, folks, I'm going as a Presbyterian today. There's a message on the answering machine for you, Mrs. Cameron. Someone named Dodie Finch."

Then we saw Jamie Campbell with the Hamiltons and Casey Borders, heading down the street toward town. They looked to be dressed for church too. I stepped over to them and asked who was staying with Millie and if I could help.

It was Jamie who answered. "Tricia and Tim are with her, just while we go to church. She isn't often conscious yet, Sara. Doc Pete and I have decided it would be best for her to gain back some strength before she has company. Please don't go to see her until Zach and I feel it's safe for you. I'll call you after church. You and I need to talk."

He turned back toward the group and lengthened his stride to catch up with them.

Margot looked very worried as she took my hand. "Come on, Sara, you can help with dinner and then we need to figure out what we're going to take to the community Thanksgiving celebration. I think most of the town will be there, even if they're having a family gathering later. It's less than two weeks away and everyone is getting excited about it. The children are working on a pageant with costumes."

When we got into the house, I touched Thad's shoulder. "Would you listen to Dodie Finch's message and find out what she wants? I'm not sure I'm ready to see her yet."

"Yes, ma'am. Jamie called her last night to let her know you were here. It may be about Millie or maybe Dave's scientific stuff. Dodie told him the college went into Dave's office the first weekend after they found out he'd been murdered and shoveled his papers and books into boxes, no labels or anything. They went into his lab and dismantled it except for a few boxes. Dodie never understood what he did at school and it's like a foreign language with no dictionary or translator. I guess the lab assistant, Caroline, was so upset she went home to Montana.

"Anyway, I'll go listen to the message and see what she needs. Remember, I worked for Dave too, for more than ten years, and never knew what he was up to. I still have trouble believing it. We don't know how much Dodie knows about his government job, most likely, nothing. If she wants to see you, I can go with you when you're ready and I know Zach will need to go too."

The house was full of wonderful odors as the pork roast and dressing baked in the oven. When Zach got home from church we were sitting at the kitchen table with cookbooks and loose sheets with recipes jotted on them.

Margot was filling me in on the plans. "Yvette has promised to arrange the roasting of the turkeys and everyone gets to bring whatever they would like to have to go with them. She makes the most divine dressing. I wonder if the herbs in Millie's garden survived the fire. She and Hank used to grow all the wonderful herbs Yvette used."

I reached out to take Margot's hand. "I remember. And I remember their generous hospitality when I came to town last spring. So many devastations have come to this town. How have you survived?"

As she glanced over at Zach, Margot said, "Sometimes we thought that we wouldn't. I was downtown, standing on the steps in front of the hardware store talking to Thad, the afternoon Mrs. Crosswick shot Hank Greer. He and Millie were walking back from lunch, hand in hand. I saw the surprised look on his face as he fell at Millie's feet. He never regained consciousness and it took him weeks to die.

"It was the worst time of all except for the fires. We never knew whose home would be next. They would sneak into town late at night to set the fires and then leave before anyone saw them or they would go out into the country and destroy a beautiful home that belonged to a rich Pittsburgh family. Thad was about the only person who could communicate with them and I lived in terror for his life and mine. We were at war with our own neighbors, rich against poor, townies against the hill people."

Thad stepped into the kitchen as Margot was talking. He reached out and took her trembling body into his arms. "Hush, Dear One, we must hope it's over now and that we will find peace again." He looked over at Zach. "Would you excuse us for a few minutes? I think Margot needs to walk to the end of the road."

As they left by the back door, Zach sat down at the table. "Are you OK, Sara? This has been a helluva homecoming for you and we've been here less than two days. Is there anything I can do for you?"

I sat with him as I tried to explain. "In a way, I feel responsible for what happened to the people of Campbell's Point, because my house and land was the first arson set in anger; even though it was an outsider quarrel. It was the death of Mr. Crosswick when he tried to protect his home in the hollow up behind my place that set off the conflict."

Suddenly, the blind terror of the escape down the mountain road came back. I was whimpering as I tried to explain what had happened. Tears streamed down my cheeks as Zach reached to help me up. "Come on, you need a walk too. Turn down the oven and we'll take off the other direction. Margot and Thad need some privacy right now and you need some exercise."

It did help, but his legs were so long I had trouble keeping up. "Slow down a bit, Zach. Don't forget, you're ten inches longer in each leg than I am."

He smiled down at me and slowed his pace. "Sorry, I was thinking about something else."

"Or someone else?" Now it was my turn to smile. "You seem different this morning, happier somehow. I hope a nice thing has happened to you."

"Well, I got offered the job helping Yvette in the kitchen when she does the turkey caper. She said she needs a strong back but I'm hoping she'll take the rest of me too."

"She's a very special young lady. She carries some scars, as all of us do, but I'm quite thankful to her for her care of dear Isabelle while she was growing up on the streets.

"Not to change the subject, but I'm really concerned about Margot. Tim told me about Hank's shooting but I didn't know Margot actually witnessed it. I was thinking about all the years she was part of the Greer family as their servant before she married Thad.

"And what of poor Millie, with her daughter dead now and her husband murdered, all alone and living with those memories in their beautiful home, with that monster, Lars?

"I feel as though I just want to run away, run and run until I drop in my tracks. I feel as though my body is betraying me.

"I'm getting soft and Jacques always used to tell me my only freedom was to be in top condition so that I knew what my body could do. I miss him so much. I wonder how his recovery is going. By any chance did you know him?"

When I glanced over at Zach, he was grinning. "Slow down, Woman. Don't you ever stop chattering? Remember, we're kin. You don't have to tell me everything all at once. I hope you'll be a part of my life for a long, long time. Now, I'll race you to the end of the street."

We arrived at the barricade breathless and laughing. A flock of late migrating crows flew up in a whirr of wings and legs, chattering and complaining at the disturbance. The fallen leaves scattered in swirls around our ankles. It felt good to take big gulps of air as we stopped to rest.

I pulled off my sweater and tied it around my waist as Zach held up a shiny key on a chain. "We need to make time every day to get some exercise, even when the weather's bad. Here's the magic key to Dr. Campbell's shop. Since he's back in school, all the machines are pushed back in one corner and there's plenty of space to work out. Thad says a lot of the guys in town take advantage of the place. I wonder what the girls do?"

"When I came to Campbell's Point the first time, Millie told me that she taught Yoga classes. Do you think she'll be able to do them again?"

"Not for a while, Sara, but maybe it will help her to heal when she can share her skills with her friends again. Come on, we need to get back or we'll miss dinner. No race now, just move 'em out, cowgirl."

We got to the kitchen in time to help with last minute preparations. Zach mashed the potatoes while I set the table for seven. Thad had invited Tricia and Tim to join us when the Hamiltons got back from church, and they arrived in perfect time with the seventh guest, Jamie Campbell.

It didn't seem quite right to say something mundane like, Nice to see you again, Dr. Campbell. When I looked into his eyes, I sensed the tremendous depth of his anguish. I felt as though someone had gut-kicked me from my blind side. The only person who heard my gasp was Zach, who was standing beside me when they entered the back door into the kitchen. His glance was puzzled and then veiled as he reached out to shake Jamie's hand.

Zach had learned something else about his brother's wife that I would not have revealed on purpose. The stress of the past few days had heightened my empathic powers to the point that I was being physically assaulted by another's pain. The psychic line between Jamie and me was so thin that the spillover had been instantaneous.

After a moment I was in better control. "How's Millie today? When may I go to see her?"

41

Jamie glanced at Zach. "We're guardedly optimistic. She isn't able to eat yet, but her color is better and her temperature is stable. It's going to be a long convalescence, Sara; he nearly killed her."

He had told the first unvarnished truth about her condition and I was in no position to handle it. I turned away from him and ran, stumbling down the hall to the front door. Moments later, Zach found me doubled over the porch railing.

He must have known what I was going to do because he had brought a damp towel, and waited while I cleaned up.

"What can I do to help, Sara?"

"Take me someplace where I can scream."

He nodded. "I'll go get your cloak and boots."

I climbed into the truck and waited for him.

"Where would you like to go?"

I whispered, "I want to go out to my farm to the stone bench."

"You'll have to tell me how to get there. It's like the trip to Foresters' except a little farther up the mountain, right?"

"Yes, we'll need the four-wheel drive to get there."

Zach's voice was gentle. "It must have been a beautiful place before the fire. Tim was telling me about the trees and how much you loved them. Were you going to live up there all alone? Somehow, you don't seem like such a recluse. People are much too important and special in your life."

I settled into my seatbelt and began to tell him about the Campbell farm and how I had hoped to remodel it to be a wonderful Hospice with special research facilities, a place for doctors and nurses to be renewed along with their patients.

"Your brother Mike wanted to be involved in the project. We spent hours making plans. He was such an honorable and gentle man. I wish you had known him in later years. We were separated for thirty-five years before we found each other again in May this year. I wept for his loneliness but wasn't given the chance to make it up to him. He died in my arms a few months before we were to be married."

Zach was driving with care, watching for deer in the growing dusk. "How did Cade come into the picture?"

"Last summer when Michael was set up to have the operation for his aneurysm, he called Cade to come and help protect me. The thing with Dave Finch had escalated to the point that my life was in real danger. The worst thing was that they didn't tell me the truth about Finch until it was almost too late. Jacques Grayson finally told me just before Michael's memorial service."

We passed the turnoff to Foresters' and then Renquist's cabin. It was dark when we stopped at the bottom of the hill leading up to the parcel of land that was to be Liriodendron Retreat Center. I hadn't been back since the fire.

The recent snow covered the desolation in a white blanket of modesty. The rectangular outline of the stone bench that had stood behind the house under the trees was softened with the rounded edges of the snow.

As the moon began to come up behind the hill, the trees that had survived, threw thin, twisted shadows. The scent of desolation drifted down from the charred, surreal landscape.

I turned to Zach, tears glistening in my eyes. "This was only one of the things Dave Finch did to me. He stalked me for the year of my mourning after my husband died, and made four attempts on my life, putting the blame on Andretti and dear Nelson. Then he tried to kill me by tinkering with my climbing gear.

"Because of him, several of my closest friends and working partners were murdered or maimed. I have somehow managed to find forgiveness in my heart even for my husband Henri, but the hatred and disgust I feel for the treachery of Dave Finch is a terrifying, constant reality in my life."

I wrapped the cloak tight around me as I slid to the door and got out. The long, uphill walk was difficult in the snow and the paths were mere indentations in the snowscape. I swept the snow from the bench and sat down facing the place where the house had been. The foundation, so sturdy and beautifully crafted by Jamie's father, stood in stark relief. Shards of glass were sticking up at awkward angles through the snow. It was so silent. There were no night creatures in this desolate place. Even the owls had moved on to other hunting grounds. I couldn't even cry.

What welled up inside was the grief of the ancient Gaelic lament Jamie had sung here for his baby sister Melanie Jane and that I had sung for Michael as he died in my arms. I turned to face up the hill toward the place where Mr. Crosswick had died trying to save his home. I sang the lament for him and for my beloved Michael and for all the people who were harmed by the treachery of Dave Finch.

43

When I finished, I curled up on the bench.

Zach came to sit with me. He didn't speak or touch me. He was simply present, and I felt his validation of my pain. We stayed there for a long time and I felt a gentle peace descend and enter my heart.

I sat up as I said, "We must go. I have no intention of becoming a permanent part of this wounded landscape. Let me tell you what will happen in the spring.

"The whole mountainside will be covered with morels and tiny plants. They come, following the disaster of fire, as a first renewal of life. And in the summer, there will be acres of pink fireweed spires and wildflowers that thrive in the sun. And under the ash, thousands of tiny seeds are waiting. They've been waiting for decades to sprout and thrive in the new environment. There will be new trees and in many places, although a tree seems dead, it will sprout from the roots to renew the forest again.

"I hope the people of Campbell's Point will have the resilience of nature, and will love one another again."

On the trip back to town, deer were on the move, walking in the moonlight on the road, and we saw other smaller creatures doing their foraging under the protection of night. In the quiet of the big truck, we heard growling sounds.

With a big grin, Zach turned to me. "Man, am I starving. Do you suppose they saved some supper for us?"

We slipped in the back way and warmed up our waiting meal. What a lovely evening to sit with friends in front of a cheerful fire.

CHAPTER SEVEN

Next morning brought the surprise of damp, murky fog. The sounds of the town wakening were muffled, subdued under a shroud of gray. There would be no sunshine today.

Margot came with a note from Jamie. I wasn't sure that I even wanted to read it but she waited for my answer.

> Sara, I will be leaving for Pittsburgh at seven o'clock. Doctor Cameron will be coming with us and will take you to see Dodie Finch while I attend my Monday classes. I know that this will be a difficult visit for you, but we feel it must be done now. There are some objects brought from Dr. Finch's office on campus that we believe belong to you. JW

I looked up at Margot. "Please tell Zach I'll be ready."

A cold chill struck as I began to dress for the day. I decided to wear the warm outfit Michael had given me for the trip to Finland. As the time drew closer for the meetings, I almost regretted my decision not to go. It would have been an opportunity to see my colleagues, to share in the joy of research and to find satisfaction in the proof of my ideas.

Then I had to admit to myself that only one decision could have been made at the time. It would not have been safe for me to go, as long as Dave Finch was alive. Now, I didn't know if Caroline would be going in my place. I was sorry that she was taking his death so hard.

Zach came from Thad's office with an attaché case and an elegant metal toolbox. He was all business.

"I see you're wearing warm clothes, especially boots. That's good since we'll be working in the garage on a cold, concrete floor. I'd rather not have to carry the boxes inside to work with them."

45

I was puzzled, until it occurred to me that Zach might have been sent to Pennsylvania not only for my sake but also to close some of the affairs related to Dave's work for the government. It was a strict no-no to keep papers at the place of your cover job, but Dave might have gotten careless after so many years.

From what Thad had told Jamie, the college had moved Professor Dave Finch out of his office and laboratory, lock, stock and barrel, and had dumped the boxes in Dodie's garage. We certainly didn't want any confidential or top-secret papers tossed into the trash.

I sighed as I saw days, not hours of work, sorting Dave's professional papers. I was the only one with the skill and knowledge to understand the scientific and technical part, since we'd worked together for twenty years on our scientific research. When we finished the material from his college office, there would be his private office to sort. I was exhausted just thinking about it.

Jamie arrived on the dot. I chose to sit in the back, closing my eyes to the tawdry jumble of outskirts businesses: adult video stores, car lots and day-care centers. I longed for the simplicity of mountain country, the endless miles of trees, rivers, and crags rising to the sky, the clean, pure air filled with the cries of the hawk. I was napping when we pulled into Dodie's place. Jamie left for his class while Zach and I went in to begin the day's work.

Zach handed an official-looking envelope to Dodie and waited while she read what it contained. She said softly, "Thank you, sir. I appreciate your kindness in this time of difficulty, especially because of the circumstances of his death. Please come this way."

Dodie hadn't spoken to me. I found it rather strange but bided my time. She began with a wave of her hand.

"Sir, let me explain where I think things are. Every time I come out here I'm so overwhelmed it's been a nightmare. I haven't even made a start.

"I think the boxes in this corner came from his personal files. You'll probably want to start there. One reason I asked you to come was because of the equipment and tools. I have no idea what they were for or who should have them."

She turned to me. "Sara, there are some things labeled with your professional name, Dr. Sara Harvey, as well as several in the same box labeled Rebecca Jane Campbell. Do you have any idea who that might be?"

She turned to leave. "I'll be inside if you need me."

I was puzzled. Dave Finch would have had no way or reason to think that my name wasn't Sara Harvey. When we met at Paris language school, my name had already been changed. When I began the research connection several years later after I returned to the States, I always corresponded with him through the drop mail because my husband Henri Lambert ordered it done that way. Dave Finch should not have known about my husband's name or where we lived.

I had a frightening moment as I realized that if Finch had wanted to though, he could have traced me in several ways through the official channels of his position and connections with the CIA. If he'd traced my life back before my fifteenth year, he would have had a tidy piece of information for blackmail of my husband. I didn't like the implications of my musings. I was glad to get to work on the tremendous task ahead of us.

We set up three card tables at one side and a makeshift table of sawhorses and boards and began to work through the stacks of papers. Dodie asked me to save what I thought a fellow professional in our area would wish to have and then to bag the rest for disposal. She was planning to have someone come in to shred them when we were finished.

The whole chore, the process and the memories, was just like the one surrounding the disposal of my husband's public and private papers. I became a machine, a zombie; sorting by key words and letterheads. I was watching a professional and personal life flow through my hands as if it were a biography of a man's life.

We took a break at eleven. Zach was rough sorting for me, based on what he understood of Finch's job. However, he seemed to be looking for something specific, and sometimes, out of the corner of my eye, I would see him put something into his case, or into a special box. My instincts warned me not to ask what he was doing.

About one, Dodie told us lunch was ready. I was surprised when Zach said we'd eat while we worked; that we were in a strict time constraint and would work until we were done. Apparently, he'd figured something out, because he worked more quickly now and seemed to know better where he needed to search.

On the other hand, perhaps he'd already found what he was searching for. It was four o'clock when he stopped for a break. He put on surgical gloves and picked up three green research notebooks, put them in a plastic bag, and then into his attaché case. He began to sort through the boxes from the laboratory, only opening the lids to see what they contained. He set aside several full boxes by the door, including the ones Dodie had pointed out earlier in the day. Then we returned to our sorting.

I was so exhausted when Jamie returned for us at six, that I collapsed in tears as he stepped into the garage. He looked at Zach, a silent question in his eyes.

Zach answered. "I found what we were looking for. We need to get to Forensics before they close at eight o'clock tonight. You were right, Campbell, I apologize for not believing you from the beginning."

Somehow, I was out of the loop and didn't care. When Dodie came out to the garage, I showed her how much we had accomplished. I turned to Zach and asked, as bravely as I could, "Will we be coming back tomorrow to finish?"

"Do you want to finish the job for Dodie?"

I knew I must say yes, though how I would summon the strength to put in another day, I didn't know.

"I'd like to try. I know what a traumatic job it is, since I've done it so recently in my own household. Yes, of course. Will someone bring me back tomorrow?"

Zach looked at Jamie. "Will you be coming in?"

"Yes, I'll be in tomorrow. Only fifteen more days and I'll be finished with the semester. I'll be glad when it's over." Jamie's answer surprised me since I thought he was happy and interested in his new studies.

Zach asked Dodie, "Will you be here to let us in?"

Dodie looked weary and unhappy. I wanted to reach out to her and hold her. I had no idea what had happened to her since Dave's death, but it sounded as if the College had been strangely unsupportive. I wondered if he'd left her reasonably well off.

I figured out the answer was no, when Dodie replied.

"I need to get back to work tomorrow. I had to take today off without pay. Come inside and I'll give you an extra key. Will you want to work in his library office too, sir?"

"Yes, ma'am. We need to work with his computer and his personal files. When will you be back in the afternoon?"

She thought for a moment. "They won't let me go before six o'clock. Perhaps we can go out to supper when Jamie gets here to pick you up after class."

"That sounds fine. If all goes well, we'll be ready for the shredder by then. We'll need some paper boxes for the important things you'll want to keep. The shredder guy does boxes and all. It's quite a show."

Zach steered me to the door and helped me into the back of the car. I wrapped up in my cloak and was fast asleep even before the men did their errand in town.

Margot tapped on my door at six-thirty the next morning. I moaned in protest as she came in to make sure I was up.

"I wanted to pack a lunch for you since Dodie won't be home, and you need a good breakfast before you go. Any requests?"

"Whatever Zach wants for lunch is OK." I climbed out of bed. "Oh Margot, we worked so hard yesterday, I don't know if I can do another day like it."

Margot smiled. "If it helps any, Thad says the men already found what they were searching for. They should have their proof in a few days. What you and Zach are doing now is a simple kindness for a woman who was caught in a trap she couldn't escape from except by death. His!"

She took me in her arms and held me for a moment. "Now scramble or Jamie will be late to class."

I was thankful for the giant thermos of hot tea laced with sugar and milk. The second day was even more difficult than the first. I was stiff and sore from standing on the concrete floor and utterly exhausted. When we stopped for lunch and surveyed our progress, we knew that if there were no surprises we should be done by evening.

I finished up the paper files while Zach downloaded and erased Dave's computer hard drive, and gathered up all the disks. His tool kit made a simple job of the locked desk drawers and I heard him let out one whoop and a string of relatively mild swear words. He must have found something else of importance. I was down to the last two boxes when Dodie got home. She went to change clothes as the last box went to the shred pile.

I'd made a note for each box, with my recommendations for disposal. I felt like I'd been through a war and somehow survived. Dodie could never have managed to do the job. Zach was finishing up in the office when Dodie came out to thank me.

"Sara, I could never have done this alone. Thank you from the bottom of my heart. Now perhaps I can get on with rebuilding my life."

Jamie came in and we decided to go to a small place around the corner for a light supper. Zach looked weary and sad but he managed to keep up his end of the conversation.

When we took Dodie home, I asked what her plans were for Thanksgiving. She had none so we invited her to come to Campbell's Point for the day. Jamie invited her to make a base at his house and they'd go to the community service and dinner together. When she asked about Millie, he was guarded in his answer but said she was healing slowly. Zach walked her to the door.

When he climbed back into the car, he said, "God! What a brave woman; now let's hope she has some happiness ahead."

I was dozing when we got back to Campbell's Point. All I could think about was a hot shower and crawling under the covers. I wondered if I would ever be warm again.

CHAPTER EIGHT

I was allowed to more than sleep the clock around. When Margot knocked, she had a gentle smile as she announced that Thad was on his way home for lunch and it would be on the table in ten minutes. She pulled the curtains aside and opened the window. The weather had turned mellow. The last of the leaves were a translucent, ethereal yellow. It wouldn't be long until they were blown away by the wind.

The last of the migrating birds were hurrying to eat a little more before they continued on the hardest leg of their journey. From their actions, I guessed that a front would sweep across from the northwest soon. Only the sassy, resident cardinals acted as if nothing had changed. They would rule the woods until spring and they knew it.

A question was working itself around in my head. I'd gone to bed thinking about it. In the tens of thousands of pages of material from the office and laboratory, and the boxes of equipment from the laboratory, I'd not seen a single piece or line that could be classified as government business. The home office was the same. Where had he kept it?

Zach buzzed in just as we sat down to lunch and I could feel him watching me. I turned to him and began my question. "Zach, why...?"

He put his finger to his lips. "We'll talk about it later, Sara. Thad gave me the rest of the day off from the store. Let's go to town and play hooky. Both of us could use a shopping trip this afternoon."

We had a lovely lunch and then took off for Pittsburgh in my big green truck. I was glad Zach drove, since the truck was too much for me to handle. Imagine my surprise, when our first stop on the way into town was a truck sales lot.

He grinned. "Tim told me you really needed to have this taken care of, so I scouted for a smaller truck for you this morning. I even found some that don't smell like a dirty old

51

man. I have a feeling you're in need of some independence. Let's make this your start."

We wheeled in and met the dealer. I was enchanted when I learned that a woman ran the place. She knew exactly what I wanted. Within a half hour I'd taken several for a run and picked one out. It was black with silver trim and wheel flaps with wild horses instead of girls with pointy boobs.

As I climbed out, I asked her, "Any chance we could trade the green monster for this one?"

She grinned. "I was hoping you'd ask. I've been salivating over your rig since it came on the lot this morning. I've got a homesick Texas gal who'll take it in a wink. She's a former competitive barrel racer, and ready to head out to the Texas Roadhouse at the drop of a Stetson. I can even give you some generous add-ons for yours, or cash difference. That green one's a mighty fine truck, it cost somebody a bundle."

Paperwork over, she handed me the keys as she smiled at Zach. "You're a very lucky lady to have someone like him lookin' after you. Have fun, you two."

The check she handed me was for ten thousand dollars; the same amount Cade had given me in St. Louis when I was on my way to the Idaho ranch. Zach heard the catch in my breath as I accepted it.

"Want to drive?" he asked, as we got ready to leave.

"No, you can be first." I handed him the keys. "Just for today, I'm going to enjoy being 'a very lucky lady'. What's next on the list of surprises?"

"Shopping for clothes. We both need some things for the Thanksgiving party. You've got some good work clothes but your party things are non-existent."

I smiled at him. "I guess you know more about me in some ways than I do myself, Zach, since you did my packing. I'm sure what's missing can tell you a lot about a person's state of mind. Partying has been the last thing on my mind for several years and I've been in and out of black for most of it. I know exactly what I'd like to find, let's be brave and head downtown. What I want is pretty old-fashioned and not likely to be in a mall store."

By four o'clock, I had my dress in the right color, with shoes to match. I found another pair of sturdier winter boots, a down jacket and some sweaters while Zach picked up some work clothes, dress slacks and shirts and a pair of mud-mucking boots.

I had to ask him, "Whatever are you going to do in those

boots? They look like they're just waiting to slog around in Abe Forester's hog lot."

He shrugged his shoulders and grinned. "It's a surprise."

I requested one last stop, at a store specializing in period costume patterns and material. I bought enough material for two full-length dresses for the Christmas season. One would be glorious emerald green velvet, the other, an apricot satin, perfect with my red wig. Yes, I decided I would wear it, if things went well. We put the precious bags into the truck and prepared to face the traffic going home.

I touched his hand. "Thank you so much. It's been a wonderful afternoon. Tell you what, let's not fight the traffic right now. Could we stay in town for supper and drive home a little later? Let's find a place to sit and talk. The neighborhood looks safe. Let's walk around the block and see if we can find a snack."

We found a small family restaurant without a happy hour, blasting TV or smoking. We settled into a corner booth to enjoy orange juice and homemade sugar cookies.

"May I ask you a question, Zach? Do you believe that it's possible for a woman to be deeply in love with more than one man at a time? Is it the same for some men and their women?

"The difficulty comes when we must decide what we will do about it. I've been fortunate because most of the men I've loved and still love gave me support and protection without taking advantage of me. One even loved me without my knowledge. Antonio Andretti watched over me for twenty years, while he waited for me to be free of the bondage of my husband, Henri Lambert. He wanted to marry me and died saving my life.

"Jacques Grayson has been a precious part of my life off and on for ten years. He was my official guard, and protector and recently my working partner. He was my spirit mate. In his case, I was the one in love with him. After Lambert died, I begged Jacques to accept my love but he refused. I still carry a special love for him in my heart.

"Of course, there's the enduring love I have for your brother, Michael Cameron. It's a love that has stretched from the time we were young teenagers. When we were lost from each other and for all those years in between, not a night went by without my praying for him and for his soul.

"During our short time together this last summer, our love grew to depths I could not have imagined. When he died, my grief was so all encompassing that I thought I would die. In fact a part of me did die. But a part of me still loves him now and will until eternity.

"I think Cade knew this and accepted it. We were drawn together in our grief, but our love has given us a deeper and more mature relationship earned by our misfortunes."

Zach asked, "And what about Jamie Campbell?"

I sat in shocked silence. Then I whispered, "How did you know? Surely he would not have said anything to you about me. He has been a perfect gentleman under difficult circumstances. Our love was immediate and instinctive. We are both struggling to find a path we can walk with honor."

"Sara, no one told me anything. It's a misfortune of my profession to be adept at assessing people even when I don't wish to pry or to be involved. Thad told me about Jamie's story and how helpful you were to his healing.

"Jamie's feelings for you are deep, protective and nurturing; it's almost as though you have known each other before. I've never come across a relationship quite like it. I'm fascinated and humbled by it."

I wasn't prepared to talk about Jamie. "Zach, I'm exhausted. I can't think straight any more. Let's get on home. I want to sit in front of the fire and eat leftovers and pick out recipes for next week's Thanksgiving dinner. I need to try to be normal for a while, whatever that may mean."

"OK, let's go. I'll tuck you in for a nap on the way back. And Sara, the answer to both your questions is yes."

No one seemed concerned when we were late for supper. In fact, the homemade vegetable soup and wheat bread were better than anything we could have ordered in the city.

The little migrants had been right. When I wakened in the night, the wind whistling around the corners of the old house rattled the shutters. The last of the leaves careened against the windows, making tapping sounds as their petioles hit the glass. By morning, the strange reflection of brightness on the ceiling gave away the snow. Well, it was time, and I was ready to settle into my refuge for the winter.

Margot and Thad had been most welcoming. They wanted me to share in the months before the baby came. Margot's mother was dead and she needed someone to assure her that everything would be all right. After her many kindnesses to me, I wanted to do this one for her.

When I came downstairs, Tim and Zach were in the

kitchen tucking away big bowls of oatmeal. They were dressed for outdoors and I wondered what they were up to.

Tim's grin was biggest. "Ma'am, we'd like to borrow Black Beauty for the day. That's one sweet truck you got yesterday. I can't wait to try it out."

I wasn't planning to go anywhere so I said yes. "Well, if you get it covered with mud, you have to wash it before you bring it back. When I take it to town I don't want it to look like I've been out in the tulles 4-wheeling."

"Thanks Mrs. Cameron. We might be late. Don't wait supper for us."

The guys looked like guilty little boys so I smiled and told them good-bye. It would be nice to have a day at home alone with Margot. Maybe I could get one of the dresses cut out. We laid out the cookbooks again and made our choices for the Thanksgiving potluck, made shopping lists, and then settled down by the fire with big mugs of tea. I put several extra-nice logs on the fire and put up the screen. We decided the day called for a nap before lunch, a delicious luxury and one we both needed.

After lunch she put bread to rise while I cut out my green velvet dress. It was to have a high neckline and long sleeves and a full dancing skirt. It would be beautiful with the golden chains of the Cameron wedding necklace. Surely we would be celebrating his return by then.

About three o'clock, the clouds were lowering and bringing the day to an early close. I wanted to stretch my legs and work out a little, so I decided to walk down to Jamie's workshop to stretch and do some kata.

Thad said it was all right for me to be there and he had brought me a key. I put on black tights and a turtleneck top, tucked a scarf into my jacket pocket, and told Margot where I was going.

It felt good to be moving out at a swift pace and I made a vow to be better about exercising. When I slipped the key in the workshop door, I wondered what might be inside. I'd heard the story of Jamie's accident, and the death of his father in this place. Since the riots and the town's retaliation against Jamie and his business because he was my friend, there was little need for the equipment. There was no business. The place didn't even smell of wood shavings and varnish, only a little of machine oil and cold dampness.

It was not heated and I shivered as I flipped on the bank

of lights farthest from the door and made note of the size of the space I would have to work in. I decided to do some careful stretching first and then to begin the Russian kata Michael had taught me during the days before his death. The busy time just past had kept me from thinking about him, but now, I was overwhelmed with sadness as I finished the second sequence. My back was facing the far door and my eyes were closed as I worked.

Suddenly I felt the air move from left to right across my face. I decided to continue the routine and to ignore whomever it was for the time being. If he meant to do me harm, I was defenseless.

A few moments later, a soft-spoken voice asked me in Russian if he might join me. "I haven't seen these done for many years. Please allow me to share some instructions that I remember from my childhood."

I turned to answer in Russian, and was surprised and puzzled. Of all the people in Campbell's Point, he would have been my most unlikely guess. It was Casey Borders, dressed to work out. I hadn't realized how big a man he was or how physically attractive. I'm afraid several emotions must have been competing on my face.

His expression was one of cautious waiting. I had the feeling he was revealing a part of himself that could put him in great danger in the wrong circumstances. I had to make a quick decision about how I would handle the situation. I thought that in Campbell's Point, only Thad and Zach knew that I spoke Russian, and used it in my work.

Perhaps I could gain some information about his home by his idiomatic use of phrases. If he'd been gone a long time, it might be even more revealing.

I began my conversation in diplomatic Russian. "Of course I would be pleased to have you offer suggestions. Would you like to warm up first?"

It would give me a chance to watch him and to decide how to proceed. He nodded and began a disciplined warm-up routine of a kind I'd never seen before. Then he turned to me, bowed and spoke in Russian, "Shall we begin?"

The next hour was pure joy. Casey Borders was a fine teacher and he had some important corrections for the routines I'd learned third hand from Michael. His patience and gentle comments encouraged me to do my best for him. I hadn't felt that way since Jacques had worked with me on the night maneuvers.

We were finishing the seventh one when he turned to me and said, "Ma'am, you should stop now. I don't wish to wear you out, and I'm sure you have other obligations this evening. You have given me much pleasure. Perhaps we may work together again?"

He stepped forward, his tone serious and his manner more guarded. "It would be best if you didn't speak to anyone about our working out together. I would not wish to bring trouble to you."

He turned away and moved toward the far door. I was amazed at the fluidity and grace of his motion. He would have been almost impossible to see outdoors in the dark. Slipping on his coat, he disappeared out the door.

I spent a few minutes cooling down and stretching, and then left for Margot's warm kitchen and cheery fireplace.

My mind was busy trying to figure out what was going on in this tiny town. Margot said Mr. Borders appeared a week or so after Hank Greer was injured. He set up a modest office in the building across the street from Gary's Grill and began to help the people who had depended on Hank for their needs.

The one tremendous crisis came when the townspeople found out that he would be defending the "Crazy Lady", Mrs. Crosswick, when she returned from the sanitarium. He was a stranger and they didn't know where he stood on the basic issues tearing them apart as a community. I decided to ask Thad as soon as I could, if he knew where Borders came from and more important, why.

Margot had the luxury of a separate room for her sewing and other creative projects. When I got home, I gravitated there to work on my dress and to allow the Penards some privacy for their evening by the fire.

The sewing machine could be left up and pieces of material put out on the bed in the order they would be sown together. I was still working when the men returned with my truck. I didn't even go to find out where they'd been.

Soon I heard the washing machine start and they were in the kitchen, still in some kind of noisy, male-bonding mode. I'd had enough of men for a while and decided to go off to bed without going to the fireside to say goodnight.

After a long, hot shower, I still couldn't seem to get warm. I wrapped a blanket around my shoulders and collapsed to my knees by the side of my bed. I began to pray; for Anna's soul and for Cade and the success of the mission, for my beloved Michael and for my little town of Campbell's Point with all her problems and sadness.

Suddenly, I sensed someone standing behind me. His presence was infinitely comforting. I turned to find Jamie looking down at me. I rose and went into the shelter of his arms as he whispered, "Zach is giving Tim and Tricia a ride to the farm and then he promised to wash the truck. I told them I'd walk home. Sara, we need to talk.

"Slip into some clothes and we'll sit by the fire. I think Thad and Margot have gone to bed and we'll have some privacy. If we don't finish this evening, I promise to come back for you tomorrow and we'll go up to the farm."

We were in no hurry. Our conversation was gentle and filled with comfort. We talked about my loss of Michael and my marriage to Cade. He told me of his sadness over his friend Jenny Cameron's death, and then of his anger and grief when he was jilted by my daughter so soon afterwards.

No one had told him that she was not my real daughter. He was in class in Pittsburgh when she and Barney came to tell Yvette goodbye and he had missed seeing them. I shared the complicated story with him.

He took my hand as we sat by the fire. "I'm sorry about the circumstances of your real daughter's death. How cruel for all of us that we didn't know the truth. I had no idea that Jenny searched and found the woman she believed was your daughter to make her beloved Uncle Michael and you happy, not to cause you grief."

He got up from the couch to stretch. His look of compassion took my breath away. "What about you, dearest Sara? You're alone again, since Cade is dead. What are you going to do now?"

My God! What was I going to do? Jamie had been through hell because of me already. Was he trying to tell me that he wanted me now that I was free?

For my own safety, I didn't dare tell him that I believed Cade was still alive. But the cruelty of not telling him would be devastating to us both. I tried to think of the right thing to say, not lying but not revealing the truth about my situation or any information that would jeopardize the security of the Finnish mission or its people.

"Jamie, I don't know what I'm going to do. I've been given a safe haven for a few months, at least until Margot comes to term. Right now I can't think any farther ahead. I'm exhausted and find myself crying a great deal. I need rest and the comfort of my friends."

He sat back down beside me. "If you promise you'll save time to go to the farm tomorrow, I'll let you get back to your night's rest. I have some plans to discuss with you because I know you'll help me make the right decision. I'm glad you're back. You're good for my soul and I need your common sense and gentleness right now."

When he took my hands in his, I could feel his anguish and I began to share his pain, whatever its cause might be.

"Good night, Dear One. Sleep well."

I heard the front door close. I stepped to the upper window to watch Jamie walk down the street toward his house. It must surely be a lonely and unhappy place after all the happenings of these last months. I was ready to undress and return to bed when I glanced out to see Zach coming back with the truck. He wasn't dawdling. In fact he was moving fast. He didn't stop to take off his coat as he came up the stairs two at a time and rapped on my door.

He seemed surprised to find me fully dressed. "Are you all right? When Thad called a few minutes ago on the cell phone, he was fit to be tied. The security tapes from this afternoon had pictures of you working out alone at Jamie's place. And then someone came in on you. Why did you keep working, with a stranger at your back? You're crazy, Sara."

"Sometimes it's stupidity and not courage driving my survival instincts. However, although there were some interesting surprises, it was someone whom I had met and had no reason to fear."

Now Zach shrugged his shoulders. "Thad told me Borders spends a lot of time in there. He carries a cell phone to answer his business calls. What did you two talk about?"

"There was no chit-chat. We were discussing the moves in the exercises we were doing. He's a fine instructor. I wonder what he did before he became a lawyer."

In the silence of the big house, we heard Thad come out of the office and head up the stairs. He would have known Zach was back since he'd made such a racket.

He didn't waste any time in pleasantries either. "The photos just came in on the computer from Mountain Home. There were several sets of the six men, one set in military uniform. One of the six is the man we know as Casey Borders."

Zach let out a whistle. "Damn! How far is it to the

nearest border crossing? I'm sure he'll head for Canada since Yvette told me he speaks French."

He turned to me and grabbed my shoulder. "This is no time for fun and games, Sara. Did he say anything that would help us know where he's going?"

I pulled away from him, gasping in pain. "No, he didn't."

Never would I reveal anything about this apparently marked man. He'd helped to save Millie Greer and I had a feeling he wanted to be free of the trap he was enmeshed in, to have peace and gentleness in his life, whatever small amount of it was left.

Why he came to the workshop and what alerted him to his imminent danger, I didn't know, but I knew his chances of survival were shrinking by the minute. I wasn't going to be responsible for taking any of his last few hours of life away. Besides, he might escape.

I rubbed my aching shoulder and turned to Thad. "Am I allowed to see the other portraits? Perhaps there are others at Mountain Home that I might recognize."

We went down to the office and I waited while Thad sent out the warrant for Casey Borders, with a picture to put all the Canadian border stations on alert. He sent a report to General Ryan and then called up the file with the pictures from Finland. I was thankful that they were almost through with their assignment.

I asked Thad, "How many others are they searching for?"

"General Ryan said a while ago there were two they didn't recognize. He knew Casey Borders as Chuck Binder. He's a top military lawyer who usually worked to defend military personnel when they were accused of crimes on leave. He was on a case when he left Mountain Home during the summer while you were there. That's why you didn't recognize him here in town. General Ryan can't believe Binder is a traitor."

I whispered, "Could these men be merely lovers in Wilhelmina's stable and not Russian spies?"

Thad looked at me with compassion. "No, they sent several other sets of portraits including a series of the men in uniform and the blackmail ones. Borders and the two others were in full Russian regalia including medals and swords; younger but unmistakable."

I sighed and sat down beside him at the computer. "Let me see the other two Russians."

He showed me only the pictures I needed to see, skipping

the ones of the American men, one of whom I had loved and trusted and one of whom was the Alex in Michael's note. I was not told the third man's identity.

I gasped as the first alleged Russian spy came on the screen. I'd dealt with this man almost every day in the ladies' gym. He took care of the swimming lessons for the children and wives and watched over the intramurals and games in the gym. He was in charge of the weight rooms and exercise classes.

General Ryan might never have had reason to deal with him. What a perfect place to gather information, since the military wives and kids would talk to each other about the comings and goings of their husbands and fathers. I gave Thad the information and his name.

The second picture took me longer. Finally, I recognized his eyes and ears from someplace quite recent. Through half-closed eyes, his hair blurred into a green cap and his lower face was covered with a mask. He was one of the anesthetists from sickbay, the one present when I was taken from the tarmac of the landing strip and put under sedation for several days. I gave his description and where he worked to Thad. I had no idea what his name was. The third portrait on the screen was of Casey Borders. It was unmistakable.

The pictures of the three Russians haunted me. I went to make some hot chocolate for us while Thad contacted General Ryan again. The return message said they both lived on base and had worked that day. The men would be apprehended at once.

It was Casey Borders I feared for. He would not survive the night. I'd given him an extra few hours by not reporting our Russian conversation, but it would not be enough.

The phone rang at three o'clock. Casey Borders had been stopped by Canadian authorities and denied entrance on a paperwork infraction. They followed him when he turned around at the border crossing, and watched as he tried to go across on foot several miles away in a wooded area. He was shot as he tried to escape the dogs sent after him.

The final message at four o'clock was from General Ryan, reporting that the other two men were in custody on the base. He included a message for me. It was a generous one, considering the way I had treated him.

Mrs. Cameron,

I want you to know how many lives will be saved because of your loyalty to duty. Thank you. The mission is finished. The operatives will be home as soon as possible.

General Ryan

I turned away from the computer and glanced at Zach. His look was guarded and without joy. I left the room in tears.

CHAPTER NINE

It was still dark as I drifted in and out of restless dreams. As always, I didn't know what triggered the gut-wrenching nightmares, but one engulfed me now. Margot must have been right outside my door. She came and held me as I sobbed in her arms.

"Jamie thought you might need me this morning," she whispered. "He called a few minutes ago to ask me to come and sit with you. Thad and Zach have already gone to the store but they started our morning fire. Come down and we'll sit and enjoy it after I fix you some milk toast." Her gentle, lilting French was soothing to my heart, as we sat in the warmth of the kitchen, with bowls of toast and hot milk.

I turned to her as we finished. "Is Jamie all right? He's had as many bad things in his life these past few months as I have, and I feel responsible for most of them. Knowing how close a friend he was to the Greers, it must have been terrible for him to watch Hank die and then to see Millie in her most recent travail."

Margot shook her head. "He's in survival mode. He's trying hard, but his heart is broken by what's happened in Campbell's Point. His family was a part of this town for many generations too."

"How do you think it will end for the town?"

She stepped to the sink with our empty bowls and shook her head again. "I really don't know, Sara. It won't be easy, but Thad and I are not going to leave and Yvette has promised us she will stay. She's found a home and her peace here too." Margot smiled now. "That is, unless the blooming romance with Zachary Cameron persuades her to go away with him."

"What?"

"Thad told me Zach is entranced by her. He's been going downtown at four in the morning to be with her before the town's day begins. He's going to help her with the turkeys

63

for the holiday feast."

"Zach is a good man. I can't think of a nicer, more gentle and generous man and I think he's in need of a woman now; a permanent one to complete his life. Perhaps he could leave the military and start some kind of practice here. I think he's a psychiatrist but I'll bet he knows how to bind up broken bones and dole out flu shots too."

We went to the living room to sit in front of the crackling fire. I was exhausted from my shortened night. I fell asleep in the warm room, as Margot worked on her knitting.

When Thad came home for lunch, Jamie and Zach were both with him. Margot must have been warned because the table was set for five. It was a lovely meal, with hot chicken soup and dumplings and big bowls of peaches. The men went off to the library while we cleaned up.

Jamie came into the kitchen as we finished our work. Thad had gone back to work and the house was quiet.

"Where's Zach?" I asked him.

"He went down to my place to work out for an hour or so. He asked me to stay, so we'll finish our last night's visit here, if that's OK."

"Would you like a mug of tea, Jamie?" As I turned to him, Margot went down the hall. I hoped she would rest a bit and dream happy baby dreams.

Jamie accepted the mug I gave him and we sat down at the table. His voice was gentle and full of concern. "How are you, Sara? I've been very concerned about you since you made the trip to Dodie's. It must have been exhausting and filled with difficult memories."

I sighed. "I feel as if I've been dragged by my heels face down through the main street of Campbell's Point. I'm so exhausted. Will there ever be an end to all this?"

Jamie shook his head. "I wish I knew. I do know that I couldn't have survived without the Penards and the others who believed in me even when things were at their worst.

"The hardest thing for me during this time though, was to have to come to terms with the truth about my damaged hand. Modern medicine and I were supposed to produce some miracle to make everything right again. Now, I've had to admit that a doctor, especially this one, isn't God!

"To make things worse, my first semester in Music Therapy has been a disaster. With all the distractions, I don't know if I'll even pass the first set of final exams. What scares me and disappoints me most, is that I don't care.

"I dreamed about it for so long and I burned a lot of bridges in the medical community. I'm torn between guilt and anger. The music therapy curriculum and practice is so dominated by rules and regulations, even worse than general medicine.

"I'm at loggerheads with my professors all the time about how things should be done. I'm too old to kneel at the feet of teachers who don't even know the meaning of the word handicap, let alone have any feeling for the students and clients they are supposed to be helping. I'm trying to get up the courage to quit."

We sat in gentle silence as I thought about his situation. I had no advice, only compassion for his plight. "What will you do instead, Jamie?"

"Well, something has been offered to me and I'm inclined to take it. Doc Pete's wife Laura has been begging him to take a break and go on an extended cruise for three months. He's worked for years without a vacation and they aren't getting any younger. He's asked me if I'd consider looking after things here while he's gone. I'd like to stay in Campbell's Point and be a part of this town, like my father and grandfather and his kin. I might need a second person to cover the things I can't do physically, maybe a physician's assistant. It would give me a chance to decide whether I'm willing to be a backwoods GP."

"You can't really call it that when you're less than an hour from Pittsburgh. What about another doctor, someone who needs a break and a breather in his life? What about Doctor Cameron?"

"Doesn't he work for the military?"

"Yes, but on contract. They need breaks too and I think he might be a person to consider. Some new interests in town might entice him to stay a while."

Jamie smiled. "You mean Yvette?"

"Margot hinted as much, earlier today."

He got up from his place and stretched. "Let's go see if Margot is awake. I'd like to sit by the fire before I go to see Millie."

I reached for his arm. "How is she, Jamie? When may I go to see her? Why are you so protective of her?"

Jamie's expression was guarded. "It isn't Millie we're protecting, Sara, it's you."

"I don't understand. Why are you protecting me?"

He motioned to me to sit down at the table. "How much

do you know about Zach?"

"Not very much at all except that he saved my life and he was assigned to help Tim drive across country to Pennsylvania. He's apparently going to stay a while here, though I'm not sure why."

"Zach told me that when he was at your bedside after the airfield rescue and spent several days with all your files, he recognized the classic symptoms of Post Traumatic Stress Disorder, but more important, he found some clues about their cause. When he spoke to General Ryan about it, they decided on a course of action.

"Doctor Cameron is a psychiatrist trained in this area. He usually treats returning prisoners of war. One important key in your specific case is the discovery of the perpetrator. He's working on that question now and when the results come back, we should have some answers.

"You must make the decision about whether you want to be helped. You're the person who must go through whatever treatment he chooses. He's discussed it in detail with me and has asked me to be present and to help.

"If we're successful, the terrifying nightmares should stop. You'll be able to gain perspective and some measure of joy. I love you too much to stand by and watch you suffer any more. I hope you'll agree to allow us to work with you."

Just as we finished our conversation, Zach came bounding in the door. His arms were full of bundles and he was grinning from ear to ear.

"I haven't had so much fun in years. I remember as a kid that everyone in town joined together for a Thanksgiving celebration." He sighed, "Those were simpler times weren't they?" He took off up the stairs to drop the bags in his room.

Jamie smiled. "Well, there goes Margot's nap. Let's go see if there's anything we can do to help her, and then maybe we can sneak away for a walk. They're forecasting rain and then snow for tonight."

"How deep? What I'd really like to do is go out to the Forester farm to visit my favorite children. I promised I would begin *The Secret Garden* the next time I came and I brought a wonderful copy from Idaho with the original illustrations. Let's see if Zach might remember where he packed it."

He told us which color crate to look in, and we found the book on the first try. I squirmed just a little at having to ask permission to leave town. I was surprised at his answer when we returned to his room. "Yes, of course you may go. Black Beauty hauls three with comfort, may I join you?"

While I changed into my favorite story-reading jumper, Jamie called to let Kylie Lou know that we were coming and when he asked if we could bring something with us to share for supper, she suggested a box of apples.

I decided to let Zach drive and Jamie helped me into the middle seat before he climbed in. I tucked the book deep into a pocket of my cloak and found my fur-lined gloves from our recent trip across country. They reminded me of how many things had happened in such a short time.

I remembered what Jamie had said earlier and spoke to both men. "My answer is thank you, and yes, I want to be helped. I promise to do everything within my power to cooperate. Now, while we wait for whatever must happen, let's go and be children again."

It was a magical evening. The children were looking forward to the long holiday. They were dressed in their warm play clothes and after chores and supper, we settled in to read to one another. I was concerned about the very first part, when little Mary is made an orphan, but with a good bit of explanation, the grownups kept things in perspective. You needed the contrast of what kind of life she came from and what she was like in India to appreciate how much she changed with the help of Dickon and all the animals.

Everyone was asked to read a little, grownups and children alike. I was pleased with Abe and Kylie Lou's progress and proud too of Tim and Tricia who'd carried on in my absence to help her parents with their reading skills. Tim said the next GED exam was a few days after Christmas, and he hoped to take it then. He was looking straight at Tricia when he promised it because it was his goal to achieve it before he asked for her hand in marriage.

Next, Abe took down the Bible and we settled in to hear the story of Samuel being called by the Lord. The evening was good for us all, especially Zach, who seemed to wink back tears several times as he held little Lane Crosswick on his lap. I wondered if he might have lost a girl child sometime in his past.

The weather held off until we got back to town. The first rattles of sleet drummed on the street as we pulled into Jamie's drive. I smiled down at him from the seat of the truck.

"It's been a good day for kin, Jamie. Thank you. Let me know how your plans develop. We'll see you tomorrow."

He looked up with a gentle smile. "I'll be over to get you after lunch, Sara. I think it's time you went to visit Millie Greer."

Most of the older Victorian homes clustered together at the south end of Main Street in Campbell's Point. Thad's house was the last one in the row. He'd lived there alone, while he built up his business and waited for Margot to be free to marry him.

She was a servant and companion for Millie Greer's handicapped daughter until her death several years before. Margot had pleaded with Thad and Jamie to let her help with Millie's care, but the men said they didn't think it was wise or best for her own health. I didn't know what I would find at Millie's bedside, but I wanted to help her if I could.

Doc Pete's house was in the next block toward town and Jamie came to walk me down. I was surprised when Zach came out of the library to join us as we left the house. He took my hand as he said, "Tim Campbell told us a little about how you helped with Jacques Grayson and I trust you with Millie. Just promise you'll let us know if and when you need us."

We made a detour and went down the street to Millie's garden. The gaping hole where her house had stood was surrounded with the stark blocks of the stone foundation. Patches of snow were scattered about the yard and gardens, but I remembered the location of the lavender in the herb garden. I brushed aside the crystalline clots from last night's sleet and broke off a branch. Wrapping them in a bit of damp paper towel, I slipped them into a small bag.

When we reached Millie's room, the men put their chairs by her door. I thought I was prepared, especially after the trauma of Jacques' struggle for recovery, but this was entirely different. Instead of the miasma of jungle filth and illness, I was confronted with terrifying, total emptiness.

Millie was no longer present in the room, but far away, somewhere in her own protected world. I had to look to see if she were breathing, to believe that she was alive. I felt a tremendous need to call her back into her body, the body betrayed with such violence. I didn't look at her physical injuries; they were somehow secondary to the desperate need to reunite her body with her mind, soul and spirit.

I knelt and began with the Lord's Prayer. It is the last thing people lose on their death journey, and the first one regained in recovery, if it is to be. I hoped she could hear me even if she couldn't tell me so.

Then I rose, went to the window and opened it for a moment, to let in the cold crisp air.

"Millie? It's Sara. I've come to stay with you a while, to sing, and to tell stories about the world outside. It's a glorious, sunny, winter day. The sky is bright and clear; the ethereal blue of the forget-me-nots in your summer garden.

"There are tiny chickadees hopping on the snowy ground picking at the seeds thrown down by the bossy cardinals who like only sunflowers. The feeder is emptying fast but someone has come from the cottage to fill it.

"It's Tricia Forester, who comes each day to make sure your dear cardinals are being fed. She's used the snow shovel to clear a path to the feeder. Her work has uncovered the corner of a lavender bush and broken off a stem."

I leaned down to Millie and put the lavender branch near her face, sending the fresh and honest scent into the air as I crushed the sturdy leaves with my thumb.

"There's music coming from the open door of the cottage. I wonder what it could be."

I was trying frantically to think of a simple song, when I heard from the hallway, the gentle sounds of "Frère Jacques". Jamie came into the room along with Zach and the three of us sang the children's round for several minutes.

I turned to Jamie. "Would you sing one of your songs to her while I take a break?" I stepped to the door with Zach while Jamie sat by her bedside. He began one of the lovely songs he'd sung for me in St. Louis when I was hospitalized after I was attacked.

Then I returned with my Psalm book and began to read a few of the songs of praise and thanksgiving. After a while, I stepped to the door and began to sing the children's duet from Hansel and Gretel. Jamie joined me and we sang about the guardian angels who would protect her from harm. As we knelt by her bed, I whispered, "Dearest Millie, we love you so much. Please trust us and come back. We promise to guard you and to keep you safe."

I left the curtain open in her room and tucked the blanket around her shoulders. "I'll come to see you again

Jeanne Anderegg

soon, Millie. Rest now My Dear and dream of your jaunty cardinals, calling, and flitting from branch to branch. They're waiting for you to come out to them."

I stood for a moment looking down at her bruised body, and said one last prayer for her recovery.

The three of us decided to walk on downtown. I was in desperate need of exercise to work off the tension of the last few days. I trembled as I realized how dangerous it had been for me to be in Jamie's workshop alone.

We would never know now, why Mr. Borders made the visit while I was there. Was it accidental or intentional, or even whether he had come to do me harm and then changed his mind.

For some reason, the death of Casey Borders continued to affect me in a deep and personal way. It had always been difficult for me to understand the need to kill people without allowing them a chance to defend themselves and their apparent actions. I wondered how many times the wrong people were killed, or were framed, as Antonio Andretti had been.

Now, I was weary to the depths of my being. Whether my nightmares were caused by the trauma of my work or by the problems in my personal life, I didn't know. What lay ahead in working with Zach would be a difficult episode in my life, but a needed one.

The men drifted into Gary's for coffee and pie while I went across the street to the building I'd named the Yellow Mall because of the wonderful yellow and white-striped awnings along the front windows.

An hour later, I went into Gary's to see if they were still there. This time my arms were full of wonderful, lumpy packages. I had found sock yarn for making Christmas presents and some yarn to make a gift for Margot's baby.

"Are you guy's ready to head back or shall I leave you to visit and find out the community news?"

Zach got up from the booth. "We're ready to go. Let's use the back door."

As we went through the back hall beside the kitchen, he stopped by to whisper into Yvette's ear, as she bent over a huge pot of soup. Her smile hinted at a meeting later on. Gary was busy grilling steaks and didn't see the exchange. I wondered if he knew about the budding romance.

As we walked back to Thad's, the men told me they would like to begin my sessions. One of the most important

70

first steps was a series of writing exercises. They had chosen one of the small bedrooms on the second floor for our workroom. There was a window looking out over the back garden. A lovely tulip tree grew close to the house. Its branches almost reached the window. I could imagine the glorious orange and yellow blossoms that would decorate and celebrate the coming of summer next year.

We settled into comfortable chairs while Zach explained what we were going to try to accomplish and how it would be done.

"Sara, you've spent your professional life as a research scientist. I'm sure you want to know what we're doing and why and how it all works. I'm going to ask you to suspend your curiosity, because these techniques work on a different level than you're used to. We'll have better results if you can manage to do this."

I nodded assent as he explained what he wanted me to do first. When the task was finished, I had begun the new avenue to my healing.

Jamie and I returned to spend the evening with Millie while Doc Pete and Laura had an evening out. We spent some time just sitting quietly with her. I was holding her hand and touching her more often now but there had been no response.

I decided to sing a lullaby. I sat on the edge of Millie's bed, draped a small blanket around her and lifted her onto my lap. I sang, and rocked her gently. In a few minutes, I felt her move closer to me. A tiny noise came from deep inside her, a humming that vibrated on my breast. She wept as she whispered, "Mama? Mama? ... He hurt me so."

I continued to hold her and stroke her as I sang the song again. I looked up at Jamie as he whispered, "Thank God, Sara. I think she'll make it now."

CHAPTER TEN

Jamie came by to pick me up next morning after Mass and we stopped by Millie's garden to find some things to take to her. I used the small trowel I'd borrowed from Thad's garage and put a few scoops of damp earth into a small bag. Then I clipped some sprigs of rosemary, thyme and sage. We went to sit with Millie while the Hamiltons went to church. Doc Pete took Jamie aside to give him the morning report.

He looked as if he might have had a full night's sleep, after many days and nights of worrying and watching over Millie's frail body. She'd taken a few swallows of liquid and the color of her skin was the faintest of soft pink. She hadn't opened her eyes but had said a few more words.

We settled down with her. As I spoke to her and began the Lord's Prayer, Millie began to speak the words with me. I went slowly and waited for her to put the words together. At the end, she whispered, "Amen", and a hint of a smile flickered across her face.

It was time for a story and I opened the curtains wider to let a small zephyr of cool breeze from the window caress her cheek.

"Millie, I've brought the morning report from the Secret Garden to share with you. It's sunny now, and the neighbors are coming back from church with their coats slung over their arms. We are to have a lovely day and then tonight the weatherman says it will turn cold and cloudy as a new front comes through. It's supposed to bring ice and sleet and bad driving conditions.

Everyone is trying to get their business done so that they can get home safely before the storm. The old man next door is carrying in firewood to fill up his woodbin and the little children on the other side are whizzing up and down the sidewalk on their tricycles making wonderful, clanging sounds and squeals of joy.

"The cardinals are busy tucking away sunflower seeds as

fast as they can get them hulled. There are pieces of shell flying in every direction. They stop only long enough to scold the latecomers for trying to take cuts at the feeder.

"Oh, look. There's Tricia coming to fill the feeders. She only needs her boots for the muddy path. The snow is all gone now and the outlines of the winter garden are clear. The yellow witch hazel flowers glitter like jewels against the dark brown of the turned earth. In the rose garden, the rose hips are like a wonderful necklace of bright orange beads flung over the still green leaves of the bushes."

I took out the bag of earth from my jacket pocket and opened it near her face. "Can you smell the damp earth warming in today's sun? The herb garden is tucked away for the winter but the plants aren't frozen yet. There will be rosemary, thyme and sage for the Thanksgiving turkey."

I put the herbs into Millie's hand and raised it to her nose. There was the tiniest smile on her face.

"I can see in my mind's eye, all the wonderful crocuses and snowdrops, daffodils and tulips busy making roots and forming their flowers; just waiting to spring from the earth in a few months. We'll go out to sit in your beautiful garden and watch the cardinals doing their springtime antics. The sun will be soft and warm on your face and you can rest, dressed in just a sweater and take a little nap."

There was a smile on Millie's face as she spoke. "Do you think so, Sara? How nice it sounds. I need to rest now."

I was facing the window and didn't know that Zach was in the house. He and Jamie had entered the room from the hallway. Jamie stepped to Millie's bed, bent down and whispered, "Sleep well, Dear One, we all love you very much."

Zach put his arm around my shoulders. "Thank you, Sara. You continue to be a miracle worker. It's time to head back to Penards'; I'm supposed to tell you dinner's ready."

Laura slipped in to sit with Millie as we prepared to leave. When we got to the sidewalk, I looked up with a mischievous grin. "Race you back, guys."

I headed off up the middle of the street at a dead run. We were panting and laughing as we stumbled up the porch steps, ending in a tangle of arms and legs. Margot and Thad came out to check on the commotion and knew Millie must be getting better by the minute.

In the afternoon, we returned to the little room to work. My assignment the first day had been to make a list of the most traumatic happenings in my life and to put them in order from least bad to worst. This day I was to choose one and to write about it for about thirty minutes, disclosing thoughts and feelings about the event as though I were talking with a trusted friend.

It was the first time I'd ever tried to talk about some of the things. Because of my situation in my marriage with Henri Lambert, when I was not allowed to show any anger or fear or feelings, I suffered my worst injuries in my mind. There had been no one to confide in or to receive help from.

My tears were ones of relief as I finished the exercise. I stood up from the desk and stretched. "Would either of you gentlemen have time for a walk? I feel like I'm suffocating. I need to get some oxygen into my system again."

Although Jamie didn't have classes during Thanksgiving week, he did have a paper to finish, so Zach was my designated companion. Jamie excused himself and headed toward home while we took off in the opposite direction toward the end of the street. A path meandered beyond the barricade and in the last moments before the next storm, we headed out on an exploring adventure.

The sunshine was gone. A tumble of gray, scudding clouds was moving fast, piling up against the higher hills. Our coats were not warm enough and we decided the better part of valor was to get on home. The thought of a brisk, blazing fire encouraged us to jog back into town. Thad and Margot were sitting snuggled up together on the couch and seemed glad to see us as we collapsed on the floor, tossing off coats and shoes like little children coming in from play.

Zach stayed a few minutes to warm up and then excused himself to finish some paperwork. I curled up in front of the fire, my coat tucked under my head and a quilt from the couch pulled up around me. I fell asleep to the murmurings of Margot and Thad as they talked abut their hopes and dreams for their little one. When I wakened, Zach had gone downtown to supper and it was snowing in earnest.

Zach was welcome to use Black Beauty whenever he needed her. He'd taken the truck early this morning for a run into Pittsburgh. When he got back, I'd get a report on how well the truck performed in the snow. The note on the kitchen table said he'd be back by early afternoon. I was glad for a day of relative rest and went to the sewing room to work on my Christmas-green dress.

After a few hours, I got two pieces sewn together wrong and realized I needed a break. Actually, I was drawn to the little upstairs room. I was anxious to continue the exercises and surely I didn't need the men there while I wrote.

As I settled in at the desk and my writing proceeded, I became more and more upset. I could see where the line of thought was leading and I was terrified by the conclusion.

Suddenly, I couldn't breathe. I was struggling with a panic attack so violent that I grabbed a coverlet and wrapped it tightly around me. Then I stumbled to a protected corner behind one of the big chairs and collapsed. My body wouldn't stop trembling. I whimpered and then struggled to stop the gut-wrenching sobs of terror. I stuffed the corner of the coverlet into my mouth to muffle my cries.

I could hear someone coming up the stairs two at a time. It was Thad, home for lunch. As he ran down the hall toward the room, I heard him call back down, "Margot, call Jamie and get him here fast. I think he's at home studying."

Thad pulled the chair away from the wall and knelt down beside me. He didn't touch me but he began to speak to me in French. The soothing cadence reached deep into my heart. I was still cowering, my face turned to the corner and my eyes tightly shut, trembling and whimpering like a small child when Jamie got there.

He said, "She'll need a cold wet towel for her face and a mug of hot tea with lots of sugar and milk."

I opened my eyes as he turned me toward him. His body language said he was very angry. When Thad was gone he shut the door and really let me have it.

"For God's sake, Sara. How many degrees does it take to learn how to follow orders? We told you not to do this by yourself. I can even guess which one you were working on. You're a total, stupid idiot and I'm terrified for your safety. We were hoping to get you through this without having to send you away."

I was up in one motion, the coverlet forgotten as it slipped from my shoulders. I crouched to face him, my fists clenched and my voice low and menacing.

"What did you say? How dare you imply that I'm crazy? You're not going to send me anywhere. Get out of here ... Get out of here, now!"

My fists were clenched in anger as I swung them at him. I was looking for something to throw. The only thing moveable was the jar of lavender branches and blooming witch hazel that I'd brought from Millie's garden. It was full of stinky, slimy water. I screamed in anger as I hurled it at Jamie, just as Zach stepped in the door. They both ducked and I heard the glass shatter on the wall outside the bedroom. I was so angry that I was growling as I moved in a half-crouch to circle the men. I picked up the straight chair to attack them, when Zach held out his hand.

"That's enough, Sara. Give me the chair."

He took it from me and replaced it by the desk. "My Dear Sara, you get an F for following orders and an A+ for anger. Do you realize what you just did?"

I stood, feet planted, my body ready to fight. What was he getting at? My mind struggled to process thoughts while the adrenaline of anger swirled through my body and then began to dissipate. I turned away from them and unclenched my fists. My body began to relax, and I didn't cry.

It was deathly quiet in the tiny room. They waited as I turned back to them and reached out in supplication.

"Please forgive me. Please don't abandon me now."

I heard Zach whisper, "God! I hope Cade gets home soon. His woman has suffered enough."

I moved to stand in front of him and looked into his eyes.

"We both know Cade's dead. When I told you I believed he was alive, it was only cruel hope. Sometime I must ask Johnson why he didn't put the locket in the box and why he sent the message to me. Even your prayers were a set up. Cade is dead. He won't be coming back. Not ever."

Zach chose not to give me a direct answer. "Go get your workout clothes on, Sara. We're going down to the shop to work until we both drop in our tracks. I'll meet you at the door downstairs in five minutes."

There was a deadly earnestness as we hurried down the street with Jamie. He needed to get back to his paper and we were in desperate need of physical work.

Jamie came into the metal building with us and turned on the heat. It seemed even colder inside, dark and gloomy and the floor radiated cold.

I had a wave of regret as I remembered the recent afternoon I'd spent with Casey Borders, working together with such gentleness and joy. Now he was dead, because of Wilhelmina Porter. I didn't know if I could go into her house before it was disposed of. How many lives had been shattered by her lust and greed? It made me ashamed to be a woman.

I shook the ruminations from my brain and settled down to stretch. I'd never seen Zachary Cameron in fighting mode and I was surprised at how well-trained his body was for someone who sat at a desk every day as a psychiatrist; or did he? He'd said that part of his job was to save fair damsels in distress. I guess it could fit many job descriptions.

We settled in to spar and I knew at once that he was no civilian. I was fascinated when I figured out what he was doing. He knew from my files what sort of training I'd been given. He went through the moves and kata with deliberate and calm intention.

He encouraged me to fight harder and with more resolve. The more force I used, the more he adjusted, to act the foil. He never was the aggressor. Instead, he was giving me a chance to work out my fear and anger with a person I trusted. At the end of an hour, he said, "It's time for a break. I wonder if the water's turned on in here."

We searched and found a bathroom tucked into a corner by the front door. We let the water run until it turned from brown to orange to pale yellow. There was a rack with large paper cups and I drew one full for Zach. As I handed it to him, I whispered, "Thanks."

I drank my own water and we returned to work.

He asked, "Had enough, Sara?"

I shook my head. "No, I have some unfinished business to take care of now."

This time there was no rhythm or pattern, only an increasing feeling of anger and violence against fate, and against men. Zach kept in balance with my motions and whispered encouragement as I struck out against him.

I knew it wasn't about him. Instead, it was about all the times I'd been punished for standing up for myself, or for pleading innocence and not being believed. It was about being attacked by an unknown assailant who left me with a broken body and spirit.

It was about the unfairness of finding Michael and then losing him again, of finding out too late about Andretti's love for me, and then losing Cade, the last stabilizing force in my life. The litany of life review had no redeeming features and left me filled with anger, misery and grief. I fought until I collapsed in total exhaustion.

Then from somewhere, a blessed feeling of peace came to

surround me. I said to Zach, "I'm glad I trusted you, Zachary Cameron. Thank you from the depths of my heart."

I was exhausted and very hollow. "I'm starving. Do you suppose it's too late for lunch at Gary's?"

He sighed in relief. "Let's sneak in the back door to the kitchen. I'll bet Yvette would cook us a couple of steaks."

It was almost dark when we got back to Penards'. Zach went to clean up and change and slipped out again. I expect he and Yvette would have their evening together.

I smiled at Margot. "I have some stitching to take out. If you'll excuse me I'll get at it."

I didn't get very far before I had to crawl into bed. I slept so hard I didn't waken until the smell of Thad's early morning coffee announced a new day.

The new day was not attractive. A low ground fog turned the town into a roily confusion of shadows and sounds without substance. It reminded me of the old movie sets in London, with the fog obscuring all the evil imaginable. However, my mood was far from matching the weather. I came down to join Margot and Thad at breakfast. I knew not to ask about Zach's whereabouts. Undoubtedly he was down at Gary's keeping company with Yvette as she made the morning rolls and started breakfast for the grill's daily visitors.

We were finishing up breakfast when the phone rang. It was much too early to be a social call. When Thad picked it up, he listened for a minute and then said, "Let me go in the other room where I have my accounts. Hang on."

I was ready to work on my sewing project so I followed Thad down the hall. I never eavesdrop. For some reason, though, I found myself slowing down as I passed the library door. Something about the way Thad had answered the phone made me extra vigilant. I had the feeling he wanted to talk without the rest of us hearing the conversation.

I stood rooted in place in front of the door as I heard Thad say, "For God's sake, Cade. We've been worried sick since Johnson said you were dead. I didn't want to believe it was true. The Italian police report said they found only one body, Anna's, and I could still hope. Where are you, man?"

After a long pause he continued. "What do you want me to tell her? OK. We'll see you when you get here."

I hurried down the hall and stepped into the sewing room just before Thad came out of the library. I couldn't believe what I'd overheard. Now I must pretend I didn't know.

Jamie came by about ten and asked me to come with him to visit Millie. I left a message for Zach. I wanted to make a quick trip into Pittsburgh as close to twelve as he could make it. He would want to come, and I would need him if things went according to plan.

Millie was sitting up in a chair eating breakfast when we got there. Music was coming from a small player by her bed, a joyful performance of Mendelssohn's Concerto for two pianos, written when he was still young. It was a perfect statement of new beginnings for someone we all loved.

Jamie had brought her a single pink rose, The scent of summer wafted about her room as he leaned down to touch her cheek. So that was how this story might play out. Jamie, Jenny, Millie and Hank had grown up together in Campbell's Point and had been friends since childhood. Now, the two remaining friends were in deep need of each other.

Laura and Doc Pete came in later and we discussed with Millie what she might like to do about her living arrangements. She understood what had happened to her big house. Her plan was reasonable. She wanted to move into The Cottage so that her beloved gardens and her birds could surround her. Perhaps even before the Hamiltons left on their trip, she would be well enough to move in.

She was tucking away creamy, scrambled eggs, and toast covered with strawberry jam. She looked up. The gaze from her dark amber eyes was for Jamie alone, as she asked, "Would you build me a new home, Jamie? We'll use the foundation stones from the old place but not the same site. We'll bulldoze all the old past into the basement hole and cover it over. The landscaped area will honor the Greer family and begin the healing. I'm going to be all right now. Will you be a part of my life?"

He knelt down to take her hand. "Yes. I'll build your home, and we'll live there in peace. Millie, will you marry me?"

She smiled as she answered, "Of course, Jamie. Now, I'd like to get up and take my first steps. I'm going to need stamina when we start planning and building, and, I want to go to the Thanksgiving celebration."

We took Millie's plate and helped her out of bed. She was wobbly but I saw determination in her eyes, as the future meant more to her than the past.

I had to hurry to get back to Margot's before twelve. Zach was waiting, expectant but without questions. He was a real pro and I appreciated it. I switched my coat for a sweater and grabbed a cookie from the plate on the kitchen table. "I need to make one last phone call and then we can leave."

I called to alert the jeweler I'd contacted about the Andretti box, to meet us at the police station where it was being held in the safe. I knew they wanted it out of there. I did too. They'd said it could be worth millions and I wanted it cycled into my portfolio as money, by the time Cade got back. It would give us another option for our plans.

On the way into town, I related the story about the jewels and the terrible murder of Andretti in St Louis. Since Zach was part of the family, he needed to be told about some of our twisted paths.

I was surprised by his comment when I finished the story. He said, "Dave Finch lied when he wrote up the incident in your files, and probably all the rest too. No wonder you people were so misled. We've got to get better checks and balances in the Service or some other snake will self-destruct and cause another disaster like yours. I need to talk to General Ryan about it when I get back.

"I still don't know how you survived, Sara. I guess it wasn't your time to go." He reached over and touched my hand. "I'm glad you're still around, or I wouldn't have met Yvette, or you or Johnson or the folks in Campbell's Point."

I struck pay dirt when I chose the professional gemologist from the registry of their national society. He was bonded and had good leads for the sale of the jewels and their box.

I'd seen the fake one Dave had ordered made in St. Louis and there was no comparison with the real box, which was exquisite, with swirls of beautifully cut and polished rubies, sapphires, emeralds and diamonds. They were arranged in an ancient Celtic pattern of love knots that divided the parts of the crystal lid. I took some pictures of the box and at the last moment, I decided to keep the necklace.

I thought I could be allowed this much remembrance of a gallant man, Andretti, who had tried to watch over me during those terrifying years. It contained over a hundred perfectly matched, creamy white pearls, with a clasp of golden Celtic knots promising eternal love. I thought of him designing it with love, as he waited to propose marriage after my husband's death.

Jacques had told me that there had been a love note in the box. It was now missing because of Finch's perfidy. Vicious, blind jealousy or greed must have driven Dave Finch on his destructive path. I could imagine his violent rage when he couldn't figure out a way to steal the valuable box from the police station. The police had warned me that he'd tried several times to get it without my personal signature.

We finished our business and I signed permission for the box to be removed. When everything was fully appraised, we would know what part the government would get. The appraiser promised he'd do his best to save as much of it for us as he could. Since we had no idea about some of the stones' origins, he would have his work cut out for him.

As the truck and escort went down the street, I couldn't help my sigh of relief. "Thank you, Zach. Another portion of my past is now laid to rest.

"I was going to ask if we could stay in town to eat, but I'm exhausted. Let's go home and sit in front of the fire and eat whatever we can find among the leftovers."

Zach's smile was gentle and patient. "I'll think about it as we dodge traffic getting out of town. You buckle up and I'll sing you a happy song." And he did.

CHAPTER ELEVEN

It was only one day until the big Thanksgiving celebration. Everyone planned to come to the service and pageant, and most would be coming to dinner. We didn't know how many from the hills might come but they would be welcome too. Their children came to school every day, now that things were better among us.

Tim dashed in the back door to get Zach. They were on their way to take Millie to spend part of the day out at Foresters' while they did errands for Yvette. The kitchen was already filled with the wonderful smell of baking pies.

Margot looked weary and worried, but with the men gone we could rest between tasks. We were having a second cup of tea, when I saw a wave of pain ripple across her face. I took her hand. "Margot, what's wrong?"

She began to weep. "I think I'm losing my baby. I've had spots of blood and cramps. I'm afraid to tell Jamie."

"You've got to tell him. He can't help if you don't tell him. I want you to go stretch out on the couch and I'll call him now. He's started working office hours with Doc Pete."

I helped her into the library and then made the call. Within five minutes, Jamie was at the back door. I left them and returned to the kitchen to look after the food in various stages of preparation.

In a few minutes, he came into the kitchen. "Sara, the only safe thing to do, is to get Margot to Pittsburgh right away. Thad is coming to take her. Could you get a suitcase ready for her? Don't let her move, until we're ready to carry her to the car. My Subaru will be best to carry her flat. Could you go along in the back with her? I called the hospital and they'll be waiting for you.

"Tricia is coming over from Gary's long enough to take care of finishing the food in process. I don't want to frighten Margot, but it's pretty serious. I wish she'd told me sooner. Call me when you get her admitted and settled in."

I packed her suitcase and within fifteen minutes we were on the road. She was terrified. Aside from her broken arm, she didn't know anything about hospitals. Thad was fit to be tied and I was thankful that Jamie had arranged for us to go into the hospital on the east side of town.

By ten o'clock she was checked in. The doctor made his report to us. I liked him. No nonsense, but with enough compassion to know how upset the young people were. He said she would need to stay a few days and as soon as we said good-bye, he would give her a sedative. He smiled as he assured us that she would get the best care they could provide. We called Jamie and then headed for home.

Thad's hands on the wheel were white with tension and he was fighting tears. "That baby's the most important person in our whole lives. I can't bear to think about what will happen to Margot if she loses her. I know we were pushing our luck, being older and everything, but we wanted her so much. We waited so long."

I smiled as I asked, "How do you know it's a girl?"

"Because that's what we wanted and the Lord surely heard our prayers."

He dropped me off at the house and went down to reopen the store. He planned to close early and head back to the hospital. The house seemed so empty and lonely. All of us were looking forward to the holiday and now everything was topsy-turvy. I didn't even light the fire in the fireplace, but went back to the sewing room to work on my dress.

Several hours later, Zach and Thad came in together. In a few minutes, Thad came to me with his duffle bag in hand. "I don't know when I'll be back. Pray for us, Sara."

I took him in my arms. "Do you want me to come too?"

He shook his head. "No, there's nothing we can do now but wait and hope. I'll call you when we know something."

He hurried out the back door to his truck. It was already dark. The driving would be difficult with all the oncoming lights of the people driving out of town for the holiday.

I went to the kitchen to find something for supper since I hadn't eaten all day. Zach was sitting at the table doing paperwork. He looked weary and worried.

"I'll need to get back to work for Yvette soon. She's up to her elbows in dressing right now and sent us home to get us out of the way. Then, Tim and I are going to deliver the turkeys to the ladies who volunteered to bake them.

"I'm sure sorry about Margot. Are you going to be OK,

Sara? I know you're worried about her. Why don't you come with us and help? It will take your mind off it for a while."

I thought about it. "Yes, I'd like to help. Do I have time to make a sandwich? I haven't eaten since early this morning."

It was good to get out with other people and do something besides worry. We finally finished the deliveries at seven o'clock and dropped Zach off at Gary's. Jamie had left a message with Yvette to ask Tim to go pick up Millie. Mrs. Buchanan was in labor a week early and he needed to get out to her farm.

As we climbed in the big truck to go back to the house, I felt a real need to be with women. I needed Kylie Lou and Millie and Tricia and all the little girls.

I said to Tim, "I'd like to ride out to the farm with you. The women will want to hear about Margot and I need to be with them now."

He grinned. "Sure, you can visit while I pick up some more stuff for tomorrow and you can help with Millie."

By the time we got up there, children were heading to their various beds. Millie was curled up on the couch looking weary but content. The Crosswick children were scattered around her, Steven on one side, sound asleep, a book still clutched under his arm. The two little girls were asleep, with their heads cradled in her lap.

She looked up when we came in. "Such dear babies. I wonder if their mother will be able to care for them soon. They're such brave little things."

Tim went out with Abe to load stuff into the truck and I had a few minutes to tell the women about Margot. Knowing how devastating my own miscarriage had been, I hoped Margot wouldn't have to go through it. Kylie Lou had lost three babies and knew much more than her share of grief. She looked weary tonight.

As soon as Tim and Abe came in, we said our good-byes, bundled Millie in a quilt and the men carried her to the truck. She was sound asleep before we got to the notch turnoff. We delivered her to Doc Pete's and then Tim took me to Penards'.

"Do you mind staying here all alone tonight, Sara? You could come and stay with us if you want. Jamie shouldn't be too long. Mrs. B's had eight and it probably won't take long to hatch this one. Zach's probably at Yvette's."

"Thanks for the offer, I think I'll just go in and crawl into bed. It's been a long day."

The porch light was on and the hallway was lighted. I figured Zach went out after dark and left a light on for me. As I reached for my key, he came dashing down the hallway, duffle bag in hand. "Hey! I'm on my way to Jamie's. See you sometime tomorrow. I made a fire for you."

He stopped in front of me and gave me a big hug. I was a bit surprised he wasn't going to Yvette's. Then he finished his message.

"Oh, by the way, some scruffy-looking guy came to the door a little while ago asking for you. He looks like he's been sleeping in his clothes for days and he needs a shave, and a hot shower. Be careful, I believed him and let him in."

His voice dropped to a whisper. "Sara, how could I have forgotten? His hair's just as red as ever. 'Nite, Sweetheart."

He continued his flight out the door into the bitter cold as I stood in the hallway, stunned by the news. After all the weeks of frantic worry, of not knowing where he was or if he were still alive, was it possible that Cade was there in the house waiting for me?

I dropped my cloak on the hallway bench and began to search. He was in the logical place; sound asleep on the couch in front of the fire. He looked so weary that I hated to wake him up, but I needed to touch him, to feel his body next to mine, before I'd believe he was really home. I got a quilt and laid it over him as he slept. Then I lifted it enough to slip underneath and into the curve of his body.

I whispered, "It's just me. I'm freezing cold. May I trade a quilt for a warm snuggle?"

He moved a little and a small moan escaped. "Thanks Sweetheart. Sleep tight." He was sound asleep again.

Something wasn't right. I turned toward him and began to stroke his face and head, then his body. I hit the cast as I went down his left arm. No wonder he was sleeping on his right side, propped against the back of the couch. His back seemed to be all right but as I unbuttoned his shirt and moved my hands down his belly, I found two more bandages. I slipped off his slacks and moved my hands over his feet, legs and thighs. Everything seemed fine and in good order, even in sleep. I returned to the nest of his body.

I could feel his arms tighten around my waist as he stretched under the cover. "Well, do I pass inspection, My Love?" He was laughing now, and so was I.

"You wretched man! What a way to get your cheap thrills. Kiss me, Cade. Kiss me a thousand times for each moment you were away from me. I missed you so."

In the middle of the night, I wakened long enough to realize that the fire was almost out and the house was getting very cold. The wind rattled the shutters and whistled around the nooks and crannies of the old house. I lay there in my husband's arms and snuggled closer.

When he stirred in his nest, I whispered, "I'm hungry. Let's go find a snack and then get cleaned up. We need a proper bed and lots of blankets for the rest of the night."

We decided there would be many too many pies at the Thanksgiving dinner, and chose to cut one of Margot's wonderful cinnamon apple pies. Big triangles went into pottery bowls to warm up. They warmed our hands and let the odors of the spices waft to our noses as we watched the growing pools of melted ice cream run down the mountains of apples and crust. We fed each other from our treasure bowls until we were full.

Cade needed help getting cleaned up. He wouldn't be shower-ready for weeks. As I sat him on the bathroom stool and began to wash his face and then his back, there was only a momentary thought about the bath ritual Michael and I had shared.

My life had moved on. The past had taken its rightful place; not to be forgotten but to be appreciated for what it had taught me about my self and what it had given me as a gift to share with the living.

The silver locket around his neck gleamed in the light as he kissed me. "I told you I would bring it home to you, Sara."

"Let's go upstairs to my room. It's the only double bed besides Margot and Thad's and there are plenty of blankets up there."

We settled in again and didn't waken until the phone rang about nine o'clock. As I went downstairs to answer it, Cade settled in and returned to his dreams.

"Penards'"

"Sara? It's Tim. Thad just called to tell us Margot's going to be fine. She needs to stay until Sunday and then he'll bring her home. Gotta make some more calls. I hear your old man got in last night. We'll see you guys this afternoon."

I couldn't believe the good news. I was so relieved I was crying as I thought about starting breakfast for Cade. Then, I decided to wait for him to get up. After I put the logs in the grate and started a nice fire, I curled up in front of it with a mug of tea to think about the change of events.

Next time it was my turn to be sound asleep in front of the fire when Cade came downstairs wrapped in a blanket. He dropped it on me, and settled in beside me as he whispered, "I'm freezing cold. May I trade a blanket for a warm snuggle?"

I wakened enough to let a smile flicker across my face as I opened my arms to him. "Thanks, Sweetheart. I love you."

Next time awake, we knew we'd be in serious trouble if we didn't get moving. The children's play was at two o'clock, and I couldn't miss little Susan's performance. I changed my mind about the dress I'd bought for the day, and finally settled on slacks and sweater. About the same time, Cade came out dressed in borrowed clothes. His things were still packed away among the boxes loaded from the Idaho ranch, and I couldn't find anything on the first try.

"Well, at least the guy who let me in last night is about the same size. By the way, where is he and more important, who is he?"

I detected a hint of jealousy in his tone and couldn't resist teasing him a little. "Didn't he tell you?"

Cade was a bit petulant. "I had to beg, to get him to let me in. It was strange, I think he knew all along who I was, and was teasing me. At the time, I just wanted to find you."

My smile was gentle and somewhat motherly. "Sounds to me like normal behavior for a couple of brothers who haven't seen each other in many years."

I watched a wonderful swirl of emotions dance across Cade's face. "What? I haven't seen or heard from that little runt brother Zach since I left home. Sara, are you sure?"

"Well, all I have is his word. When he told me last night that you were here, the last thing he said was, 'How could I have forgotten? His hair is just as red as ever.'"

"What's he doing here?"

"It's a long story, one for an evening in front of the fire. Perhaps he'd like to tell it while you get reacquainted. Cade, he's a good man and a real gentleman. But watch out, he's a professional fighter for the military. It's interesting, he doesn't teach them fighting, he's teaching them about themselves. I'd guess he's the one who decides whether the guys in trouble go to the brig or get court-martialed. His other specialty is returning POWs."

"My God! Is he a shrink? How did you find out?"

I took his hands in mine. "We need to go or we'll be late. I promised Susan Forester I wouldn't miss the pageant.

"I'll tell you about it later. Zach pleaded guilty and asked for the indulgence of the court when I accused him of being one, yes; I think he's a shrink."

We hurried out to Black Beauty and I handed Cade the keys along with travel instructions. I planned to be taken care of for a long, long while.

"This yours?"

"Yes, I traded the green monster for it plus got 10,000 dollars refund. I put it away for the future, uncertain what it might be. I didn't want anything from our life together to be left to remind me of my loss."

I reached for his hand. "Cade, do you have to do another assignment like the last one, ever again?"

He smiled. "I'll tell you about it later, in front of the fire. We have some important decisions to make and we'll need to think about the options and their possible consequences.

"Now, let's go celebrate the holiday. I'm ready for prayers of thanksgiving and little ones doing a happy skit and then my plate mounded up with turkey and all the trimmings."

As he pulled into a parking space by the gym, he leaned over and shared a passionate and possessive kiss before we took our offerings for the Thanksgiving dinner and shared our public faces with our new friends.

Kylie Lou and Abe had saved places for us close to the makeshift stage. All the other Foresters were lined up in a row on a bench pulled up to the table. We were lucky to get into such good company, and so close to the food. My mouth was already watering with the wonderful odors wafting from the turkeys being carried in by the husbands of the various ladies who'd taken on a roasting project.

I glanced up to see Jamie Campbell enter with a very lovely lady on each arm. One was a radiant Millie; the other was Dodie Finch. Dodie looked so different that I hardly recognized her. Her hair was tinted a beautiful chestnut brown, the long tresses were braided and wrapped around her head like a crown. She was wearing a stunning, gray-blue, woolen dress that hung to her ankles around her elegant black boots. Only one piece of jewelry adorned her body. A large, cream-colored pearl hung from an intricate chain made of links of silver.

I slipped over to greet her. "I'm so glad you were able to come. It looks as if something very wonderful has happened in your life, Dodie. We'll visit later."

Her smile was self-assured and for me, mysterious. What could have happened? Well, perhaps she would reveal it later; anything that helped her was a gift from God.

The little pageant was a rousing success. A lot of ad-libbing added to the fun. We were ready to begin the buffet. People were circulating, visiting and gathering up children, when a couple of strange men came in the far door. They looked rather disreputable and as they came into the room I watched one man stagger as he took off his coat and struggled to get it hung up. Cade was visiting with Abe Forester while Zach carried in platters from the kitchen. Tricia, Tim and I were visiting by our table.

The drunken stranger drifted to our group. I gasped as he grabbed my bottom. Not a pinch or a squeeze; he was holding on tight with his whole hand and was totally out of line. Tim knew something was wrong.

The stranger whispered in my ear. "Well, Honey, nice party here. Wanna sit with me?"

His breath would have killed a cow and he had a day's growth of stubble on his face. In the old days, I would have decked him. Instead, I turned to him with a sweet smile.

"How nice to see you. Please refresh my memory. What is your name?"

He leered at me. "Name's Chucky Chandler. This here's my pal, Russ."

My voice was measured to his sodden brain. "Well, Mr. Chandler, please remove your hand. If you touch me again, I shall turn you into a soprano. And when I'm finished, my husband, Commander Cade Cameron will string you up by the heels and gut you like a rutting buck."

I continued to smile, thinking of the deed done. I watched as the color drained from Chucky's face. His muddled, drunken brain tried to process what I'd said. We heard a tinny, shrill squeal. It sounded like a piglet picked up by his ears. Then there was a louder, strangled yelp as Chucky turned to his buddy and grabbed his arm. "We're outa here, Russ. Go man!"

Now everyone turned to watch as the men stumbled and staggered toward the door, grabbing coats and hats as they ran. They hit the outside door just as Sam Saunders opened it from the other side. They fell in a heap at his feet and then scrambled up, running away as the door shut behind them.

Tim was standing beside me with eyes as big as Frisbees. "Are you all right, ma'am? What did he do?"

I smiled as I answered, "He made me an offer I chose to refuse."

Tim hadn't seen the grab but my husband had. I looked up into Cade's eyes just as he signaled thumbs-up with a big grin. Zach saw it too but his face hinted at something more important; perhaps pride in me because I'd gained a new respect for myself, and a new way of handling the trials of everyday life.

Dinner was perfect. After a short time the noise level lowered as people ate. Then the friendly buzz rose in the room as visiting began again. There was a round of applause for Yvette and her many helpers. She asked everyone who'd contributed food, time or talent to stand up, and everyone in the room could stand up in good conscience and clap for one another.

She'd planned ahead and when the meal was finished she began to dish up plates with lids for the people in the community who were not able to come. She included the injured and homebound, those who had to stay to take care of others and those too shy to come. She included a large box for the young kid at the 24-hour store. He had eight brothers and sisters and a bunch of grandparents to support.

The names and addresses were written on the covered plates and they went into boxes for Tim's crew of high school kids to deliver. They headed out with much laughing and giggling and I figured their party was just beginning.

I was ready to head for Penards' to sit in front of the fire, but Jamie had come by our table very early on to tell us they needed to take Millie home to rest, and invited us to come by later. I was so curious about Dodie's change of circumstances that I had to go and find out her secret.

They were circled around a crackling fire when we came in. Millie looked weary but contented. Everyone had been so kind to her and had asked how she was getting along. Word was out about her engagement to Jamie and her new ring glistened in the firelight.

It was Dodie who had stolen the show at the dinner. The mystery lady made a great hit with all the eligible bachelors in town when they found out she was a recent widow.

Just as I was going to ask, she smiled and explained. "I had a high school sweetheart who was very special to me when I was growing up in Nebraska. We lost track of each other when we went away to different colleges and then, I was stolen by circumstance to be Dave Finch's wife. Hal Richards found out about my husband's death from a mutual friend, and came by to see me a few days ago.

"When I opened the door and found him standing there, I burst into dreadful sobbing. He came inside and we grieved together for all our years apart. Sara, he said his wife died of cancer last year, but I think he's ready to love again. I can't believe my good fortune. He has kept his precious loving spirit and he wants me to be a part of his life."

I got up from my chair and went to sit by her. "I'm so glad for you, Dodie. I wish you happiness in your life now."

She continued, "I met such nice people today at the celebration. Doc Pete has asked if I'd like to come to Campbell's Point for the time they're gone on their trip, to house sit for them and keep the books for the doctors. By then I'll know better where I might want to live.

"Dave left me penniless. Even the house doesn't belong to me. I'm supposed to be out by December first. I'll need to work to keep food on the table, and I'd like to do it among friends. I told him yes."

I smiled as I remembered her good friendship over the years and I was glad that we would be able to see more of her. Her mention of the doctors made me wonder where Zach was. Everyone assumed that his interest in Yvette was mutual and progressing and that they were together tonight. So we were surprised when the doorbell rang and it was Zach, duffle bag in hand, looking downcast and abandoned.

He sounded frustrated and hurt. "When I took her home after the party, she wouldn't let me in. She said she wasn't ready for a relationship and to leave her alone."

He shook his head in puzzlement. "And then, when I was walking away, Sam Saunders drove by in his squad car and got out. He scared the hell out of me. He pretty much said if I ever hurt her he would kill me!"

He still didn't sit down; just paced back and forth. Jamie moved to him and began to lead him down toward the hall. "Zach and I need to talk a few minutes in the library and then we'll be back to visit. Maybe you ladies would be kind enough to fix some hot chocolate for people."

Dodie and I went into the kitchen and found what we needed. After a few more minutes of polite visiting, she decided to head out for home before it got any later. There were big hugs all around as she left the house. As soon as the men came back, I gave Cade the sign it was time for us to leave too. I offered Zach a ride home to Penards'.

He shook his head. "No, I need to walk. You could take my bag home, though, so Sam doesn't pick me up as a vagrant. Where do they throw them since there's no jail?"

He was not a happy camper and needed some time to himself. I don't know what Jamie told him but I figured it was about Yvette. I also suspected it had been a real shock.

"Come on, Cade. You need some rest before tomorrow. The town grapevine at the party said you and Zach are going to run the store for Thad until he gets back. The Friday after Thanksgiving is the busiest day of the whole year."

I was exhausted and ready to collapse after the long day. I felt the first flakes of snow hitting my face as we pulled in the drive at Penards'. I sent a traveler's prayer out for Dodie and a heart-healing prayer for Zach as we headed upstairs to collapse into bed.

CHAPTER TWELVE

Thad usually opened the hardware store at seven-thirty, but today, because there was a big holiday sale, he'd planned to open at six o'clock. Cade and Zach were up and long gone before I was ready to start my day. My biggest projects were to finish the green dress, and to get busy with my Christmas knitting. I'd planned to make boot socks for both Zach and Cade.

After putting on a big pot of soup and mixing up a batch of chubby, raisin-filled oatmeal cookies, the rest of the day was mine. I didn't know who would be eating where, but I was prepared. Zach might be there since the path he'd made to the kitchen of Gary's Grill would not be used anymore. I was sad for them and wondered what had happened to frighten Yvette away.

The other thing hanging fire for Zach was related to whatever he'd picked up at Dodie's and put in his case. I shivered as I thought about what it might be and how it might impact me. I decided to let it all go, to let things happen as they would anyway. My worrying wouldn't help.

The whole day went by without a phone call or interruption. I worked through lunch and didn't miss it. I was still full of turkey and dressing and wonderful pie.

The soup was simmering on the back of the stove when the men got home at seven o'clock. They were ecstatic over the day's success, including the computer not breaking down and the wonderful amount of stuff they'd sold. They couldn't wait to call Thad and tell him how much they'd cleared for him.

They were tossing down soup and fresh bread and laughing about the things that happened during the day. Neither of them knew anyone in town, so they were the innocents in the stories. Cade pulled an envelope from his pocket and began to read ladies' names and their flirtatious pitches to Zach.

He was imitating their coo as they sidled up to the counter to pay. "Oh, Dr. Cameron. What are you doing here? We thought you were filling in for Doc Pete with Doctor Campbell. I'm planning to come in on Monday to discuss this weird rash I have. Lucy Smiley says you're the most eligible bachelor in town and the cutest thing she's ever seen."

Then Cade took Zach's part. "Ma'am, I'm indeed going to help in the doctor's office starting next week. We're just helping out here at the hardware store until Mr. Penard gets back. I'll be disappointed not to care for you personally; however, rashes are Dr. Campbell's specialty. Thank you for your business, Mrs...."

Cade put just the right amount of breathy sensuousness into the answer. "Ms. Byrd. Please, call me Birdie. I'm unattached and available, Honey."

Cade and Zach broke up over that one and half a dozen more. Then Zach got serious. "Wait until they find out I'm a shrink. They'll change all their symptoms to fit needing me, you just watch. The air base job may look mighty good by the time I have to go back."

Cade answered with a seriousness of his own. "What do you do for them, and how did you find Sara and me? Come on; let's go sit by the fire while you tell me about it."

I decided they needed some brother time together so I went back to the sewing room to work on the green dress. It was taking much too long and was beyond my level of sewing skill. Maybe Tricia would give me some help. There were only a few weeks until Christmas and I didn't see how I could be ready.

And then, I realized that this was the first Christmas of my very own, with Cade and Zach as special family. Everyone else was gone, my grandparents, parents, Michael and our daughter Roslin. I felt so abandoned and sad that I was weeping when Cade came to find me.

He opened his arms as best he could with his cast, and folded me into a loving embrace. His touch was gentle and somehow different. He kissed my eyes as he whispered, "Don't cry, My Love. We'll do the best we can and God will take care of the rest."

The brothers were long gone when I wakened. At least this was the last six o'clock opening for them. On Monday, Zach would begin working a training shift with Doc Pete in preparation for the switchover in January. Jamie had classes Monday through Wednesday until almost Christmastime. I was relieved when he told me he'd decided to finish the term. Cade was going to continue helping at the store. He couldn't lift anything but he was a whiz at the computer checkout. He'd always wanted to have a builder's supply store and being a plumbing contractor gave him a lot of knowledge about what builders would want and need.

Then I returned to more difficult realities. We had no home and Cade and I needed time to talk about our future. We weren't willing to hang up our boots and sit by the fire the rest of our lives, but I hoped we could make a living doing something safer. Not just a little, but really simple, safe and sane. Maybe the store could be the beginning for him.

I was working in the kitchen about noon when the doorbell rang. Penards' house was at the end of the street, not the kind of place strangers would drift to. I had a momentary stab of fear, but talked myself out of it. Besides, this wasn't my house and not many people knew we were here.

Nonetheless, I was whispering a small prayer as I went to answer the door. A dark blue Subaru was parked at the curb. What brought joy to my heart was the lovely German shepherd sitting on alert at the edge of the porch. It was surely Violet, because standing right behind her on the steps were Johnson and General Ryan.

I had a moment of panic as I wondered why they had come so far in difficult traveling conditions. They looked exhausted and worried. I opened the door and Violet waited while I gave Johnson and the general a very unmilitary greeting. As soon as I touched General Ryan, any hard feelings between us were forgiven and I knew that we would get on with our lives together.

It was Johnson who didn't quite manage to keep his concern from showing. "Sara, we've been so worried about you. Cade said on the phone yesterday that we needed to come. I wasn't sure what was wrong. Where is he?"

General Ryan spoke up, "And where's Zach?"

There wasn't any reason not to tell the truth since there would be no way to hide the men in our small town. Why the thought came to mind, I don't know; but I didn't like the feel of it.

A bit of the "Ice Queen" returned as I decided what to do.

"Please come in. I'll call the store and let them know you're here. Let me take your coats and get you settled, the fire is ready to light. Please make yourselves at home while I put on fresh coffee. Have you had lunch?"

I dropped to my knees and hugged my dear Violet, whispering sweet French love greetings. In the swirl of the weeks since our trip from Idaho, I'd forgotten Johnson's promise to deliver her when her training was over. But it was supposed to be contingent on my having a place to live. I was puzzling over it as we went down the hall to the kitchen.

By the time I returned to the men, I knew what Johnson had done in addition to the normal training. Violet was trained to hand signals. Now, I wondered why he'd done it.

General Ryan rose from the couch. "Mrs. Cameron, I hope it won't be too much of an imposition. We need to stay in town for several days during our meetings and Penard offered us a place here since he and Margot will still be at the hospital. He'll be back for the meeting tomorrow.

"Ma'am, we flew overnight from Mountain Home to Wright-Patterson and drove from there. I'm exhausted. I need sleep more than food right now. If you'll show me where I can bed down, I'll be out of your way for a few hours.

"Oh, by the way, here's a sealed note for you that came to my office right after we cleaned up the Russian spy case. I have no idea what it is or who it's from."

I put the envelope in my apron pocket to open later. I took them upstairs to rooms at the end of the hall, found clean towels for them and left them to their naps.

Johnson had done the transfer ceremony so Violet would obey only me. She never left my side during the afternoon. We slipped out for a walk after dinner was under control. How wonderful to have her with me again. In the middle of a mad, zany dash to the end of the street, I had a terrifying thought. Was Violet brought here to protect me while Cade and Zach were taken away to do another job? Suddenly the day was not so beautiful and my heart turned to stone.

I stooped down to clutch Violet in my arms as I whispered, "Please, no. I can't bear it. Please don't take my family away. Please don't let them be harmed again."

When we returned to the house, Johnson was sitting on the back porch steps and witnessed my bitter tears. He reached for his handkerchief and sat me down beside him.

"All right, Sara. What's the matter? Why are you so upset?"

"I'm terrified. Why are you here? I'm afraid that you've brought Violet to protect me while General Ryan takes Cade and Zach away to die … I can't bear it."

His smile was gentle and patient. "Ah, Sara, that's not our plan at all. The general came to meet with the district agents to help choose a successor to Finch. He let me come to deliver Violet to you and to give me a few days to look around and meet Abe Forester. I'm ready to move from Mountain Home to somewhere more peaceful and quiet."

I was so relieved I kept on crying as I let the news sink in. "Is that really true? We'll go in and call Abe so you can get together. Are you involved in the meeting tomorrow?"

"No, thank God. I'd like to have the pleasure of taking you to Mass in the morning, and then I'd like to go see your place and meet Abe. It looks like the weather should hold off another day or two and you and I will get into the back country to check some places out. I remembered you mentioning R & J Realty. I called them from Idaho and they're lined up to take us out on Monday."

I turned to him and smiled. "Johnson, would you do something for me?"

"That depends, ma'am."

"In all the time we've been together and all the things we've been through, I've never known your first name. What is it?"

"Ben."

"I'm glad you're here, Ben. How have things been since you got back from Italy?"

"I still have nightmares about the mission. The shootout at Andretti's place was the closest I've come to dying since 'Nam. I don't want any part of it any more."

I got up from the steps and we began to walk. Violet took up her place at my side as we went down the street to the barricade and the path beyond. I touched Ben's shoulder as I asked, "Would you be willing to tell me what happened?"

He hesitated and then motioned for me to sit on the log by the side of the path. "I've given my report to General Ryan, but haven't spoken of it to anyone else.

"It happened so fast I really don't remember much except the blind terror of seeing my two friends and work partners gunned down before my eyes; knowing that if I'd been in the front, I would've died too. I feel so guilty because Anna died instead of a worthless old man who wouldn't have cared; one who was waiting to die and to be with Cara.

"I dropped Skorski in his tracks by reflex and dumb luck. It was almost dark and there were no lights on in the house. There was blood all over them. As soon as I checked and decided everyone was dead, I tried to gather up all the papers and rings and things so no one would be able to identify them.

"I crammed everything into my pocket and climbed over the wall. I had trouble getting back into the States because I'm just temporary military now. I finally got to the base the morning you found me. I hadn't slept in a week of travel.

"General Ryan arranged for two operatives stationed in Germany to take care of the job in Finland. Thank God he didn't send me. I wasn't in any shape to do anything after watching my friends die, and when I got back to base and saw how torn up you were about Cade, I was almost ready to try the runway thing myself."

"Ben, why didn't you take Cade's locket?"

"I did. It must have fallen from my pocket as I went over the wall. I knew how important it was to you, I'm sorry."

I sighed. "It kept me sane. I believed Cade was still alive, especially with the rose bouquet you sent by way of Tim."

"That was pretty much a blind guess on my part. Cade told me a little about the code on the way over in the plane. I was coward enough to try to keep your hopes alive a few more weeks, even though I believed he was dead."

Ben continued, "General Ryan told me he finally convinced the people at the Italian hospital about Cade's identity and they escorted him straight to the Embassy and then home. Cade told the general he has no idea how he got to the hospital. He'd lost so much blood it was touch and go whether he would survive. He looks good now. It was a relief to see him this morning when we got to town. It's a miracle he's alive."

"Ben, he was wearing the locket when he came home to me. An Angel of Mercy must have found it and put it on him when he carried Cade to the hospital steps."

We sat a few moments in silence. Then I said to him, "I'm sorry about Anna."

His laugh came out with a funny snort. "Sara, I don't know why you believe I was messing around with the boss's wife. He would have killed me and cut me up in small dice to feed the dogs. I wasn't the one. It was the kid, the third helper, who got Anna sent to the institution. I did care, but there was nothing I could do to save her from her own lust."

I let that news sink in. I felt guilty that I'd even suspected Johnson of adultery. I got up from the log and brushed the leaves from my clothes. "Come on, I need to finish getting supper ready. I'm so glad you're here and I hope that when you start looking around, something perfect turns up."

General Ryan had come downstairs after his nap and curled up on the couch in front of the fire to sleep some more. He looked so weary. I dropped a quilt over him and left him to rest.

I took Johnson aside. "Is General Ryan all right? It's not like him to be so tired."

Ben hesitated a moment too long. "I guess it's all right to tell you. He was one of Wilhelmina's American lovers, along with Michael and Skorski. The general's wife left him because of the scandal and they were in the middle of an ugly divorce. Then the stupidity of the whole thing hit them at the same time. They decided not to let Wilhelmina destroy their marriage. They're both exhausted now from it.

"I hope the meetings are short and that you'll let him have a day or two of peace and quiet before he has to go home. I think he's filed for retirement but they're so short of officers he may not be able to leave as soon as he'd like."

"Thanks, Johnson. It helps me to care for him, knowing what's going on. Now, I think the men are back from work. Let's go and hear about the hardware store day. You won't believe how happy Cade is. He's always wanted to have a store and I'm sure he must be very good at it."

As we visited in the kitchen over bowls of soup and bread, General Ryan slept on in front of the fire.

Johnson and I slipped out to early Mass, leaving the weary retailers and General Ryan to get in a few more hours of sleep before their meeting at ten o'clock. We took Black Beauty and Violet waited for us, curled up on her quilt on the front seat. I knew the Foresters would invite us for dinner, so I arranged for the General's meeting group to go down and let Yvette cook for them. It would be the first time Zach had been there since his rebuff.

Ben Johnson and Abe Forester took to each other right away, especially after they started talking dogs. Kylie Lou and I smiled and went inside to enjoy the children. I reached out to hug her. "You're one of the special reasons I wanted to come back to Campbell's Point. It seems like a long time since we met in the woods behind the house.

"When I did some reading about the use of tansy, it mentioned not only the hazards but the poor number of successes. Is that what happened?"

"Yes, I was afraid to try again. Abe was so frightened by what had happened to me. He said we would never do anything to abort a child again; we'd accept what God gave us."

"Did you agree with him?"

"I agreed to carry this child to term if God willed it. We'll use the method you taught us, when I'm fertile again."

"Are you concerned about this baby being all right?"

Kylie Lou shook her head no. "Before, we were going to a doctor on the other side of the mountain. This time I went right away to see Doc Pete and I trusted him to tell me what to do. He sent me to a place in Pittsburgh for women with special problems. They say everything looks fine, but I'm going into town to have the baby."

"What do you think about Jamie trying the doctoring for Doc Pete? He was so disappointed with the music therapy program; he won't be sorry to quit."

Kylie Lou sat down in her favorite rocker with baby Pam in her lap.

"I don't have a good feeling about it, but I know he needs to try it. I'm sorry about the music therapy, but I knew it wouldn't fit his soul. Sometimes we have to stand by and watch people we care about make mistakes, and he's still in a bitter and desperate fight to accept that his hand will never be useable and his medical career has been ruined. I don't know how it will turn out or who will win."

I shivered with fear as I thought about Jamie's tortured soul. She continued with the family news. "Tim's going to take the G.E.D. right after Christmas. We should have tried it too but I haven't had time to study and work with the hardest parts, like fractions.

"I love the Crosswick children but adding three more to my family was more work than I expected. I don't know how I'll manage when the new baby comes, but something will work out."

Baby Pam was in her lap, a thumb firmly planted in her mouth. Her huge brown eyes watched every move I made.

"Is there anything I can do to help with dinner?"

"No, everything's ready but we won't eat until about three when the kids get here from town."

I smiled. "Why don't you two catch a little nap and I'll look after the crises for a while."

She pulled a quilt around her shoulders and wrapped Pam up with her. They were both asleep in moments.

A little later, Abe came in to say he and Ben were going out to drive around some of the back roads. Old Mrs. Biden was moving to town to live with her daughter and her farm was going to be for sale. They were going to take a look at it.

The children were playing outside in the warmth and sunshine of the late season. There were still places with several inches of mushy snow in the shade of the north slopes and plenty of slushy, muddy sloughs to tempt the little ones to stomp and roll. They were a terrible mess when Tim's truck pulled in and they rushed to cling to him.

Violet and I greeted them as they came onto the porch. I said to Tim with a smile, "I expect you can guess who's in town for a few days. He brought Violet to me, and he came with a hankering for some peace and quiet. I think he's ready to bolt the noisy ranch at Mountain Home. Abe took him out to look around."

Tim grinned. "Hey, that's great. You'll like him, Tricia. He's a real gentleman. Let's go get these little ragamuffins cleaned up before your mom sees them."

I smiled at my favorite young man. "She was napping with Pam when I came out."

The kids went inside and I had a few moments to sit and enjoy the day with Violet. I wondered if I would ever have a place of my own, with the simple things I'd always wanted. The winter resident birds were busy flitting about, the chickadees pecking and picking at the damp ground. The squirrels were chattering and scolding as they carried nuts from one place to another before they decided where to bury them, sometimes changing their minds and digging them up to move them to yet another hiding place.

A deer stepped out from the forest's edge to graze on the vegetables still in the garden; beet tops and a few ears of corn. It was a spike buck, sleek and healthy for going into the winter. I hoped he would escape Marvin and his friends.

All the Forester children came out on the porch looking much cleaner and more Sunday-like. My Lady Susan came to snuggle in my lap. "Will we get to hear more from the Secret Garden today, Aunt 'Becca?" As she smiled up at me,

I wondered where she'd come up with that name. No one knew about my childhood name except Jamie Campbell.

"We'll have time to read a bit after dinner. Why did you call me Aunt 'Becca, Sweetheart?"

She smiled, her little mouth puckered into a kiss. "Please don't be mad. You just seem to be a Rebecca, I call you that when I make up stories about you and your adventures."

I smiled. "Oh? Perhaps we should be reading your stories to the family."

She giggled. "Not yet. I can't write much yet but I can do my name. Want to see?"

She took my hand to lead me inside, as Ben and Abe came up the drive. They looked so happy I wondered what they'd been doing. "Well, what did you see?"

Johnson could hardly stand still. I'd never seen him so excited.

"Sara, I can't believe how beautiful this place is; the wildlife is so abundant, there's so much wild country, and they've done a decent job reclaiming the strip mines. And it's so quiet. I can see why you love it."

After supper the family settled down to hear about the next adventures in the search for the Secret Garden and then we heard the story of Daniel in the Lion's Den, complete with the sounds of hungry, growling lions.

Violet was a perfect lady all day and I was very pleased and proud of her. She was quick to settle any problems with Abe's dogs and they treated her like the princess she was. The children loved her and took turns petting her and playing with her on the floor. I taught them a few French phrases to use with her and they were so proud to be able to say they spoke "a little French". It had been a perfect day and I didn't want to go back into town.

It was Johnson who got up from his place and said we'd enjoyed the day but needed to get back. It was dark when we got to the notch turnoff and we needed to watch for deer in the road.

On the way back he told me about the flock of turkeys. They'd counted forty birds. They'd seen several does with their young of the year and several species of woodpeckers he'd never seen before. He turned to me and took my hand.

"I would never have thought to come here if it hadn't been for you. Do you realize how many lives you've touched, Sara? Everyone is better for having known you. Thank you, from the bottom of my heart."

The men were clustered around the kitchen table when we got back. Thad said Margot was safely tucked in bed. We sat down to catch up on the day. The meeting went well, the voting was done, and General Ryan looked relieved. I think the general was honoring my request to be out of the loop for a while. There was no reason to know about what transpired and he didn't speak of it.

He turned to Ben with a big smile. "Well, Johnson. What about this country? Think you might like to move up here?"

"It's beautiful, sir. I've already found three perfect places for the dogs and we haven't even dealt with R & J yet. Sara and I are going out tomorrow morning with him. You knew she's part owner of the operation?

"But the best surprise of all is Abe Forester. He's a fine man and I'd like to work with him. He says he's interested in being a part of it, so a place close to his would be most convenient."

I spoke up, a little chagrined. "Sounds like I got rid of the Green Monster a little too soon. But I'll bet Tim can persuade Abe to let him borrow the farm truck to help you move, especially if I loan him Black Beauty. Maybe you could be settled somewhere by Christmas."

Then General Ryan turned to Zach. "Well, Doctor, now that you've had time to think about your options, are you coming back with me; or taking a chance and staying here with the woman you hope to marry, your newly-found brother and sister-in-law, and a chance at a new life? Damn! Doesn't sound like much of a choice, does it?

"We'll miss you out there in the God-forsaken desert but I may not be there much longer anyway. I've requested retirement as soon as possible. My wife and I are going back home to Memphis to settle down, garden, play cards, and enjoy the grandchildren. And if by some chance I get bored, I'll come up here and harass you people while you're working in the new school."

I was puzzled. "What did you guys cook up today while I wasn't here to defend myself? And if you say, 'We need to talk', Cade, you're right."

Cade got up from the table. "I agree. Let's go for a walk before you get all the wrong ideas. Ben says you're an expert at drawing wrong conclusions, always bad."

I went to get my cloak and boots and gathered up Violet and her leash. It was a beautiful evening. I looked up at the sky and hoped the weather would hold one more day.

We headed to the end of the road to the fallen log. I smiled as we settled down to a few moments of silence and peace. Everything in the last few weeks had turned out so well, I chose to expect more good stuff rather than looking for something bad to happen.

Margot was tucked in bed at home with instructions to let people do things for her and to rest as much as possible. Millie would be moving to The Cottage in the next week, and Dodie would come over on December first to begin her training with Doc Pete and to stay in the house with them.

"All right, Cade, it's time to tell me what's going on about the school. But first, we need to figure out what we're going to do about a nest of our own."

"I know. That's what this is all about. Thad was pleased with the job Zach and I did for him. He knows Zach will be training with Doc Pete now, but Sweetheart, Thad wants me to work for him in the store pretty much full time at least until the baby's born in late spring. If everything goes right, by then I'll have enough contacts to begin a builder's supply to complement what his hardware carries.

"It will give us time to start planning and building our house. Would you let me do that for you? I know how many ideas you have and how much work you've done to learn about green building. Let's do it together."

I could hardly believe what he was offering me. After all the years of living in administrative housing and being told what to do and say, it was hard to believe I might have my own home. The freedom of it took my breath away.

"Cade, do you really want to? I'd love to help. Tomorrow, Randy Renquist will get to deal with me again. I'm sure he'll love it. We'll need a temporary place to stay until it's done. Zach and Ben can stay with us until they get settled themselves. If I could help run two ranches I can handle this."

"Consider it done, Sweetheart; now, about the 'school'. What General Ryan has been asked, is to set up a place where special, highly-placed people can come, one-on-one, to get very specific training in languages. The kind of colloquial-based stuff you're so good at. The important thing is the solitude and safety of the mountains and being away from D.C. Other times it may be the reverse, an elite ESL training for a specific task and person. Interested? I told him it was absolutely up to you."

I sighed, as I thought about the questions that needed to

be answered before I could decide.

"I have three questions."

He grinned, "Mind like a steel trap! Shoot."

"That's the first question. How dangerous is this going to be? Do we have to provide guards and protection for them?"

"No, they'll bring their own people with them."

"Would we have to feed and house all of them too?"

"I don't know, but I would expect so."

I got up from the log and began to pace. "What kind of support help will there be?"

Cade was following my train of thought. I hadn't worked with him on a project before and it was important to hear his answer before I made up my mind.

"It depends on what's needed. There would be a pool of teachers depending upon what language we need. Thad speaks French, German, Chechen and Russian. Zach is fluent in French, Thai, Japanese and Korean. Johnson speaks French, Finnish, Russian, and Vietnamese. You speak French, Italian, Finnish and Russian and I speak Italian, French, Finnish, Russian, and Arabic. To be useful for the ESL, he wants you to start the training you were offered last summer. The paper work is done and you could walk right into classes. What's the third question?"

"Whom do we work for? Are we still in the military?"

"It's strictly a contract job, sort of like what I am doing now. We have some military privileges but not the hassle, and anytime we decide to take a break, or don't want an assignment, we can say 'no'."

I sat down again beside My Beloved and took his hand.

"There's a fourth question."

"What?"

"How much do you want to do it? It'll take a lot of work and you know the government doesn't pay anything close to what the job is worth. Besides, I have a feeling we'll be asked to spy at the same time, if they go according to their usual game plan.

"Cade, I'm not going to take this just to get General Ryan off the hook, whatever one he's on; especially not if he's going to retire as soon as he can. How do we know we'll be taken care of as well by someone else?"

Cade was squirming a little and I could tell these were issues he hadn't considered. "I don't know who his replacement will be."

"How soon do we have to give him our decision and is it

105

final? For instance, could we say 'no thank you' right now and then put in a bid for the job at a later time?"

I saw new respect in his eyes as he answered. "I see where you're headed and I think I like it. I was feeling guilty because we were sneaking out of our patriotic duty. Could it be someone else's turn? Can we live with that?"

"Dear Heart, if we want to live, we may want to consider it. The situation in the Middle East is deteriorating by the hour and that's your specific area of skill. I don't want you to be involved.

"I'm going to be selfish and say I don't want to do it now. Whether it develops later is for another time and place. I want to enjoy my life with you, to build a home and make it a place of safety and peace for both of us, after all the years of terror and danger. I love you too much to allow you to be in such danger again."

My kiss carried an air of finality. "Who's going to tell him?"

"I'll do it."

CHAPTER THIRTEEN

Cade and Thad were the only ones up early next morning. They headed off for the store while the rest of us lay in late until we heard Margot stirring. I went down to say hello and suggested she let us bring her a cinnamon bun from Gary's. I thought the men needed a chance to enjoy the local routine before they went back to Idaho. She stayed in bed with a smile and a cup of tea.

Zach needed to be at Doc Pete's at nine and Ben and I were to go property hunting at nine-thirty, so we headed out for breakfast at Gary's. Things hadn't changed much since the first time I'd gone in last spring. The farmers weren't in any hurry, and their beloved caps were a lot more grubby and sweat-stained after the summer's work. Tricia's sunny smile welcomed us as we ordered cinnamon buns all around and one to go.

When we went to the register, Zach handed an envelope to Tricia and asked her to give it to Yvette. He turned away and went up the street to begin his new job.

General Ryan said he was off on a long walk around town. He looked more relaxed and almost happy. He didn't seem upset about our turning down the assignment of the new language school. Ben and I headed back to take Margot's bun and then, took Black Beauty to R & J Realty.

No nonsense from Renquist this time. I gave him clear instructions about what we needed to do and in what order. Ben's search came first so the morning was spent looking at property for the dog operation. I was along for the ride, but I was also getting a feeling for the different areas around Campbell's Point and where people chose to settle.

I didn't like most of the new houses plopped down with no thought to their place in the terrain. The builders had destroyed many trees instead of keeping them in place, not only for their beauty but also for their soil preservation importance. Ben found three more possible sites and said he wanted to think about it until the next morning.

In the afternoon it was my turn. Renquist said, "Mr. Cameron called this morning to talk about what you're looking for. Any chance you might be interested in renting the lawyer's place? He's been trying to sell it since the fire, with no takers. I'll bet he would jump at the chance to get a little out of it, especially if you said you might rent with the option to buy. Do you know anything about it?"

"I only know about his lawsuit against Abe Forester. I had no reason to see the place. It's sited so there's no evidence of it from the main road. I don't think there's even gravel on his track. I'd be interested in it for location's sake. I do love the area and it would be near my friends."

After we got out there, we decided not to try the dirt track in. We walked the last couple of hundred yards, partly up and partly side hill, then up onto a plateau.

The house faced south and nestled into the side of the hill as though it had been born and raised there. The trees had been trimmed with care and only one had been removed, to allow the sun to enter the living space. It was the most beautiful, organic house I'd ever seen. The combination of native stone and unpainted oak slabs was fascinating. There were no hard angles. The windows were openings from the house's heart that reached to the hills and sky.

"What a magnificent place. I can't believe he would leave it or that no one wanted it. What happened to the lawyer?"

Renquist answered. "He's been out of the country on an assignment, Turkey I think. He's been gone since June. The story I got from Penard was that he'd spent most of two years building it, doing everything he could by himself. The stone came from the ridge behind the house. He hauled and mortared every piece himself and used the oak slabs from the trees he cleared for the pond.

"It was to be a home for him and his wife. I guess when she realized he was serious, and meant for her to live in the woods away from her social life and friends in Pittsburgh; she bolted, and ran off with his law partner.

"Anyway, the biggest problem is that he wasn't finished with the most important parts, there's no power or heat. He ran his equipment with a generator. It's going to cost a bundle to put gravel on the dirt path he used and it needs to be graded to keep it from washing out. The place is too expensive for most people who want a second house in the country. It has too much acreage and you gotta admit it's not the usual house."

"Well, Mr. Renquist, I'm anxious to see the inside."

I had the feeling I'd been in this house before. Her mark was on it, as surely as if she'd signed her name on the front door. When we entered the kitchen, I knew I was right. Her signature cabinets with the sinuous curves, hung from the walls and ceiling like sculptures. The stone island this time was pale green to compliment the slight gray-green of the wood stain on the cabinets.

The lawyer had put light maple floors throughout, which increased the feeling of open space. Hidden from the outside by the slopes of the various portions of roof was the protective top for the interior patio, with the possibility of glorious starlit nights. I was in awe of her artistry and talent.

I turned to Ben. "This is one of Jenny Cameron's houses. The men must come to see it. I hope they'll want it as much as I do. What a tremendous honor it would be for us, and tribute to her, if we could own and live in one of the houses that she designed. Mr. Renquist, what is the asking price?"

"You haven't changed a bit, have you ma'am?" He turned to Ben, "No willy-won'ty about this woman, Mr. Johnson."

He dug into his pile of papers. "He's asking two hundred fifty thousand dollars, but it has eighty acres plus a year around creek, a pond and some outbuildings."

I had enough money of my own to cover the purchase and I wanted the house more than I could explain to anyone, except myself. It was a part of the Cameron family heritage and its unearthly beauty and charm made me want to weep and to sing at the same time.

"How soon could you get a building inspector out here?"

Renquist grinned. "Don't miss a thing, do you, ma'am? Actually, he's already been here. He says the guy did a better job than most professionals. Everything is more than up to code."

"Do you think the price is fair?"

"Yes, ma'am, more than fair. When you get the rest of it done, it will be worth a bundle."

I glanced at Johnson now and smiled. "Would you be willing to help us finish it up and live with us here until you get settled in your own place?" I knew Ben's grin meant yes.

"Mr. Renquist, I would like to buy this property. Let's make an appointment for tomorrow morning at nine o'clock to sign the papers. That will give you time to get things in order. It has been a pleasure doing business with you."

Ben spoke up then. "Thanks for showing me around this morning. I think with the new developments I'll be putting my dogs at Foresters' since it's just down the hill. Never know though, I may be needing a place too, a little later next year."

Now, Renquist actually smiled. "If you bring me much more business Mrs. Cameron, I'll have to give you a cut or put you on the payroll. Your brother-in-law is looking for a place too."

My heart was singing as I thought about the project ahead. "I need to get home, gentlemen. I have dinner to fix."

Everyone was there for dinner, even General Ryan, who was returning to Idaho early tomorrow. I began to tell everyone about "Jenny's House". I called it that from the very beginning. After dinner, Cade and I began to make lists of things to do.

One happy speculation was whether Tim could come to help with the heavy work. Cade wouldn't have safe use of his arm for several more months and we would need to get the house ready to live in during the worst of the winter.

I looked forward to some serious wood splitting since we would probably be settled around a wood stove to keep warm as well as to cook on. Thad took Margot off to bed and Ben took off for a walk. We stayed to work on plans and lists for our new project.

Tuesday was an incredible day filled with anticipation and then fulfillment. Cade took the morning off from the store to come and sign papers. Then we headed out to the house. I was coming to appreciate his trust and openness about money.

We set up a special account for the new house and allotted what we thought would be a generous amount for finishing the basic building requirements. We decided to get along with one truck and I planned to shop for a Subaru as soon as I could get to Pittsburgh. We wouldn't use the dirt road to the house until we could make some grade changes and get some solid gravel footing for it.

Cade's first sight of the house was from the same vantage point we'd reached on foot the day before. "Jenny's House" was even lovelier with the darkening sky and lowering clouds of approaching snow. It nestled down into the hillside like a mother hen brooding her chicks. Even the naked branches of the winter forest lent a sculptured look to her solid beauty.

The glorious abandon of the glistening yellow witch hazel in the understory lit up the hillside. The rock outcroppings were dotted with lichens in shades of green, yellow, rust and red, all freshened and swollen into full form by the winter's moisture.

We stopped to catch our breath and I knew Cade must be realizing for the first time, the tremendous loss of talent the family had suffered because of Jenny's untimely death. He had never met his niece, since he'd left home before she was born.

I already had the notebook out and we made notes of the things to be done right away and those we wanted to do in the future. The driveway grading and gravelling stood at the top of the outdoor list. A small, garden tractor with a snow blade was second.

The indoor list began with several wood stoves. I wanted soapstone ones to augment the fireplaces that would eat up wood by the cord. We moved through the various rooms and tried to visualize what they had been designed for. The one we chose as our bedroom had a lowered ceiling that curved around the sleeping area and dainty, raised fireplace.

The biggest immediate problem was electricity. I hated the idea of stringing wires from the road. It would spoil the look and would be viciously expensive. There were no appliances in the kitchen, not even a wood cook stove, and of course, no furniture. It was gloomy and cold inside and the task became more formidable by the minute.

I spoke to Cade as we finished the assessment. "Let's go out and see what's in the outbuildings and check out the pond. I need to know if he planned to use solar. There may be a pad for the collectors and a special shed set away from the house for the batteries. What about the plumbing?"

Cade shrugged his shoulders. "It looks like he was planning to use composting toilets. He didn't put in any of the usual wastewater drains in the bathrooms and the kitchen isn't plumbed for modern water handling. There's only a hand pump at the sink. I can understand his wanting to live in the woods but I can also sympathize with his wife for not wanting to move in here, especially with the way he was expecting for her to live."

He took me in his arms. His kiss was gentle and

111

comforting. At least he didn't say any more then, but gave me the chance to realize the enormity of the task ahead and to work through my disappointment first.

We stepped out into the darkening day and found the work shed, a very nice animal shed with two well-used horse stalls, and a large woodshed with at least ten cords of prime oak, split and ready to use, along with neatly bundled kindling. The lawyer's ax, splitting maul and wedges were neatly stored in a wooden box of oily sand.

There was no sign of a garden or landscaping. It probably was not his intention, judging from his handling of the trees around the house. We found the pond, out of sight over a slight rise. I recognized the hand of the Corps of Engineers in its design. It was much larger than I could have imagined for the terrain and was already filled to go into the winter. It should make fire insurance much cheaper.

As we walked up behind the pond toward the top of the ridge, something about the skyline caught my eye, something that didn't quite fit. When we approached closer, my steps slowed, as I realized what it might be.

It was a grieving cairn like the one I had made for Michael's bairn. It had a wooden cross, lashed together with a wide leather band tooled with Celtic symbols. Portions of a flower wreath still graced the top, and as we knelt beside the stones we found a large wooden block nestled among them.

The message was carved into the wood, along with a magnificent carving at one side. It was of a Scottish warrior woman with her sword raised, her wild hair and billowy cloak streaking out behind her in the wind.

In Memory of my beloved Jenny
Jennifer Rose Cameron
April 10, 1966---May 31, 2001
May she dwell with the angels

I whispered. "He didn't leave because of the fire, but because of the death of his lover. Poor man, I wonder where he is now. Oh, Cade, how sad."

Cade raised me to my feet and we clung to each other on the ridge of the beautiful mountain, looking out over the ripples and twists of the foothills as they made their way off into the growing darkness. Surely the lovers had done this many times during the house building.

Darkness would come early this day because of the clouds. We needed to get down onto the road. Our trek back to the house to lock up, and then down to our truck, was done in thoughtful silence. As we climbed into Black Beauty for the return trip, I leaned over to Cade and kissed him.

"My Precious One, I love you so much. God has been good to us, Cade. I hope we can repay him in some way."

The deer were already taking shelter and the wilderness stood silent. Nothing moved except a huge owl starting early on his hunt before the snow sent him to his roost.

As we pulled into Penards' back driveway to park, I moved closer to Cade. "I hope you'll understand. I'll always be glad I found 'Jenny's House' and bought it; especially after what we've learned just now. I'm glad she spent some happy time in her life here. She was such a talented linguist as well as a talented architect and engineer. I'm glad to be able to honor her this way.

"There's something else we need to do for her and for Michael; find Tony."

Cade grinned at me. "Sounds like another story from the annals of Cameron history. I'm sure Zach will want to hear it too. Let's wait until we can get together, maybe tonight?"

"That's fine. I'm starving. I wonder what Margot has simmering on the back of the stove. I'm glad she seems to be better. That baby means more than the world to them after what they've been through.

"Have you counted up how many babies are incubating among the people we love; Kylie Lou's, Gloria's, and Margot's? I'll have to begin making baby shower gifts. First though, I need to get the Christmas gifts finished. It's less than a month until Christmas and I'm hardly started."

I was chattering happily as we went in the back porch entrance to the kitchen. Cade caught me as we shut the back door and gave me a kiss so passionate and loving I was breathless with joy. "What's that for, Commander?"

"Just because I love you so much that it hurts."

"That's what Abe Forester said about his love for Kylie Lou, the first time we met. I'm honored, Cade Cameron. Let's not waste a moment of it."

It was three-thirty and we had plenty of time to share our love before supper.

When I went down to start supper, I reached in my apron pocket and found the envelope General Ryan had given me several days before. With all the things going on I had completely forgotten it. I took a few minutes to open it and read the note inside. I was devastated by the news it contained.

It was from Casey Borders, written in the evening after we had worked together at Jamie's. What a tangled and twisted web his Russian handler had woven for him.

An immediate change of assignment was made after the house in Finland was entered by our operatives. He was to kidnap me and bring me to Russia as a hostage and cryptography expert.

In his note he said that he couldn't do it to me and that he decided to try to escape to a neutral country before his handler knew that he was gone.

He hoped that I would be safe from harm and he wished me well. He also asked for my prayers for his safety.

I was weeping when Cade came into the kitchen. I wasn't ready to share my grief then or perhaps ever. I had been right about my assessment of his character and his situation. I prayed for his soul and for mine.

CHAPTER FOURTEEN ZACH SHARES HIS STORY

It was about seven o'clock Tuesday evening when I headed down to Gary's Grill. It would be busy now with late dinner guests, and Yvette had several hours to work yet before I'd know if she'd changed her mind and would see me.

Tricia was still working her long shift and took my order. While I waited for my supper, several townspeople stopped by to say hello and to welcome me to town. Word had gotten around fast that I'd be working with Dr. Campbell while Doc Pete was gone.

I was glad that I'd decided to work in Doc Pete's office. The more I settled in, it felt right. I respected Jamie's skills as a doctor, but wondered if he realized how difficult his job would be. The handicap of his unusable hand wouldn't go away. These next four months would be important for both of us and we would need each other's support.

When my order came, Tricia gave me a big smile and tucked a sheet of folded paper under my plate. I was afraid to open it. Maybe I was being too persistent, too fast. Maybe Yvette would say no again.

Well, I would keep trying. Our times together in the early morning hours had been the most special and precious of my whole life. We had laid the gentle groundwork for a deeper relationship. I knew I wanted Yvette to be my wife, this woman and none other. I could wait; I would wait for her as long as it took.

It was a good thing I'd ordered a simple supper. Yvette's famous potato soup was gentle going down but I was so nervous I could hardly eat. I must have looked miserable because Tricia came back to the booth and whispered, "Don't worry. She loves you. Open your note."

I finished my soup and then picked up the note. I was glad for the semi-darkness when I finished reading it.

My Dear Doctor Zachary Cameron,
Thank you very much for your offer to walk
me home when I am finished. I will come to
you when I am ready to leave.
Sincerely, Yvette Sorley

P.S. I think that I love you too. Y.S.

That rascal Tricia came back to the table to offer me dessert along with a packet of Kleenex. I accepted both.

When Yvette came out from the kitchen, she looked like a queen. She greeted her favorite customers, some of them in French.

As she worked her way over to me, her smile became even more relaxed and happy. She put her cloak on the opposite bench and sat beside me in the booth. The warmth of her body turned my mind to mush.

She smiled at me. "Well, Dr. Zachary? Would you like to stay here and visit or shall we begin our evening with a walk in the snow?"

"Let's walk, Yvette. I need to stretch my legs," My voice dropped to a whisper, "and I need to see your glorious hair cascading down in joyous abandon."

It was a beautiful winter night. As we stepped from Gary's, the snow was coming down in gentle swirls. The flakes were as large as God allowed. One fell on Yvette's nose and I kissed it off as I reached to take the combs from her hair. She took my hand. "Let's run, Zach. Run like the wind until we can't run any more. I'm so frightened and so happy I can hardly bear it. Come quickly."

I'd been so convinced that she would turn me down. Now I was frantic, thinking about what I would do next. I'd promised myself I wouldn't try to seduce her, that I would be honorable and chaste and other high-minded stuff. But here she was, like an angel flying beside me, with melted snowflakes glistening on her eyelashes. Or were they tears?

"Wait, Yvette. We don't want to lose your lovely combs."

She stopped in the middle of the snow-strewn street. Her breath came in tiny gasps, as I took the combs from her hair and put them into my pocket. Her hair fell in a golden cascade around her shoulders as I gathered her into my arms. She was trembling as I bent to kiss her.

It was the closest we had ever been, our bodies clinging beneath her cloak. I realized what a magnificent body she had, lithe and strong and she was much taller than I had realized.

"Yvette? Do you have any idea how much I love you? How much I want to be a part of your life? How much I want to be the father of your children? May I kiss you?"

Her face turned up to mine was radiant and she didn't hesitate as she nodded yes. My kiss was gentle. I didn't want to frighten her away again.

I whispered, "Will you marry me, Yvette?"

I could see tears glistening in her eyes. "Zach, no one has ever kissed me like that before. No matter what happens, I'll always remember your kiss."

I held her closer. "What do you mean? What could possibly happen to our love?"

Her voice was filled with sadness as she answered.

"Come. It is time for you to know about Yvette Sorley and her past. Perhaps then, you will not want her any more."

Sam Saunders had hinted at her difficult life, and the wise young lady, Tricia, knew something had made her friend Yvette very sad. I had felt it too.

I was sure of one thing though, I wanted her to trust me, to feel safe in our love. I knew what would happen if we went to her place to talk. I feared my body wouldn't be as honorable as my promises.

I took her hands in mine. "Yvette, we shouldn't go to your apartment. We need to find a place where we can talk, but be protected from gossip. Shall we go down the street to Penards'? Sara and Margot will be there to protect you."

She had a thoughtful look on her face. "What a wise idea, Zach. Yes, I can do that. Perhaps Sara would be willing to be with us when we talk. I trust her wise ways."

We turned and walked back past the Grill as the latest guests were leaving for home. Several couples waved and offered us evening greetings as they went to their snow-covered cars. I glanced at my watch and was glad it was only nine o'clock. I knew Sara was not one to stay up late. I hoped they weren't in bed yet.

When we got there, we hung up our coats in the hallway and joined them. Cade was sitting with Sara and Violet in front of the fire. There were papers and drawings spread out on the table in front of the couch.

Cade rose to greet us "Good to see you, Yvette. It's a mighty pretty night to be out walking."

It was hard to miss the question in his voice, but Yvette

just smiled. She was showing talents I wouldn't have imagined. God! She was beautiful.

She spoke to Cade. "We would like to borrow Sara for a few minutes if we may? We need her wise presence."

Sara nodded to him and left the room with us. Knowing Sara's intuitive powers, she probably knew what was about to happen. I could feel her protectiveness and loyalty to Yvette, as a woman and as a friend. She took Yvette's hand as we went down the hall.

"Let's go into the kitchen. Would you like something to drink?"

Yvette glanced at me and smiled. "Yes, thank you; something cold. We ran part of the way and I'm very warm."

Sara and I settled into our chairs and Yvette remained standing as she began.

"Doctor Zachary Cameron has asked me to marry him. I cannot in good conscience allow him to want me, unless he knows about my life.

"You probably put two and two together, Sara, when Isabelle told you about taking Roslin Marie's identity and escaping to Paris. Yes, I picked her up off the streets of Paris, dirty, hungry and terrified of what she'd done.

"Every lovely young girl believes that she can make a living as a prostitute in a big town. Well, it doesn't work that way, especially not in Paris. I tried to persuade her to go home and ask her parents' forgiveness, but she was a willful and stubborn child and refused for fear of what they might do.

"So I took her in, fed her, found clothes for her, and gave her a place to sleep. Most important, I kept her safe, healthy and clean. Most houses were bad places and the girls didn't last the year out, but my place was different.

"She was good at her job and many of the men tried to persuade her to marry them. My clientele was high class and I was making good money.

"My downfall came several years later, caused by an unpleasant rivalry with another woman who was jealous of our success. I learned too late about the highly-placed police official to whom I hadn't given enough bribe. Perhaps no amount would have been enough.

"She turned in a false accusation against me and I was sent to prison for two years. I protested my innocence, but it was hopeless. I spent the first year in the brutal nightmare of the penal system. Prostitutes in prison are treated worse than murderers and there was no escape.

"It was difficult to forgive. I spent hours on my knees in prayer. One of the guards tried to protect me from the worst of the brutality and I will be forever grateful to her. She did something else that saved my life during the worst of my despair.

"A cooking school, as a gift to the city of Paris, gave one scholarship each year to a woman in prison. This guard entered my name for consideration. When I won it, I was able to spend the next year going to school in the daytime and my nights in prison. When my school was over I was free to go back into society, my debt repaid.

"Several students in the cooking school asked me to marry them, but I wanted to come to America and begin a new life. I decided I would never touch a man again or keep dreams of marrying and having a home and a family.

"Then, Zachary Cameron came into my life. I was tempted not to tell him, but I could not start our life together with bad secrets between us.

"So, my dear Zachary, the woman you have called an angel is in fact a former prostitute, madam, and a criminal who spent two years in prison."

She was weeping as she turned away to leave the room.

"I'm sure you can no longer want me now, so I will leave you to your happy lives, your evenings in front of the fire and the happy sound of laughter as you play with your children when you come home from work. Good-bye, my dearest Zachary, I would have loved you well."

I rose to block her path. "Sit down Yvette. It's my turn to speak now, and for you to listen."

Her eyes widened in surprise but she obeyed. Sara reached out to hold her hand as Yvette sat beside her.

My heart was filled with love for this brave woman.

"Thank you for being honest about your past; you were right to tell me, but not for the reasons you felt you needed to. It's important for people to be able to share their story with someone, to speak the words and to share their pain.

"Yvette, I love you in spite of your life circumstances as well as because of them. You are a precious, loving soul and I want you to be a part of my life.

"For as long as God allows, I promise to love you, protect you and cherish you. Please trust me and trust my love."

She sat in quietness, hand in hand with Sara. She must confront her moment of truth. Either she would accept my love and begin a new part of her life or she would deny herself the happiness she deserved and desired, giving in to a false sense of justice and shame. I could do no more; I could only wait and hope.

She rose from her place and stood in front of me. I could hardly breathe. My heartbeat was so loud I was sure that the women could hear it.

"Dearest Zachary, I accept your proposal. I would be honored to be your wife." Her smile was gentle and her kiss was filled with promise.

I was surprised when Yvette stepped back from our embrace. "Now, my Zachary, love of my life; it is your turn. I want you to tell me what happening has turned you into such a melancholy soul. I think something very difficult happened to you in your past life and now you must tell me about it and then we will lay it to rest."

I was stunned. I turned away from her, and looked straight into Sara's eyes. They were brimming with tears. I wasn't prepared for this. I'm a man. I'm supposed to be strong and able to handle anything and besides; I'm a psychiatrist, for God's sake! I'm supposed to heal other people, not myself.

It was my turn to hesitate as I tried to decide whether to tell these women what had happened to destroy my life and my happiness. Then, I saw no alternative. Yvette had opened her heart to me and I could do no less.

No one in my new life knew, except General Ryan. It was why he'd hired me, when I was destitute and filled with grief. I settled down at the table with the ladies.

"She would be five now, about the same age as little Lane Crosswick. Her hair is black, like mine, and covers her head in a halo of dainty curls. Her smile lights up a room and her laughter is like the sound of angels at play.

"She is the most precious person in the whole universe, and my wife took her away. I haven't seen her in almost three years, not since the trial. I don't know where she is, or whether she's still alive. I don't know if she thinks about me when she goes to bed at night and says her prayers."

I turned away from the women. I felt only bitterness and hatred for my wife; there were no tears.

"My wife Jane married me for the prestige and money she thought a doctor would provide. After we were married, she announced that she didn't want children and actually refused to have them.

"She wanted the rest of the marriage bed though, as well as the beds of many other men. Her adultery was brazen and without conscience. It was a pure accident of God that it was my seed that brought forth my beautiful daughter."

I reached into my pocket and took out the last picture of my baby, Laurie. It was one of us, when she was two, feeding the ducks in our favorite park. When Sara looked at it, she gasped at the likeness, as father and daughter knelt on the ground, hands outstretched with bread for the birds. She handed the picture to Yvette.

"From the moment my wife found out she was pregnant she became more and more hostile and terrifying in her anger. I feared for the child's safety every instant of every day. After Laurie was born, I was the one who gave her the touching and loving every baby needs.

"Jane finally went over the edge. She made friends with a woman who persuaded her to divorce me. But she didn't leave it there; the two of them framed me for molestation of the other woman's child.

"Because of the collusion between them, I didn't have a chance. The court did everything to destroy my reputation and livelihood except revoke my license to practice medicine. They simply didn't have the evidence or the power to do that. But they made me leave the state and forbade me from ever seeing my daughter again. They might as well have shot me, or sent me to the gas chamber, and my wife knew it. It was her final act of cruelty.

"General Ryan hauled me up out of a ditch in a blinding rainstorm outside Memphis and took me home. He saved my life and found me a job at the base in Mountain Home."

I turned away from the women; tears now streaming down my face. "Stop! Stop it!" I whispered to myself. "Men aren't allowed to cry."

My fists were clenched at my sides as I walked toward the door, my head down and my eyes closed in misery. I ran into a solid wall of women. Sara and Yvette were standing in my way, their linked arms blocking my path.

Sara spoke. "That's far enough, Zach. Now it's time for you to hear us out."

We went back to sit down as she spoke. "To lose a child and not know where she is or whether she is still alive, can be a living death. And knowing that you are forbidden to search for her or contact her, is the ultimate cruelty. I have lived the nightmare too.

"Zach, listen to me, sometimes the only thing we can do is pray. Pray for your daughter Laurie's safety, her good health, and that she is being cared for. Against every feeling in your mind and heart, against every feeling of hate and misery, you must pray for Jane. She is no longer your wife, she forfeited the right to that, but she is still the mother of your child."

"I can't. I hate her for what she did to us."

Sara whispered to me, "Yes you can and you must, or you will lose your soul in the depths of a hell you have made for yourself. For everyone's sake you must try. Every waking moment, you must try.

"I was singing a lullaby to my baby girl when she was taken from me in the convent. Every night I sang it, during all those years when I didn't know where she was or how her life was turning out. It brought solace to me in my sadness."

She began to sing, and Yvette came to take me into her arms. They were both singing now and I felt the amazing resilience and power of these two women, as they took their own sorrows and those of the world into their hearts and returned them as a benediction of peace and loving.

Yvette kissed me again as we stood together. "Now, dear Zachary, I claim you as mine. I promise to love you, protect you and cherish you, now and forever."

Sara took her hand. "Yvette, I'm so happy for you both. But now we must be practical. Your workday begins at four and bedtime is long past. I'm sure Margot would ask you to stay the night if she were still up, so do stay with us and Zach can walk you to work in the morning. There's a second bedroom upstairs by my room. Let me get you some towels and make sure the bed is made up."

The women went down the hall hand in hand, whispering together. I went to the front porch to enjoy the still falling snow, and to thank God for answering the first of my prayers.

CHAPTER 15 SARA CONTINUES THE STORY

Everyone slipped away in the morning while Margot and I slept in until deliciously late. I needed a day of artsy-craftsy Christmas handwork, knitting and sewing. We kept the fire going and the soup pot simmering all day.

Jamie came to supper with Zach. We put supper aside for Cade and Thad, who would be late coming from the hardware store. Business was booming and they extended the hours for the holiday season for the many people who worked and didn't have time to shop during normal hours.

Cade was contented and happy. He looked ten years younger. He was getting along with his cast much better than I had, and he never complained. The last time I changed his abdominal bandages, he'd told me what the injuries were. If he hadn't turned sideways by instinct, he would have been killed instantly. I could hardly keep from losing my supper.

After we cleaned up the supper dishes, I was expecting a quiet evening in front of the fire. Instead, Zach and Jamie asked me to return with them to the upper room. I wondered whether the reports were back and when they would share them, if indeed they planned to. I was surprised when Jamie closed the door to our work room.

The green laboratory notebooks lay on the desk in their plastic bag. Next to them, sat a bag with the rectangular wooden box I'd seen in Finch's garage; the box with my birth name, Rebecca Jane Campbell inscribed in the upper left corner.

Jamie began the session. "We've received the information we need to finish our report to you. Zach and I haven't been able to agree on how the information should be shared."

I rose from my chair. "And what was the disagreement about? Perhaps I can save us all some difficult moments."

I took a deep breath and continued. "In fact, perhaps you would allow me to speak first. I'd like to tell you about what

123

I learned on the morning when I made the foolish mistake of working through a session alone.

"I assume that Zach was sent to Pennsylvania to shut down Professor Finch's position as district supervisor and to retrieve whatever government documents there might be among his professional and personal papers.

"Your earlier comments to me about my personnel files and Dave Finch's entries to it, suggested that you thought a different interpretation of our group's problems was in order. Information given to you by Dr. Campbell provided you with the clues to narrow the search.

"While I was helping with the sorting for Dodie Finch, I couldn't help but see you put aside some research notebooks and equipment. At the time I had no idea what they might mean or why you would want to send such things to Forensics unless a crime had been committed."

I needed to sit down with the men. I was still so appalled and frightened by my experience with the writing and recollecting that it made me physically ill.

"Would you excuse me for a few moments? I need a drink of water."

When I returned, a feeling of anticipation but also of compassion and support filled the room. It gave me the courage to begin.

"The situation I wrote about during the unsupervised session was my college days and abduction on graduation day, not the middle period when I suffered the rape and violation by an unknown assailant.

"I was recalling the years in Paris in graduate school, when I met and became close friends with Anna, Kostyan Skorski and Dave Finch. Dave and I were working on PhD programs in the same area of biology.

"We'd spent many hours together every day in our work and studies. It seemed logical and convenient to continue our relationship. We were planning to be married a few days after graduation; a very academic decision.

"Our courtship was unusual in many ways and he was not always predictable or stable. Everyone in our bunch lived hard. When work and studying were done, we did a lot of partying and drinking and wild French stuff I would never tell anyone about, ever.

"As I thought back to those parties, I began to remember things about Dave. They seemed quirky at the time, but we were all a bit crazy and believed in live and let live.

"He had a fixation about his hands. Although they were very large, his fingers were long and tapered like a musician's. His other continuing distress was because he had practically no body hair. He was terrified that someone would assume he was a fairy; not so great among tough American males going into the intelligence community.

"One of Dave's joys was dressing for masquerade parties. No one ever recognized him. His disguises were uncanny. He did them all himself after he learned the techniques from a friend who worked for a theatre group, doing makeup.

"Dave had a huge ego. When I disappeared on graduation day, he must have thought the worst; that I'd dumped him, instead of that something terrible might have happened to me, which was the truth. When I was abducted and forced to marry Henri Lambert to protect my child, I was not able to contact Dave for several years. Although he never spoke of it later when we were scientific collaborators, I can imagine he was very angry and jealous of my husband, and later, the men who worked with me and sought to protect me.

"Zach, I think I know what's in the box with my birth name. Would you hand it to me?"

I took the bag, opened it and put the box to my face. The odor coming from the box triggered the reflexive revulsion I'd suffered during my time of violation, at least until my soul and spirit had escaped from my body.

"I need a pair of sharp, sturdy scissors"

I stood and waited. When Jamie returned with them, I said, "I assume you've seen what's in here."

They both nodded yes.

I began to describe what I expected to find. "The fingers are thick, gross and stubby; covered with coarse hairs. The wrists are wide and knotted with the cords of the tendons he so coveted. The part of the gloves covering his hands and arms is heavy with wiry hair, the kind he always envied on other men. The gloves reached up above his elbows and he was wearing them the night he attacked me. The smell of them, the smell of animal lust, began the night of terror."

I opened the box and took them out. Then, I cut the gloves, dropping the small pieces back into the box. There were no tears, only a sense of finality to my task.

"Gentlemen, I suspect he wore the gloves when he wrote in the notebooks, hence there would be no fingerprints, and the resident graphologist must have had a difficult time judging whether it was even Dave's handwriting since his physical hand would have been different enough to cause different forms. I'm sure the DNA report came back with his print and no one else's."

I reached to take the notebooks from their bag. "May I see the notebook with my name?"

Zach handed me all three notebooks and a smaller codebook.

"Everything is written in code. The government cryptographers were unable to crack it even with the key. They worked for a week with every computer skill they could think of."

I smiled with relief. "It's just as well. It would have been most embarrassing for me as well as for them if they had succeeded. This is the code Anna Skorski and I devised and used for all the years we worked together. As our supervisor, Dave Finch was the only other person with the knowledge to decode and the skill to write it."

I opened the small codebook to check the beginning date and the line, glanced at the poem, and reached for the second notebook, page 100. I began to translate.

"Date: March 18, 1989. Research Subject: Dr. Sara Harvey. Title of Research: 'The Terror of Seduction.'"

The description of his experimental design was long and elaborate. The summary of the results was very short, only two paragraphs. The concluding statement expressed his frustration and anger when the experiment failed.

Because I'd been able to send my mind and spirit away from my body, he was unable to achieve his goals and discontinued his efforts. It was that night when my injuries occurred and my bones were broken. I could not ask for help or sympathy from my husband and bore the pain and horror alone.

I turned away from the men to look out into the darkness of the winter night. I felt sick in my deepest heart. My superior in the Service, my scientific collaborator, was the one who used the information I gave him as part of my job, to commit the violation of my body and spirit. He was the only one with the combination of information and intelligence to have performed the evil act.

"Do you wish for me to go on?"

Jamie came to me and took me in his arms. "No, Sara, it's over now; over for everyone involved."

"That poor, sick man," I whispered. "He must have been

insane to do what he did to another human being. Thank God I didn't marry him. I hate to think what he may have done to Dodie."

Zach answered. "She's getting help, but I suspect you two were not the only ones. As a last closure to the investigation, would you please translate just enough so that we can find out if there are other names we need to give to the authorities? We will protect their privacy but try to provide help for them."

After I'd figured out the arrangement in the research notes, we worked several hours going through the first two notebooks, translating enough of the text to find the victims' names. At the end of the second notebook, an entry made me gasp with dismay. The men were taking notes on my comments, and looked up from their work.

I felt like I'd been kicked in the gut, and could only whisper. "Jamie, did you know?"

He was silent for several moments. "Yes, she came to Campbell's Point to find me and to ask for advice. Jenny wanted the job so much and worked so hard to get it. She was devastated when he began his harassment. She was able to keep him at bay for a while, until he forced her to go to St. Louis on the Andretti mission."

He got up from the desk and looked at Zach.

"How much do we have to know? I don't know if I can bear to hear more."

Zach rose and put his arm around Jamie's shoulders. "It's time to let Jenny rest in peace. Perhaps her apparent suicide in Bermuda has an explanation now."

"Jamie, I'm so sorry." I whispered, "That's why you didn't want to go to meet Dave and Dodie Finch that day, wasn't it? You must have been devastated to learn of the connections among us. How will we bear it now, Dear Friend?"

Jamie's voice was wooden with grief. "First, we must finish this gristly task. Then, perhaps Zach will help us begin a healing process.

"The hatred I have for Dave Finch makes me feel as if I've been thrown into a vat of concentrated sulfuric acid, except I don't die. I just continue to writhe and burn."

He rose to leave the room as he looked at Zach.

"I can't do any more."

Zach blocked his way. "Please, don't go. Don't leave us now; we need you. For Jenny's memory and for her sake, this will never go beyond this room and we must minister to each other until it is resolved. Sara, would you please continue? We're almost finished."

When we got to the most recent entry in the third notebook, I felt waves of revulsion and infinite sadness. The entry was for his latest student assistant, the lovely and brilliant, Caroline Myers. I wondered if her return to Montana at his death notice had been one of utter relief. No wonder she'd been so upset.

And then it occurred to me. Perhaps as a woman of the new millennium, she was the one who managed the courage to report her harassment to the authorities at the university, and was the one who stopped his cycle of evil and violence. That could explain why his office and laboratory were destroyed and the way it was carried out. The College would want no part in the disgusting affair.

When we finished, Zach thanked me. "You are an amazing woman, Sara Cameron. I pray that God may watch over you and Doctor Campbell and give you closure now."

I hated to send Jamie away alone but he needed to get home to work on a take-home final. I suggested we gather up Cade and all walk Jamie home.

"I could use some exercise if I'm going to get in shape for splitting wood all winter, and maybe Yvette will still be at Gary's and would like a companion on her walk home."

Zach smiled. "Sounds like a plan. Let's go." He stopped off at the Grill to wait for her.

When we got to Jamie's house, he invited us to come in. He made hot tea and we sat at the kitchen table.

I had the feeling that something more needed to be done to help Jamie's healing. I looked at my beloved husband and decided to make a request. I prayed that he would trust me and allow my simple lie for Jamie's sake. I took Cade's hand in mine.

"The first time you wanted to tell me Jacques' story about the death of Dave Finch, I refused to listen to you. I thought Jacques should do the telling. I've changed my mind. I'm ready to hear it now. I need to have closure to the whole sordid affair. Jamie, will you be with me now while Cade does this, because you and I are in this together?"

Cade knew I'd heard the story from him before. I hoped that he would understand that I was doing this for Jamie. I'm sure the second telling was no easier for him than the first and it was only because I knew Jacques had survived, that I was able to listen as Cade began telling the story.

"Jacques told me he was late getting into Manaus, Brazil, because of the service for Michael Cameron. Dave didn't wait for him, but went on into the interior. He left a message for Jacques to meet him at a small village upstream. I think Jacques knew it was an ambush, but his assignment from his superiors was to kill Dave Finch, whatever it took.

"Jacques took the rickety, once-daily boat that next afternoon. When everyone got off at the end of the run, Jacques was left to find his way. The main street was only two blocks long and contained mostly bars and public houses and fronts for selling drugs and jewels.

"Jacques heard Dave before he saw him, about halfway down the first block. He was slouched on a bench in front of a tavern, singing 'Oh My Darling Clementine', at the top of his voice. He was very drunk.

"Jacques said he strolled down the block on the opposite side of the street until he was close enough to see what was happening, but far enough away not to be part of the scene. A young girl came up to Dave and stroked his knee. He wasn't so drunk that he didn't notice. He grabbed her wrist as she tried to twist away.

"Jacques said he couldn't believe what happened next. The little girl could have gotten away, but instead, she moved just far enough away that Dave staggered up from the bench. He grabbed her blouse in his hands and stripped her to the waist.

"The rest happened so fast that Jacques said he couldn't have helped even if he'd wanted to. The girl took Dave's hand and led him into the shadows of the alley and pushed him down onto the ground. She struck him with a large stone and began to go through his pockets. Two other urchins came running from the other end of the alley and they stripped him of his clothes. The girl started with his boots and discovered the knives latched into them."

Cade's voice dropped to a whisper. "Sara, she slit his throat with his own knife and then stabbed him many times with it before she left him sprawled in the gutter filth, his body splattered with mud and dung and his own blood."

The three of us sat in the quiet of Jamie's kitchen, hunkered down with the horror of this tale. No one wanted to talk. I hoped Jamie would find some satisfaction in knowing about the death of this twisted monster, the destroyer of so many lives, including Jenny's and mine. Somehow, I feared that Dave Finch's life and death would haunt us for a long time while we struggled to find healing.

I was terrified. I had to admit I couldn't bring myself to pray for the soul of Dave Finch. It was the most difficult religious crisis in my life and I needed help. I whispered, "Dear friends, help me."

Both Cade and Jamie reached out to me and we held hands in a circle around the table. All I could manage was the Lord's Prayer. My smallest prayer came from the anguish in my heart. "Forgive me Lord; it's all I can do now."

It was Cade who got my cloak and suggested we should leave Jamie to his paper. I felt my heart would break, but I also knew I needed exercise to clear my brain. It helped to be outside and moving. I urged Cade to go along the side street in an area we hadn't yet seen.

At the end of the street we found a cul-de-sac with three houses arranged in the half circle turn around. It looked like the families here were in different stages of child-raising; one with the usual trappings of trikes and bikes with training wheels, another with the usual teenage collection of various jeeps and jalopies and a basketball hoop at regulation height. The third house looked a bit dowdy and forlorn, as though the family could no longer keep the shrubs trimmed and the house in good repair. A single light in an upstairs room went out as we glanced up.

I took Cade's hand. "I wonder who lives there. I hope he isn't all alone, with no one to love and comfort him on this stormy night."

"You do have an active imagination, Sara. Maybe he's going off tomorrow to catch a plane to Hawaii for the winter."

We smiled as we headed back down the street toward our temporary home.

"Cade, we aren't going to be able to move into 'Jenny's House' for months yet, are we? Margot and Thad weren't expecting both of us to be here. When General Ryan sent me to them, he believed that you were dead and that I would need a place and people to grieve with me. Zach, dear thing, is an extra mouth to feed too. What are we going to do?"

We were walking more rapidly back down toward the center of town. It was late and Cade needed to get up at his usual early hour. He stopped for a moment and leaned down to kiss my nose.

"I'm working on it. Thad has a couple of leads and I've heard of several houses in town for rent or sale. If we're lucky, something will turn up by Christmas. Remember we promised to bed down Ben and Zach for a while too.

"We're trying to work out the schedule at the hardware store so Tim can go with Ben to bring back the dogs. What would you think about sending them out on the plane?

"Then they can load up the brown truck and find a used one for the rest of their stuff. Zach's hoping they'll have room to bring his things too so he won't have to go back. He says he's going to need a 4x4 for his house calls and he wants Tim to pick it out."

"Sounds good. You handle it. Let's jog the rest of the way home. I'm ready for a hot bath and a gentle snuggle."

CHAPTER SIXTEEN

It was too snowy next day to go more than a block or two on foot in Campbell's Point. Margot and I were extra careful as we walked to spend the day with Millie at The Cottage. We took our knitting and Christmas projects. One special project for Jamie needed a piano, and Millie had a tiny spinet in the room facing the garden.

Since I knew of Jamie's deep love of music, I wanted to try to arrange some special duets. Millie played well enough to be a pleasant foil for him and they could do it together.

I remembered planning the gift for Jamie when he was engaged to my daughter, and tried not to think about the difficult things that had happened to each of us since then.

I arranged ten of my favorite Christmas carols as duets for three hands and was quite pleased with the results. I had a lovely soft green folder with pockets for the words and music. I painted a simple wreath of holly and ivy on the front, circled it with a halo of evergreen boughs and made a line of snow-covered mountains below it.

I hadn't done anything like it in years and I lost track of time in the joy of the project. When Jamie came to walk us home, I whisked him away from my workroom with a secretive smile.

In three more weeks he would be finished with his aborted experiment in Music Therapy and free to get on with his life. I hoped he was more comfortable each day he worked with Doc Pete and Zach but knew how concerned they were about how much of the practice he could manage.

Thad and Cade stopped by the grill and brought home some of Yvette's potato soup since we'd been gone all day. Ben and Tim were ready to take off for Idaho in the morning. The main road to Pittsburgh was clear and Zach and I offered to take them in early, so he could help me find a used Subaru and drive it home. We knew about the long delays and inspections in the airports so we were going to get them there several hours early.

The pace of our lives didn't seem to slow but with everyone helping we managed to get everything done. We left the men at the airport next morning, found a suitable car early in the day and had time to swing by Dodie's to load up some of her stuff for her Saturday move. She was very grateful for the help and we shared an early lunch with her. She looked marvelous and I was glad for her.

During the week while we were waiting for the men to return from Idaho with the dogs, Millie finally got word that the police had found her possessions. They were in storage compartments on the south side of Pittsburgh. She and Jamie went to retrieve the paintings and to arrange the removal of the fragile antique furniture to safer storage.

Millie was wearing her new wedding ring when they returned from town. As each of us found out, we went to see her. I took her in my arms and wished her well. Her smile was gentle and filled with happiness.

"We decided there was no reason to wait. We both need to get on with life and to do it together. I'm excited about the new house. Thank you, Sara, from the bottom of my heart, for helping Jamie when he needed you most. We both love you very much."

That evening, Thad took Margot out to dinner and I fixed supper for the two brothers. As we finished up, I turned to Zach with a question.

"I've been hoping for a quiet family evening so I could have a chance to hear the story about your leaving the family. When we first met, you told me that you left home on graduation night and never returned. What happened?"

The expression on his face was resigned and filled with sadness. He was looking at Cade as he answered.

"My father, after many years of either mistreating me very cruelly or ignoring me for weeks at a time, told me on high school graduation night not to come home. He said if I did; he would kill me!"

I took his hands in mine. "Did you have any idea what it was about?"

"No, I only knew that he meant it. Later in my life, when I thought about it, I remembered my parents' many fights. Some bitter accusations that I didn't understand as a child came back to me when I got to medical school and tried to work through the anger of being abandoned."

He looked up at his brother. "I remember one night after Cade left, my father shouted at her that Cade wasn't his child and neither was I. That night, I watched my father beat my mother senseless."

I was watching my dear Cade rather than his brother. The expression on his face was one of misery and infinite sadness as he whispered, "I'd hoped it hadn't happened to you as it did to me. Our father's cruelty and brutality made mother a true victim of the war.

"Perhaps her lover was a soldier and they were planning to be married. He was called into active duty before it could happen and before she knew she was pregnant. In those days, unwed mothers were sent away and forced to give their child away.

"Mother may well have done the entrapment because she wanted to survive and to bear her lover's child. Perhaps she hoped against hope that her husband would die in the war."

I asked Cade. "Is that why your father disowned you; not because you married a Jewish woman, but because he believed you were not his child?"

"It made a good cover-up for what he believed was true."

I turned to Zach again. "Is it possible that you could be his child too? "Do you think she might be with her lover now? I wonder if he could be alive and in her small town? I hope she's found some measure of happiness since her husband's death."

He shook his head. "I haven't been able to think about her all these years. I didn't know whether the accusations were true or not, or who he was."

We sat in thoughtful silence as the healing options began to surface in my Cameron men.

It was Zach who spoke first. "It's past time to make a visit to Missouri, brother, don't you agree? Can you get away for the weekend? If we fly out after work on Friday, we'll have two days to do some peacemaking. Let's find out if she'll take us back and if not, at least we tried."

Cade stood up from the table. "It might work, but the only time I've seen her since I left home, was at Michael's service. She acted as if she didn't even recognize me. She was carrying a gun in her purse and she was prepared to kill everyone in the room. We'll need to be careful until we figure out what to do. Are you sure you want to open up all those old wounds?"

Zach took his brother's arm. "Man, I haven't heard that

story. You'd better fill me in before we see her. Maybe Sara would excuse us from dish duty while we talk."

I smiled in relief as I began to clear the table. "Sure, you head back there and get the fire going and I'll bring your coffee. Want me to give Yvette a buzz and tell her you're doing some Cameron family work?"

"Good idea. Tell her I love her too."

I delivered the coffee and a plate of Christmas cookies. Then I slipped off to the sewing room to finish the hem of my green velvet dress.

Next evening when the men were ready to leave for the airport, I gave a shopping list to Cade. "If the timing turns out, would you pick up these things and bring them back in Black Beauty. I assume you plan to take her and leave her at the airport. Please be careful in Missouri, I don't know if reconciliation is in the cards, but I hope so."

When Cade glanced at the list, he looked puzzled.

"Whoever are these things for, Sara?" He began to read from the list. "Prime alfalfa hay, 3 bales; Oats, one 50 lb sack and can to hold same; hanging feed bucket."

He cocked his head to the side in question. I could see his mind computing as he thought through the possibilities.

I smiled as I explained. "I have a feeling the lawyer will be coming back for Christmas. I'd like to spend some time up there decorating and doing some work before it really snows the road shut.

"I hope we'll meet him up there. If he had horses before, he'll probably bring one of them with him. Since you'll be taking the truck, you know I won't go up there alone. Somehow, I thought you'd be upset if I did."

Cade took me in his arms to say good-bye. "You're learning fast, Sweetheart. I'll hold you to your promise. We'll be back Sunday night, unless she sends us away in a hail of bullets. Then it'll be sooner."

They took off for town to catch the red-eye to St. Louis and I went to sit by the fire, to wait and worry. It didn't last long, the worrying at least, because another project needed doing while they were gone and I wondered how to start. I'd try to get the information in public records before I asked General Ryan for help.

I wanted to find Jenny's child, Tony Cameron. He must be coming up on a sad and difficult time, since his mother and father were both gone, and he might not know he had any other family. I didn't know what arrangements had been made for him at Jenny's death.

I got out the last paperwork Kostyan Skorski had prepared for me, to find the number for his financial business office in Chicago. Then I remembered Cal, in Spokane, Washington. It was three hours earlier there and he'd still be in his office. I could call him right now and ask his advice. He'd been our lawyer for years and would know how to go about it. He might even have more clout with the Chicago lawyers.

I found Cal still at the office, finishing up the week's work. We discussed what I wanted. I apologized for not having more particulars on the boy, but we got the most important dates, names and places. I left it to him.

Then I built up the fire in the living room and settled in to work on Zach's boot socks. After a few rounds, I pulled the afghan around my shoulders and slept. When I wakened, even the extra quilt Margot had put over me when they got back from supper wasn't enough to keep me warm. The house was bitter cold and the fire was out.

The men returned early Sunday afternoon. The back of the truck held my horse supplies and the brothers looked tired but contented. Cade hugged me.

"Everything turned out great. Give us few minutes and we'll fill you in on our adventure. Sara, we even got to meet our real dad."

I decided to take Violet for a walk while I waited for them. She was overjoyed to be getting outside, even though the weather was damp and unpleasant. We bundled up and walked down the street toward town. It was difficult for me not to head the other direction toward the end of the road and the woods, but I promised Cade I would be more careful and I would do it, for now.

I'd be glad and relieved when Tim and Ben returned. Violet was acting a little like she might be coming into heat and I wanted Ben to board her and to decide if he wanted to use her to raise another batch of puppies.

How could I have been so lucky? We were just to the corner by Gary's; when Ben's old brown truck came wheeling down Main Street, followed by one really slick, black 4x4. It was mighty fancy, with chrome roll bars and all the stuff I'll bet Tim hoped he could get away with. I wondered what Zach would think, since he'd trusted Tim to pick up a stodgy doctor's truck for him in Boise. Both trucks were loaded to the max and I could see dog cages and equipment stacked high in both rigs. The men waved and headed on out of town to Abe's place.

Violet and I stopped at the back door of Gary's while I left a message for Tricia to call Kylie Lou and tell her they'd just gone by. Then Violet and I jogged home with the good news.

Cade and Zach were in the kitchen rummaging in the refrigerator for a snack. Margot and I took control and shooed them away to the kitchen table while we put supper on early. Thad joined us while the men told about their visit to see their mother.

Cade started the tale with a happy grin. "When we got to town and found Mom's house, it was a little before noon. We went to the back door and we could see her fixing lunch in the kitchen. When I knocked on the door, though, it was a man who opened it. He took one look at the two of us and opened his arms to engulf us in a big bear hug. The whole time we were there, I couldn't get over how much we look like him. It was uncanny. I understand now why my father would have suspected."

"Did they get married?"

"Yes, as soon as father Cameron died. It was why she was so odd and difficult at Michael's service. Mom was terrified someone would find out she'd remarried. She feared she would lose her inheritance."

"Is she happy, Cade? Nothing could ever make up for the years of disastrous marriage but perhaps each day now is even more precious because of the short time she and her beloved have left."

"Yes, I think they're very happy. He's a real gentleman and a very neat guy. His name is Stewart Randolph. He's semi-retired from his own business. Guess what it is?" Cade was grinning as he reached for another slice of bread. "He's a building contractor."

"So you talked shop and left Zach to fend for himself?"

Zach was smiling now. "I took Mom on a long walk around town so she could show me off to all her friends. I got to tell her about Yvette and settling in Campbell's Point. She and Dad want to come in the spring to visit. I told them about 'Jenny's House' and they're anxious to see it. I said I hoped there'd be a wedding to attend."

Thad spoke up now. "Ben and Tim just got back. They'll need help tomorrow at Foresters'. Want to go out there in the morning, Cade? I'll handle the store for a few days while you help them settle in."

Cade went to call Ben, Zach went to Gary's to wait for Yvette and Margot and I sat by the fire with our knitting.

Cal didn't get back to me until Monday evening. His news was mixed and his voice was guarded. "Sara, I had a devil of a time finding the boy. The lawyers in Chicago wouldn't tell me anything until I threatened them with a lawsuit.

"Apparently, Jenny arranged for Michael Cameron to be Tony's guardian if anything happened to her. Since Michael's gone we have a problem. There's a precedent for allowing the next of kin to take over the duties if it isn't spelled out in the will. Since you weren't married to Michael yet, it will need to be his brother. Do you know how I might get hold of him?"

"Yes, he's here in town with me."

Cal continued with the bad news. "We have a big problem. The school where he's staying says he can't leave unless a military officer comes to get him. School is over Wednesday this week and he was going to have to stay the month over the holiday break because there was no one to take him."

"Where is it, Cal?"

"Somewhere in southwestern New York. When I mentioned it to a colleague during lunch today, he said some pretty harsh things about the place. Sara, he said we should try our best to get Tony out of there."

"Let me get Cade on the phone. You two can work something out. Thanks for what you've done already. If Commander Cade Cameron's rank isn't high enough for them, I think General Ryan might be willing to help."

On Tuesday, Cade took Violet to the farm and helped finish settling the dogs in their new quarters. Then, he borrowed Tim from Ben's operation and picked up Zach at the doctor's office. They headed out toward New York about dark. The weather was iffy. They were predicting light snow the next few days but it meant the going could be rough in the backcountry.

They took Zach's new truck. The back of the crew cab was filled with blankets and food. Cade packed his officer's uniform to put on when they found the place, but he'd have trouble fitting the shirt and jacket over his cast. I was frightened when I saw all the hardware being packed. He chose not to tell me any more about what they might find.

I spent a worry-filled night and day waiting for them to return with Tony. Every time the phone rang, my heart leapt into my throat and then careened into my gut.

Zach finally called at eight in the evening. "Sara, we have him and he's OK. We're going to drive straight through. I'm not sure how long it will take. I'm at the Pennsylvania line and we're trying to beat a storm. Sounds like the story of our lives. At least it's Tim's turn to drive. We'll see you the middle of the night. Keep the fire going, My Dear."

Margot and Thad waited with me in front of the fire. I think they knew how important this trip was and how precious the cargo. About midnight, the front door slammed open with a bang, and icy wind blew down the hallway. As we went down to meet them, Tim stepped in the doorway with a bundle of small, sleeping boy wrapped in a quilt.

The two older men looked exhausted and Cade's face was white with pain. I asked, "What happened?"

Cade was not smiling. "We had a little disagreement with the director about whether Tony could come with us."

Zach headed for the phone to call Jamie and I went to get my cloak.

"I'll take Tim home in the truck and bring Jamie back with me."

Thad was looking at Tim across Tony's small, sleeping form.

"I have a feeling that right now, Tim wants to stay with Tony, right?"

Tim nodded yes. "I don't want him to wake up without me being here."

He walked down the hall with all of us following along behind. When he put Tony on the couch in front of the fire, he whispered, "He's been through hell and I don't want him to be afraid it's not over."

He settled down next to his new charge and draped a quilt around them both. Tim wasn't going anywhere.

Zach said, "We need to get Cade to Doc Pete's surgery downtown to get some X-rays. Sara, everything is going to be OK now. You just switch from worry prayers to ones of thankfulness and we'll be back as soon as we can."

The two of them went back out into the snowy night. In an hour Zach was back to pack a suitcase for his brother. Cade's injured arm had been damaged so severely he needed to get to the hospital in Pittsburgh to have it reset.

I was crying as I told them good-bye at the door. Thad went with them to drive. They didn't even think about calling Heart Flight; the ceiling was about 50 feet and lowering by the minute.

I carried down pillows and more blankets for the boys, fed the fire and went off to bed. I tried to do as Zach had asked. My prayers were ones of thanksgiving for the safety of the Cameron men and for dear Tim Campbell who had helped once again when Campbell's Point needed him most.

I was in the kitchen when the men came back about six in the morning, without Cade. Zach said there would be some tough surgery to repair his arm. Cade had taken off his cast so that he could get into his uniform, and his arm was unprotected. It was shattered in several new places.

The men were ready to head off to bed when a very frightened young boy came into the kitchen. "Ma'am, I really need to find the bathroom. Could you help me?"

I went to him and reached for his hand. "My name is Aunt Sara. Come and I'll show you where it is."

When he finished, Tony didn't return to the kitchen. He headed straight back to curl up with Tim in his nest on the couch. He was asleep again in minutes.

Thad had left a handwritten note for someone to carry down to the hardware store to put on the door.

In honor of the arrival of Tony Cameron
The hardware store will open later on
today. Thank you for your patience and your
prayers. Thad. P.

I put on my cloak and warm boots and set out for downtown. I missed my constant companion, but Violet was at Ben's until they could do a proper breeding match. It was still snowing. Big fluffy flakes were piling up fast in the quieter air of the nooks and crannies.

Every fence picket had a funny marshmallow hat. The early morning light was eerie, brightened by the reflection from the snow but smothered by the batting of low wooly clouds. Not a single bird could be seen.

I fastened the notice on the main entrance to Thad's store and then hurried up the street to Gary's. Tricia was on early morning shift and I was able to tell her the men were back. I headed home with a sack of cinnamon buns.

As much as I wanted to pick up Tony and hug him and love him, my intuition said his most important need right now was to begin to trust men; perhaps for the first time in his life. He needed to believe he was finally safe among family who would protect him from harm.

I couldn't believe Jenny would have left him there at the school if she'd known what kind of place it was. What was going on there that Cal's friend had said to get Tony out of there? And why hadn't Michael been informed about Tony's whereabouts and circumstances after Jenny died?

I'm sure he would have said something about it if he'd known. The men were being protective of Tony now and we would live one day at a time until we learned more, or until it could be put to rest.

A few minutes later, Tim stuck his head in the sewing room door. "We're going to fix breakfast and then Tony needs a bath real bad. He came away without a change of clothes. Got any ideas?"

"Steven Crosswick is about the same size and so is Bobby Forester. I'll bet you could borrow a few things until we can get Tony to the store. Call out there and find out if anyone's coming into town. If they aren't, I'll let Tony wear one of his uncle's shirts for a while and you can take Tricia home when she gets off work and pick something up."

"Good plan, ma'am. I'll let you know what I find out."

I let the boys do their thing while I worked on a last minute project. When I heard them start off for the bathroom, I slipped a note in Tim's hand as he went by.

> *When you get his dirty clothes gathered up, put them in a plastic bag and don't get them wet, especially the underwear. Zach said that with material evidence, we'd have a better chance to shut the place down.*

He nodded and went to start running the water in the tub while I went upstairs to get Michael's favorite soft wool shirt. It was Cameron plaid and I thought the meaning of it wouldn't be lost on the boy.

I thought too of the times since Michael's death when it was a solace to wrap his shirt around me, as I wept for him in my loneliness. I knocked on the door of the bathroom and handed in the shirt.

Tim said, "I phoned Foresters'. Abe said he'd be in as

soon as he can. The boys are packing a box for Tony."

Then, he came to the door and said softly, "Ma'am, you must promise me that you'll let the men take care of Tony for a while. I don't want you or any of the other women to see him right now.

"Then when this is over, I'm going to need you and Margot and Kylie Lou and Tricia to hold me and cry with me while I grieve for what this little guy has been through."

He turned and went back into the steamy, warm room. I heard Tony whimpering in pain as he entered the tub.

Abe came to the door with the box but didn't stay. Tim must have told him enough that he knew not to come in. I touched his shoulder as I whispered, "Pray for us all, Abe. We're going to need it in the coming days."

It was snowing harder as I turned to go back inside. I saw Zach slip into the bathroom as Tim came out. I could hear Zach's gentle voice as he talked to Tony. He was probably binding up wounds of many kinds and I was thankful he was there to help.

The boys did a good job of choosing things for Tony. We didn't stir from the house as the snow piled deeper outside. I called Cade in the evening. The nurse answered his phone. She said he'd spent almost five hours in surgery and was resting. He needed to stay a couple of days to make sure everything was healing well.

Since the traveling was so difficult, I was glad we wouldn't need to go for him right away. I left a message for him that Tony was getting used to the family, eating as often and as much as he could stuff in and sleeping nested with Tim. I whispered, "Tell him I said I love him, and good night."

CHAPTER SEVENTEEN

Early Friday morning, I heard the men stirring. When I went down to the kitchen, Thad, Tim, Zach and Tony were in the middle of big bowls of oatmeal, brown sugar and cream.

Tony looked up from his bowl and grinned. "Man, it sure is better with cream."

He was dressed in neat working clothes and his boots were polished. "I'm going to work at the hardware store today, ma'am. Mr. Penard says there'll be lots of things I can do to help, and he promised we could go to Gary's for lunch. Will your feelings be hurt, Aunt Sara?"

I glanced up and caught Tim's eye. We winked at each other.

"Of course I'll miss having you here for lunch but I understand you men need to get some work done. Margot and I have work of our own to do today. Do you know how many days it is until Christmas?"

He wrinkled up his nose in concentration. "I'm not even sure what today is, but I do know it's a happy one."

He went back to the task of finishing up his porridge. The men rinsed their bowls in the sink. Tony watched and did the same. I smiled as I wondered what surprises might develop because of our new, small, family member.

Margot got to the hallway just as they were leaving. She was treated to a cheery grin as Tony put on his borrowed coat and snow boots.

"'Bye, Mrs. Penard. We'll see you tonight."

Later in the morning, Zach called from Doc Pete's office to tell me he was going after Cade. "He wants out of there."

"May I go with you?"

"Sure. I'll be by in about ten minutes to pick you up. You and Margot make a list of the things Tony needs and we'll go shopping before we pick up Cade. As long as we get there before three he won't have to pay for another day."

The day was perfect. We found everything we needed in one place and got in and out of the hospital by the middle of the afternoon. Cade was napping in front of the fire when everyone got home for supper. Tony was excited about his day. The whole house seemed to shimmer with exuberance as he came trotting into the living room to find us.

"Aunt Sara, you won't believe how much money we made today. And everyone came in the store to say hello and meet me and to see how I was. And ma'am, I met some boys in my class at school. They're Bobby Forester's friends."

His look turned anxious though, as he spoke to his Uncle Zach.

"I'm holding you to your promise, sir," he whispered. "You promised I wouldn't have to go back to New York."

Zach knelt down and hugged him. "A promise is a promise. Besides we need you here, especially now. We have houses to build and puppies to care for and new babies coming who will need lots of loving. You have Cameron responsibilities now."

"What do you mean, Uncle Zach?

"Ah, that's a surprise for a little later young man. We have big plans for the Cameron clan in Campbell's Point now that you're here."

"I like the sound of that. I think I'll go get Uncle Mike's shirt and wear it to supper, if it's all right? Then we can make plans."

Tony was quivering with excitement. As he turned to go, his glance fell on his Uncle Cade, sitting by the fireplace.

"Hello, Commander. I thought you weren't going to get to come home for a few days. I'm sorry those men at school hurt you so much. Will it be better by springtime so you can help build the house too?"

Cade managed a smile. "I hope so, Tony. I'm much better already since I know that you're safe again."

Tony stepped to his chair and knelt down by his uncle's knee. "Sir, thank you for saving my life. I surely would have died by Christmas."

He stood, turned and left the room with the dignity of a prince. Tim took off for Jamie's place while the Cameron brothers visited in front of the fire until supper. Tony appeared in his new soft leather boots, black sweatpants and Michael's shirt, belted at his waist. It hung to his knees like a medieval jerkin and I could tell how proud he was to be wearing it.

"Thank you, ma'am, for the new clothes upstairs. It'll be nice not to have to wear a uniform any more. It's even nicer to be able to talk when I want to; to someone who cares."

In businesslike fashion, he turned to Thad. "If you need me, I'd like to work at the store tomorrow, Mr. Penard. There was a note in my box from the farm. Bobby's mother invited me to spend tomorrow night. I could ride out when Tim takes his girlfriend home. Please, may I go, Aunt Sara?"

"I think it's a fine idea, Tony. After supper you can pack a knapsack with what you'll need. Be sure to put in an extra pair of dry socks, because I'll bet you'll be out rolling in the snow. The Foresters will be coming in to Mass on Sunday and can bring you back into town. How fun. I wish I could come too."

I was teasing a bit, but Tony was dead serious.

"I'm sorry ma'am but this is just boys."

"Well, I understand that."

Cade's eyes were glistening with tears as he got up to make the trip to the supper table. He looked so weary and he must have been in pain from his many bruises and his newly-set arm. I hadn't seen him uncovered since he'd come home from New York. He pulled a small bottle from his shirt pocket and held it out to me. "I'll have a half of one of these for dessert."

The well-remembered Blue Zingers sparkled in the bottle.

"We can do that."

As we sat down, Ben came breezing in with his duffle and sleeping bag, brushing snow from his coat and hair.

"May I throw my sleeping bag behind your couch, Madam Penard? Foresters have been more than kind but they're mighty short of space. I tried to sleep at 'Jenny's House' last night and nearly froze to death. I'll tell you, that place is going to be uninhabitable until spring."

Tony had gotten up from the table and returned with another place setting for Ben and another chair. Then with gentle politeness, he made the slightest bow.

"Welcome to our table, Mr. Ben Johnson. Tim has told me about you and your special dogs. My name is Anthony Cameron and I am honored to meet you."

Tony and Zach did the dishes while I took Cade to our room. I pushed the bed to the wall, and made a row of pillows to prop him up against as he slept on his side. He was sound asleep when I joined him a few minutes later.

It was another early day at the store. Thad and Tony were long gone before the rest of us stirred from our beds. Cade and I had spent a bad night. I kept waking as he thrashed about in his tortured dreams and I was frantic, trying to keep him from rolling onto his new cast.

I knew from my own experience that the blue painkillers sometimes caused the opposite result of their intended purpose. I slipped away to find a lighter blanket for him and found Zach up, sitting by the fire.

"How is he, Sara? I didn't like the way he looked last night. I should have made him stay another day in the hospital but he so wanted to be home."

I sat down beside him on the couch. "He's not sleeping well. His nightmares frighten me. Could it be his medication? Could you find something else for him to use?"

"Yes, of course. Let's get him up and moving around a bit, then after a clean up and some breakfast I'll settle him here with another kind. If we allow him to stay up I'll need for someone to be with him. Come on, I don't want him to fall on his arm."

Just as Tim didn't want me to see Tony's injuries, Zach wouldn't allow me to care for Cade's wounds. He did the clean up and bandaging while I fixed breakfast. When they finished and came into the kitchen, Cade's face was still wan and filled with pain and I noticed an injury at his neckline that hadn't been visible in the shadows of the night before. There was the unmistakable circle of a garrote.

I looked up into Zach's eyes and wept. "Is there no end to the violence and cruelty in our world? Where is the safety and peace our God promised?"

It was Cade who answered. "There probably won't be an end to it for many lifetimes, Sara. Our safety and peace must come from our love and caring for one another."

Zach got him settled by the fire after breakfast and stayed with him on the first shift, until he needed to go downtown for Saturday morning clinic. Margot and I took turns sitting with him as he slept, in what was becoming his favorite chair. He was resting much better now with the different medication and I was able to get some rest too.

We decided to let Cade stay downstairs by the fire for the next few days. It was closer to the bathroom and to the rest of the household. We did what we could to make him

146

comfortable. My concern increased as I watched him struggle with his injuries.

On Monday, Tony said he wanted to stay home with his uncle instead of going to work at the store. I was terrified. Many times young ones know more about what's going to happen than grown-ups and he was very worried about his Uncle Cade.

I cornered Zach in the hallway. "Is there any chance Cade might have internal injuries from the fight; something besides his arm?"

He thought a moment. "I don't know. They did a workup before his surgery but you know how things can be missed. I'm ready to take him back to Pittsburgh anyway. I'll call Doc Pete and have him arrange an admission. Do you think Tony should come with us?"

"Yes, I do. I don't want him to feel that it was his fault if we lose Cade. He needs to believe that all of us, including him, did everything possible to save him."

I was shocked at my own words. We were talking about Cade as though he were going to die.

"I'll go pack for Cade while you get the arrangements made. Tell Tony as soon as you're sure we're going, in case there's something he wants to do before we go. He's been thrown into a man's world and he should be allowed to be a man in it."

It calmed my fears to know that Zach was in charge and we were getting help for Cade. I gave Margot a hug and told her we would call when there was news. It was well after supper before I was able to call home with hopeful news.

Thad answered the phone, his voice tight and anxious with concern. "How is he, Sara? We've been so worried."

"They think he's going to be all right now. His kidney was ruptured by one of the blows to his back and they just finished repairing it. Keep praying for us all, especially Tony.

"It was good he came with us. He was very brave and didn't miss a thing. I don't know if I can handle another doctor in the Cameron family but we'll see. I guess little boys go through a hero a week while they're growing up, but right now, Zach and the surgeon are plenty big heroes to one precious ten-year-old boy.

"Cade needs to stay two or three days so we're on our way home. We'll be there in a bit. We need to feed Tony. He didn't eat all day because he was so worried about his

Uncle Cade."

I was exhausted after the worry of the past few days and barely managed to stay awake during our quick supper. When we got back to the truck for the trip home, I was the one who crawled into the back and fell asleep, curled up in a nest of quilts and pillows.

Tony chose to stay home the next day. We put him to work doing important jobs for us. The postman came to the door with a large package for Cade.

I said to Tony, "I wonder what this could be? Look, it's from Boise, Idaho. I wonder if it's a present."

I realized that it was the 18th of December and there wasn't a Christmas tree up yet. Next time Margot and I were alone, I asked her about the tree.

She smiled. "It's at the back of the garage under the snow. With all the things happening, I'm afraid we forgot about it. Perhaps Thad will help us set it up tonight and we'll have a tree-trimming party. I have my mother's old ornaments from France and we like tiny white lights. I hope that's all right."

I hugged her. "It sounds perfect. I haven't had a family tree since I left my home in Illinois. It's kind of you to include the Cameron clan in your holiday. Perhaps next year we will be in our own place and you can visit us."

"Maybe Yvette would like to come and help. I think I'll call Gary's and invite her to come after work."

As Margot headed for the phone, she said, "Let's put Tony to work on the cookies. I haven't used the old cookie cutters for years and he should enjoy decorating all the different animals."

By afternoon, the kitchen table was full of rows of animals. There were yellow ducks and red cows with white faces, white and black sheep, pink pigs, and polar bears with coconut hair. He made wonderful green Christmas trees, angels, stars and gingerbread boys and girls with cinnamon hearts.

Margot put her arm around Tony as he worked at the table. "I think we could pack a big box of cookies for you to take as a present for the Foresters when you go visiting next time."

"I'd like that ma'am. Bobby and I need to get on the mystery soon or the tracks will be gone."

He went on frosting cookies, humming carols as he

worked. When they were done, he was careful to clean up his mess and then chose one cookie as his reward.

"Aunt Sara, could you call Foresters' and find out if someone might be coming or going tomorrow so I could hitch a ride? That is, if you don't need me tomorrow."

In an hour it was all arranged and we had supper ready for the men when they returned home

Abe Forester came into town very early to bring Tricia to work. He stopped off at Penards' to round up a small, excited boy and the big box of cookies. Tony was dressed for a day of outdoor play and his eyes were shining as he dashed out the door. "'Bye, Aunt Sara, see you later."

I looked at Margot as I drank my mug of tea. "What do you suppose he meant yesterday about the tracks?"

Her smile was reassuring. "Little boys have many adventures. Who knows what this one is all about? They'll be fine. It's supposed to be a nice sunny day and they should get there and back without problems. We actually have a day to catch up on projects. What are you and Cade going to give Tony for Christmas?"

"There was one thing I had my heart set on. When we go to bring Cade back, I want to try to find some snowshoes for all of us though Cade won't be able to use them this winter, and there are several books I want Tony to have. I need to make some lists so I don't forget any of the things I promised myself would happen."

When Abe brought Tony back in the evening, he stopped in the kitchen for a cookie and some coffee.

"The boys had a big day. They helped us load up your gift from us. I hope it's in time to help with holiday meals."

He had carried the boxes of meat to the back porch. It was the pig that I had arranged as a trade for the few lessons I was able to give the Foresters before I left for St. Louis in the summer.

"Abe, you didn't need to do that for me. I certainly wasn't able to keep my part of the bargain."

His answer was gracious. "Ma'am, you've become an important part of our lives since you came. Kylie Lou and the kids think the world of you, and so do I. Merry Christmas, Mrs. Cameron."

"Thank you. We'll enjoy every morsel."

As Abe turned to go, he said, "Oh, by the way, the lawyer is back. The boys saw his tracks and I saw him this morning, riding the ridge above the farm. Suppose he knows someone bought the place?"

I wasn't sure I was happy with this news, though I knew it was bound to happen. For Tony's sake, we needed to have a closure of some kind.

"Well, he must know something's different," I answered. "Ben helped me leave some hay and oats in the shed for his horse and we put some emergency rations in a box by the new stove inside the house. Renquist was expecting him back from a six-month's assignment at Christmas.

"Ben said he spent night before last in the house and he didn't mention seeing him around the place. Surely the man won't try to stay up there. Ben said he nearly froze to death even with the woodstove going. Maybe Zach and I can get up there tomorrow to see what's going on."

Abe tipped his cap and headed out to pick up Tricia at work. It was an anxious wait until Zach got back so we could decide what to do. The minute he walked in the kitchen, I knew Abe had already filled him in.

Zach looked exhausted from his long shift and I knew he was still concerned about his brother. He held up his hand.

"Could I have some supper first? I'm running on empty and I'll probably have to go back out tonight. It's my night on call and Mrs. Peters went into labor a couple of hours ago."

The soup pot on the back of the stove was becoming a fixture. I sliced slabs of fresh bread, laid out the meat, cheese, butter and jam and dished up a big bowl of vegetable soup laced with herbs. As he began to fill up and relax, he looked up with a grin.

"Part of the Cameron marriage contract! Our women have to be good cooks. Thanks, Sara."

We decided to stay in the kitchen to visit and his first important news from the hospital was that Cade was finally heading in the right direction. They thought he could be home on Friday.

"Now, you need to fill me in on the lawyer story. You and I will be the ones deciding whether this man and Tony should meet now. I'm amazed at Tony's resilience and how well he's adapting to life with us. I don't want anything to mess it up."

After I told him about the cairn and then what we assumed from it, I realized we didn't know much at all about this man, Brian Tracker, except that he was building

"Jenny's House" with obvious skill and loving care. He had abandoned it in June, and now was back in the neighborhood.

Zach asked, "Do you think he even knows about Tony? Or that Tony knows about him?"

"I guess we'll find out tomorrow. Tony wants to go out to spend the day with Bobby again and I'm planning to take him out early. Kylie Lou and I have some things to do before Christmas. Maybe later in the day I'll go up to the house to check things out. Maybe Mr. Tracker will come by."

Zach looked concerned. "Are you sure it's safe to do that?"

"I don't know. But I think we can't wait, and Cade won't be going anywhere for weeks. You have to work tomorrow and I'll have to take care of it for the Cameron family.

"I've been suffering with a bit of cabin fever and it will feel good to have a day out in the woods. Zach, I do miss it so much. It was part of my life for many years. I hope I never have to go to jail, it would kill me to be locked up inside."

On that cheerful note we said goodnight.

CHAPTER EIGHTEEN

The day dawned late but glorious. The sky was brilliant blue. Every bird left in the territory was out feasting on favorite delicacies. I thought about Millie and her beloved cardinals and made a mental promise to stop by to leave a bag of sunflower seeds for their holiday treats.

Tony came down the stairs two at a time, with his pack and extra boots. His Uncle Zach's borrowed binoculars hung around his neck along with a pair of hunting sunglasses.

"Looks like you and Bobby have Special Forces duty today, Tony. What's going on?"

His smile was secretive. "Big game hunting."

"Oh, is that so? Do you have a notebook and pencil to write down what you see while you're scouting? And you never know when you might need to leave a secret note for someone."

He was grinning now, as he pulled the rest of his treasures out of various hidden pockets and named them off. "Flashlight, camera, matches, survival blanket and knife; what have I forgotten, Aunt Sara?"

"Let's see if Mrs. Penard might let you borrow Thad's canteen. You should never go out into unknown territory without safe water. This time of year you could use snow but it steals body heat."

"How come you know those things, Aunt Sara? You're a girl!"

I smiled. "How do you suppose all those wonderful pioneer women survived when their men were away? How did they fight Indians and storms and wild animals and have babies all alone in the wilderness? We have much different dangers now, but I still like to be prepared."

"You'd have been plenty useful to have for a wife back then. Uncle Cade is lucky he's got you to look after him now." Tony's voice trailed away to a whisper. "He's going to

152

need all of us isn't he? I was so scared when he was fighting for me. If it hadn't been for Tim and Uncle Zach helping, he would have died and so would I."

I reached for him and held him to my heart. "Precious Tony, I can't bear to think about what might have happened. But you're safe now and you have all the Cameron kin who love you and want to protect you. But, you have to promise me you'll be wily as a fox and not put yourself in foolish danger. OK?"

He was all little boy now, and started to wriggle from my arms as I whispered to him, "That's your code name, Tony, The Fox."

"Ma'am, we have to hurry. Bobby is waiting for me and we need to make plans."

"I'll get your canteen while you get your notebook and pencil. I'll meet you at the truck in five minutes."

Besides the canteen, I stopped to pick up Violet's leash, in case she might be ready to come home. I missed her and she would be a good companion for Cade while he healed at home.

Black Beauty was turning into a perfect truck for my needs and I appreciated her more every time I had a different kind of job to do. Bobby was watching for us and the boys took off running. Abe and Ben were working in the dog pens below the barn. Their friendship had grown in the days since their business alliance was sealed and I was anxious to talk to them about how things were going.

Kylie Lou came to the door with baby Pam tucked under her arm and Lane peeking from around her skirt. Their happy squeals and wriggling bodies persuaded Kylie Lou to turn them loose on me and we tumbled in a happy heap on the porch. My Lady Susan was next to join the fun and we had little girl hugs and giggles all around.

"Where's Steven?" I whispered in Lane's ear.

Her answer was a surprise. "Down helping Mr. Johnson and Mr. Forester. He really loves the dogs, especially the puppies; and he gets to help feed them when they need a bottle.

"Maybe when I get bigger they'll let me help too. Mr. Forester says I need to help inside right now and I'm learning to make bread. Come and I'll show you what Susan and I did already."

I saw Kylie Lou's eyes glistening with tears as she turned to go inside. "They're so precious. I wonder how their mother is and if she'll be able to have them back."

"I don't know, but I'll ask Zach to find out about her. I don't think anyone has heard for a while."

We gathered in the kitchen to admire the projects going on. Tricia and Priscilla were making cookies. The whole house smelled of cinnamon, ginger, anise and vanilla, and the overwhelming fragrance of the Christmas tree. The tree was up in the living room and there were ground pine wreaths with bright red ribbons, in every window.

Suddenly, my empty tummy was lurching in protest of missed breakfast. I said, "Priscilla, may I sample one of those gingerbread boys? They look wonderful and in the hurry to get Tony started on his adventure this morning, I missed my breakfast."

Her gracious nod left me free to choose one.

"Ummm, delicious, is it a special Forester recipe?"

She told the story of her great-grandmother's ginger cookies and her coming to America; part of the family's history, passed on to another generation. As I listened to her story, I saw young Priscilla in a new light. Usually in the shadow of her older sister, Tricia, I hadn't realized what a lovely young lady was blossoming as second daughter. Her hair was the same soft chestnut-brown color as her mother's and she was wearing a beautiful hand-carved wooden clip to keep her long hair out of the cookie dough.

"We'll leave you girls to keep working while we do some last minute projects."

It was about ten o'clock when we finished the most important one and stopped for a break. I decided I would take the time to go up to the house.

"Kylie Lou, would you excuse me for an hour or so? I'd like to walk up to 'Jenny's House' to make sure everything's all right, and I wanted to find some ground pine to make wreaths."

Her voice was filled with concern. "Are you sure it's safe to go up there alone? Abe and I saw someone on the ridge yesterday."

"I need to meet him and talk to him. I must decide whether he can be trusted with Tony. May I pack a lunch to take?"

She expressed her concern again. "I don't think the men would want you to go alone. At least take Violet with you. You go on down to the pens and pick her up while I fix some lunch for you and the boys. Do you know about the back way up there? It's a lot closer when you go from this side rather than go back down to the road and around."

When I returned with Violet, Kylie Lou had the lunch ready. There was plenty for all of us. She smiled. "I guess you'll get one of your Christmas gifts early."

She handed me a package wrapped with paper hand-colored with pictures of dogs. "It's for Violet. We had great fun making it for her."

Inside was a double pack arrangement that hung like horse saddlebags on each side. Violet stood very still and proud while we fastened it on and I knew she'd been trained to carry it.

"How wonderful, thank you so much. Which one of your girls helped to make it?"

"All of them. Lane and Pam helped make the drawings for the wrapping paper. Have fun, you two, and be careful."

The trail was steep and slippery from the partially melting snow. There were places where I was glad for Violet's leash to steady me. I was following two sets of small tracks going almost straight up. I recognized the print from the bottom of Tony's new boots. I assumed the others belonged to Bobby. The boys were in no hurry. Either they were playing a stalking game or they were being very careful. After the climb to each level place, I needed to stop to catch my breath.

At the top of the ridge, the boys' tracks melded with horse tracks that appeared to come by another route and led on across the ridge. I continued to follow the signs. I couldn't quite visualize where the path would come out and was surprised to find myself about a hundred yards from "Jenny's House" and several hundred feet above it; looking down on the pond, the house and the outbuildings.

Violet was on silent alert, her ears moving as she surveyed the land and buildings below. There were two flattened places in the snow where the boys probably dropped down to reconnoiter from behind a fallen tree. There was evidence the horse and rider had stopped there too. The snow was trampled and brown from the mud churned up as man and horse watched and waited.

Tucked into the bark of the fallen trunk was a message printed in pencil on a small piece of paper.

We're going in to the horse barn. Follow the tracks. The Fox

I was using my usual French with Violet. "Let's go find out what's happening."

I took my small handgun from an inner jacket pocket and strapped it on my thigh where I could reach it. My belt knife looked innocent enough nestled in the double case with the pruning shears for the ground pine.

I wondered where the horseman was and whether he had found and read Tony's note too. I looked around and found several large boot tracks mixed with the smaller prints. My heart was racing as Violet and I dropped down over the ridge, following the trail. Last evening's skiff of snow told me the boys had gone down before the horseman.

The horse tracks erased those of the little boots as the man eased down the mountain behind them. At the bottom of the trail, the tracks split, one boy going to each side of the horse barn. The horse tracks led straight into the barn.

"What do you think, Violet," I whispered, "What will we find inside?"

I tightened my grip on her leash and prepared to go in. Just as I reached to knock on the door, I heard him. Someone inside was speaking in loving, lilting French. Then he broke into a happy song about riding and horses.

His French was very fluent and comfortable but not native, as he spoke to someone named Roger. Well, if there were two of them, I was outnumbered, but I needed to find the boys. When I stepped inside, he remained with his back to me as he continued to speak in French.

"Welcome Mrs. Cameron. I've been expecting you and your faithful companion. What is her name?"

I don't know what caused me to answer as I did. Perhaps the French language we were using. "Her name is Violet. She was a gift to me from my fiancé Michael Cameron."

His answer was kind and filled with sadness. "We both have lost lovers in this unhappy year. I am not handling my loss very well."

"Neither am I." I answered with a weary sigh. "I should never have married again so soon or perhaps at all."

"No, ma'am. The Commander was fortunate that you came into his life when he needed you most."

I wondered how he could know so much about me and about my affairs, but other matters were more important at the moment.

I looked with growing interest at the back of this

mysterious man who continued to groom his horse while we talked. He was about six-feet tall, with dark brown hair cut very short. His motion, as he cared for the horse, suggested that he was not comfortable in his body. It seemed painful for him to raise his arms and move his shoulders.

He turned to speak and I saw him from the front for the first time. His once handsome face was now carrying a vicious, jagged scar, fresh enough that the still-healing flesh made an angry red mark. It began at his temple and coursed down the left side of his face to hide within the collar of his jacket. It couldn't have missed his carotid artery by more than millimeters.

I couldn't help the gasp that escaped. "My God! What happened to you? Thad said you were in Turkey on assignment, but that's not the injury of a lawyer." I whispered, "Are you one of us?"

He put down the brush and stepped forward to take my hand. "My name is Brian Tracker. I was Jenny's lover. Now I've come to see about the safety and well-being of her son, Tony Cameron. Ma'am, I have only a short time. I must leave again on Christmas. I missed him at school by a day. The Feds raided the school and they were torching three million dollars worth of marijuana cuttings when I got there. I came down here because I knew my friend, Thad, would help me find Tony."

Suddenly, Tracker switched to Russian. "We need to be careful not to frighten the boy. Thad told me a little about what he's been through, and I don't want Tony to hear anything except what will help him feel loved and sheltered. The boys are hiding, one on each side of the building and can probably hear our conversation. How do you propose we handle this?"

There was no hesitation as I continued in French. "Considering the shortness of your visit there's no time for games. I suggest you step to the door as I leave. Invite the boys in to help you finish caring for your horse." I smiled up at him. "May I assume his name is Roger?"

I watched through the window at the two small boys creeping closer to the barn door.

"Violet and I will go down to the house and lay out lunch; you and the boys come on down when you're ready."

Then I switched to Russian. "After lunch, Bobby and I will head back to Foresters' and you can bring Tony down when you're ready. I trust you Brian Tracker, and I promise to do everything I can to make your short time with him, as you would wish it.

"By the time Bobby has told all the Foresters about you and who you are, you and Tony must ride down to the farm with Roger. I'm sure Abe and Ben will take care of him for the few days you'll be with us."

My conversation returned to French. "Abe is a good man, Tracker. He won't hold a grudge against you. In fact, the letter may not even come up."

Brian looked puzzled. "What letter?"

"The one you sent, threatening Abe with being forced to shut down his hog operation."

"I've never sent a letter like that to anyone. I love this land as it is, hogs and all."

"Then you two have a mystery to solve. I'm going now."

He went out the door with me and stood watching as Violet and I moved away down the trail to the house. He turned to go back inside, and out of the corner of my eye, I caught the flash of a little boy's body hurtling into Tracker's arms.

Tony was laughing as I heard him say, "I knew it had to be you, Tracker. I remember the song you were just singing. It's the one you used to sing to me in Paris when you came over to see us. I've missed you. Where have you been?"

The boys went into the horse barn; one on each side of Tracker's big, sheltering body.

I walked down to "Jenny's House", relieved Violet of her pack, started the fire in the woodstove, and laid out lunch. In a few minutes, the boys arrived with Tracker.

Bobby piped up as we finished lunch, "Ma'am, Tony said you wanted to gather greens. I can take you to find some, where we get ours. It'll be dark soon so we need to hurry. Let's go and let them have some time alone. I'd want people to do it for me if my best friend just came looking for me."

"You're absolutely right, Bobby, and I brought Violet and her packsack to carry our greens."

He grinned and took off to get her pack buckled, while I bent down to hug Tony. "No hurry to get back. Just be sure you can see to get down the hill to Foresters'."

Tony and Tracker headed out hand in hand toward the barn. I had the feeling they were on their way to the ridge and Jenny's cairn with its beautiful marker. They had a lot to talk about.

I was really surprised then, when Bobby and I finished

our collecting task and started down the slope to Foresters' with Violet and her precious load. Tracker and Tony were already there. Tony was sitting on the front steps of the porch, hugging his knees in wiggling anticipation. Steven, Lane and Susan were having a bareback ride along the lane. I could hear their squeals of delight. Tracker led Roger, while Abe and Ben walked, one on each side, in case a little tot should fall. There was a big white truck and horse trailer neatly backed in by the barn.

Bobby and Tony's turn came next. They were very serious, perhaps because they realized they might get to help with Roger while Tracker was away.

Afterwards, while the boys and Abe went to take Roger to the barn, Tracker stepped to my side. "Ma'am, the trip down this side wasn't safe with my injuries, so I took Tony down the other side of the mountain where the truck was parked. That's why we beat you here."

He went on, "Kylie Lou invited us to spend the night and I accepted. This family is going to be important in Tony's life and I want them to know me and to trust me. She's promised to put some special salve on my scar tonight. Something that she says will prepare the flesh for the surgery they're going to attempt after Christmas." He looked weary and his face was white with pain.

I took his hands in mine. "You try to find a quiet place to rest before supper. It's been a long day for you."

Just then, Ben came and offered to take me home. I jumped at the chance to have someone else drive in the dusk of the early winter evening. Then I had to laugh when I found out what Ben really wanted; to borrow Black Beauty for the evening because he had a date with the lady who drove the library van. His own beat-up brown truck smelled of dogs. And let's face it, a bit like sweaty old men.

Supper was waiting for me at Penards' and Ben took off to clean up before he headed out for his date. As we sat down at the kitchen table, Thad handed me a note from Jamie.

Zach is busy at Doc Pete's tomorrow and it's my day off. I'll be by at nine o'clock to drive you into Pittsburgh to retrieve Cade from the hospital. Sometimes a doctor can smooth the paperwork. Jamie

I sighed with relief. "I'm glad I won't have to face that job alone. Did Jamie say how Cade was?"

"No, but Cade said he's more than ready to get home."

I started to tell Thad and Margot about our day.

"I met Brian Tracker at 'Jenny's House' today. It's a good thing I decided to trust him because he came here to Campbell's Point to see if he trusted the Cameron kin with Jenny's boy. Where did you meet, Thad?"

He hesitated before he answered. "For right now and for everyone's safety, I'll just say we're long-time friends from school days in Paris. I've worked with him off and on since then. His unusual collection of language skills is in heavy demand right now. Did he say how long he would be here?"

"He told me he'd be leaving Christmas afternoon. He has only a few days with Tony. They're staying overnight at Foresters' and riding back into town with Tim tomorrow. I don't know where we'll put him, Margot. Maybe Cade will be more comfortable sitting up at night and we can sleep by the fire. Then Tracker and Tony can have our room until he leaves."

Margot smiled. "Don't worry. We'll work something out. You just get Cade back here and everything will be fine."

The hot soup and warmth of the kitchen after a day outside literally laid me to rest. I barely made it upstairs and into bed.

CHAPTER NINETEEN

The day began with gray mist and fog. I dressed for an unknown combination of cold weather travel and overheated hospital. When I called Cade, he asked for warm clothes and a pocket full of Christmas cookies. The hollow quality of his voice frightened me. I was even more concerned when Jamie led me to a consultation room as we entered the doctors' area. His gentle voice as he spoke to me didn't help my growing panic.

"I didn't want you to see Cade without being prepared for what you'll find. He has a new bulky cast on his shoulder and arm with extra steel posts and wires across them. His bruises have gone into the usual half-healed purple and brown.

"It's going to be weeks before he'll be comfortable in his battered body. He had no physical reserves left for the extra surgery they had to do to repair the kidney. He's going to need a tremendous amount of physical care as well as psychic nurturing.

"The doctor I talked with yesterday afternoon said Cade is hanging on only by the force of his will. They can't keep him here any longer. Now you'll have to decide if you can care for him at home or if he'll have to go to a rehab facility."

I didn't have the luxury of time to panic.

"Will you be going over his charts before we go in?"

"Yes. It will take about half an hour."

"I'll be in the chapel. Please come for me there." I rose from the table and left the room.

As I knelt in prayer, I remembered how my friend Barney Bailey had chided me for neglecting the source of my strength. He'd said, "Ask your God to help you know how to heal those you love." I sat in the silence of the chapel and prayed for strength and guidance. I was ready when Jamie returned for me.

161

Cade was still in his hospital gown and robe. He sat, slumped in his chair, looking out the window into the damp grayness and ugliness of the parking lot. He looked so frightened. I knelt beside his chair and touched his face as I said, "Dear Heart, I've come to take you home."

Jamie turned to me. "I'll begin taking care of his paperwork. It could take an hour."

The nurse came in to get him ready to leave. When she finished, Cade and I sat in the quiet of the room holding hands. I was praying silently as I stroked his injured arm.

He whispered, "Sara, I was so afraid you wouldn't take me home; that you would abandon me to a nursing home. Please, would you pray out loud for me so that I can know what you're saying? Teach me to be patient in my pain and to trust your God."

The hour was gone before Jamie came to tell us we could leave. He made one stop in town to pick up some equipment, and when we reached Penards', Ben and Zach were there to help him inside.

Margot and Thad had switched bedrooms so that Cade could be downstairs and closer to everyone. He was exhausted from the trip and fell asleep almost before we got him settled in his room. Then the rest of us had a meeting with Jamie, so he could tell us how to care for Cade.

We were finishing up when Tony came dashing in the back door, with Tracker not far behind.

Tony was breathless with anxiety. "Is he home? Where is he? When can I see him?"

Jamie and Zach exchanged nods as Zach answered. "Yes, he's home. He's in his downstairs room sleeping. We drew names. You and Tracker are the ones who get to take him his supper and eat with him. It'll be your special time together. I'm sure both of you have a lot to tell him."

Jamie stood up to leave. "You'll have to excuse me. I have another house call to make before my own supper. Welcome to Campbell's Point, Mr. Tracker. I hope to have a few minutes to visit with you before you leave.

"Please forgive the casualness of the invitation, but Millie asked me to invite you all to join us for a Christmas Eve Party at Campbell House, about three o'clock. Plan to eat continually."

He grinned and began to put on his coat. I got up from the table to thank him for helping. "Wait a minute Jamie; I have a gift for you. It might be nice to enjoy it before

Christmas." I hurried to my room and gathered up the folio of Christmas carols I'd transcribed for him. I returned to the hallway and tucked it under his arm.

"Merry Christmas, My Friend."

Margot and I shooed the men out of the kitchen while we decided how to feed all the people who would be there for supper. It helped to have something to do besides worry. We'd get through this. We had to.

Cade's tray was empty when Tracker brought it to the kitchen after their supper. His voice was filled with wonder.

"I can't believe the rapport Tony and his uncle have developed in such a short time. There's an almost primeval bond between them. It's a beautiful give and take of nurturing and love."

Tony seemed more grownup and subdued when he came into the kitchen with his tray.

"Uncle Cade has asked me to read to him, Aunt Sara. He said you would know which book."

I was smiling with relief as I went to my reading box to get *The Secret Garden*. When I returned with it, the men were finishing kitchen cleanup and they made another tray with a plate of Christmas cookies and three glasses of milk.

Tony said, "Ma'am, I told him about the big package from Boise that came while he was away. He said he wanted to open it and tell us a story about it. Do you know what's in it, Aunt Sara?"

"I think so. It's a real adventure story from the Wild West, isn't it, Ben?"

Ben grinned and nodded yes. He was on his way out to see his lady friend and wished us goodnight. Margot and I settled by the fire with our last minute knitting while Zach joined us with a stack of journals to read.

I asked him, "Do you have all your Christmas taken care of, Zach? There are a couple of things I wanted to find for Tony and I need to get to Pittsburgh tomorrow or the next day. Want to come?"

"Sure, I'll go along to ride shotgun in the last minute crowds. We can go as soon as we get back from Foresters' about noon. Tracker says Kylie Lou asked him to come one more time so she could work on his scar and she wants to put something on Tony's wounds too.

"I'd like to know more about how she takes care of people, and Jamie asked me to check on her. We think the babe will be here sooner than the Foresters think.

"We have a pretty casual schedule set up for Cade's care. Tracker and I will get him ready for bed tonight. Tim and Ben will help him in the morning. Cade asked us to spare you the heavy work until he's able to get up and around by himself. We need to be careful not to wear him out, but he already looks better than when you brought him home."

He picked up a journal and began to read. In a few minutes he was sound asleep in front of the warm fire. He looked exhausted after his long day.

Tony came in to say good night. His pensive look was puzzling until he said with awe in his voice, "You never told me you fought a cougar and won, Aunt Sara. You're some lady, ma'am."

I smiled as I hugged him and kissed him on his nose. "Good night Tony. See you in the morning. Thanks for helping with Uncle Cade. He loves you very much."

Cade was still awake but ready for the night when I entered our room. As I knelt by the bed, he reached for me. "Come my little sparrow and share my nest tonight."

There were recipe books spread out on the kitchen table when the men returned. We were taking food for Millie's party and needed to get organized. She said Yvette was going to bring French party treats so we knew to steer away from that fancy kind of food.

Zach whispered in my ear, "I'm in need of some greasy junk food. Let's eat lunch on the road."

I grinned. "Good thinking, pard, let's go."

Tim was busy fixing a lunch tray as we prepared to leave. His GED review book was tucked under his arm as he went off to Cade's room for his turn to be with him.

There was giant determination in his voice as he announced, "I promised myself a hard afternoon's study. I'm going to take that exam as soon as I can, so Tricia and I can announce our banns. Do you think she would like a June wedding, ma'am?"

"I think she'll be delighted, Tim. And when you get through with your exams, we'll all work to help Abe and Kylie Lou finish theirs too."

"Yes, ma'am, we can do that. It'll probably be after the baby comes at their place. Zach says the babe isn't going to wait much longer. It's supposed to snow later today so you be careful coming back."

Margot was sitting quietly among all the confusion when

Zach turned to her.

"If anyone calls for me, Jamie's on call today. We'll try to be home by dark. Is there anything we can do for you while we're in town? I guess we all seem to keep dashing here and there and you end up staying home." He smiled at her. "Hey? Want to go with us too?"

I had to fight back tears when I saw the expression on Margot's face as she answered.

"How very kind of you. It's difficult when you don't drive and can't get places by yourself. There was one special gift I wanted to find for Thad. The man at the bookstore in Pittsburgh called this morning to tell me he had found a copy.

"I would enjoy getting away for a few hours too. Let me go get my things. And guess what? I'm hungry for greasy junk food too. It's no fun being good all the time."

She had a wonderful, wicked grin on her face as she went to get her coat and snow boots.

Since I'd made calls to town earlier, I knew exactly where I wanted to go and Margot had the address of the bookstore she wanted to visit. She told us about the very special book of French fairy tales that Thad wanted for the new baby.

When we picked it up, this copy had a wonderful pale gold leather binding and pastel silk ribbons for bookmarks. The illustrations were enchanting. Seeing her joy at finding the gift made the whole trip perfect.

My trip to the outdoor store netted two pairs of children's snowshoes and two adult pairs. If we were fortunate, perhaps Tracker and Tony would get to enjoy them one time before he had to leave. Then Bobby and Tony would have the rest of the winter to be outside in the snow and the men could take turns until we found out who really enjoyed such exercise.

Zach tackled Cade's list of last minute gifts, while Margot and I sat on a bench inside the mall and watched the people go by. It began to snow harder during the late afternoon and I was glad when we got home.

Tim and Cade were ready for some entertainment after the afternoon's study so we gathered in front of the fire to play Scrabble. It was Cade's maiden voyage out of his room and although he was a bit tottery and stiff, he made it without problems.

We'd been playing about an hour when Tony and Tracker got back, covered with snow just from their dash in from the truck. Their arms were full of mysterious packages and their grins said they'd had a successful afternoon too.

I turned to Zach when we got up to greet them. "Thank you for helping us today. I enjoyed the trip to town. Why don't you find out if Yvette would like an escorted walk home from work? Ben and I will take care of Cade tonight."

"Are you sure?"

My answer was heartfelt. "Zach, he's my husband. I have the right to care for him, even if I cry. Now go before I change my mind."

Margot took Tony and Tracker off down the hall for supper while Ben and I helped Cade get ready for bed. He was very tired but seemed in good spirits. I did indeed weep as I washed around his cast and then bathed his bruised body. We changed his dressings, portioned out his medications and settled him in bed.

Tracker came by to say goodnight. "If you'll excuse me, I'll get Tony tucked in. I'll see you in the morning, sir. Ben wants to take Sara to early Mass before he goes out to work with the dogs, and I have some things I need to discuss with you while we share breakfast."

He left the room and gently closed the door. It was about nine o'clock. In the short time it took me to get ready for bed, Cade had drifted off to sleep. I was standing, looking down at his bruised and broken body, when I had the feeling I was not alone with him in the room.

It was not an evil spirit but one of gentle compassion and affection. I closed my eyes against the mystery, and when I opened them again, my beloved Michael appeared in front of me. He didn't touch me, but I felt enveloped in his love as he spoke.

"We need to talk."

It was my Michael, without doubt. That was his favorite opening when there was a serious matter needing attention. I couldn't help my fear.

"Michael? Are you all right? I know I haven't kept you in my prayers as often as I should have. I've neglected you."

"Hush, My Dear. You've not abandoned me. I feel your love surrounding me all the time. Please don't be afraid. I haven't come for you or for anyone you love. I've been asked to come for a very important reason; to talk to you about what has happened to me.

"All those times when you were so loving and forgiving of my weaknesses and poor choices, I wouldn't believe you

166

really forgave me. I couldn't believe that you loved me in spite of what I had done to hurt you. My greatest sin was not in my actions but in my not accepting your forgiveness. I wish to accept it now.

"Dearest Sara, I've come to thank you for nurturing my beloved family, my brothers Cade, and Zach, and Jenny's precious Tony. Thank you too, for beginning the reuniting with my mother. Perhaps you will be able to mend the wounds caused by my ignorance.

"It was my father who put the witness paper with my mother's signature in the envelope. She knew nothing of it and was not involved at all in your loss of freedom. My father forged the paper to cause the final cruelty to my mother, even long after his death.

"My Dearest, I wish you and Cade happiness in your allotted time and I love you all very much. I must go now. I've been promised something special and wonderful, and I am ready now to accept it. Good-bye, my dearest Sara."

I felt his gentle, loving touch and the warmth of his body as he enclosed me in his arms for a last good-bye kiss. In moments he was gone.

I felt a frantic need to be outside, no matter what the weather. Gathering up my warmest clothes, I slipped out to the living room to dress. The only light came from the dying embers of the evening fire. Then, I put on my cape and snow boots and went out the kitchen door into the swirling, snowy night.

The snow muffled all the normal town noises. In fact it was so silent that when I closed my eyes I could pretend I was in the vast wilderness of Idaho, alone with my thoughts and with my God. Instead of heading downtown, I walked toward the end of the street. Bypassing the barricade, I went to the fallen log I had named the Talking Tree because we used it so many times to talk things out with one another. I wanted to sort out what Michael had said and to try to make sense of what had happened.

I'd never experienced such a happening before. I thought I believed in an afterlife but never thought I would ever communicate with the dead. I was frightened. Breathing deeply and slowly, I struggled to regain control.

I was facing the forest, watching the swirling patterns of the falling snow, when I heard someone coming up behind me. The approaching steps made a crunching noise in the quiet night. I was defenseless. Violet was not with me, I carried no weapons and had nowhere to run.

"Sara?"

"Yes."

"Don't be frightened, ma'am. It's Ben. Zach was sitting in by the fire and saw you leave. He would have come with you himself but he's on call now. He asked me to make sure you were safe and had someone with you. Why are you out walking on such a night?"

I turned and motioned for him to sit. "I'm glad it's you, Ben. You knew and understood my relationship with Michael perhaps better than anyone else still with me now.

"Michael came to me tonight as I was getting ready for bed. I was terrified. I thought he might be coming for Cade, or for me; instead, he wanted to talk about forgiveness.

"When we finished, he said he needed to go; to accept the promises God had made to him. Michael said he loved us and wished us all happiness. Then he whispered good-bye and disappeared.

"Michael's gone, and I think I won't see him or be able to communicate with him again. Somehow he was releasing me to live my own life. Freedom is frightening, Ben. After all these years, he's gone; I am truly alone and without him."

Ben made no comment for a while. Then he took my hands in his.

"My Cara came to see me several times after she died, to assure me that she was with her family and was happy. She too, released me to continue on with my life's journey. It was the only way I could have believed it was meant for me to find another lover or to live in peace and contentment without her.

"For a while after she died, I wanted nothing more than to die and be with her. It was why I had the courage or perhaps cowardice to go with Cade to Italy on assignment. I didn't care whether I lived or died.

"I'm frightened too, Sara, but each day becomes a little easier. I treasure the new friendships I've made here in Campbell's Point and I find my own small happiness in each day. You've been a special part of that peace and contentment and I thank you for it.

"Come on, we need to get you back to bed. Tomorrow will soon be here and I wanted to take you to early Mass. Then Tracker and I are going out to the Foresters' to talk about a pup for Tony. It's not to be a Christmas present or for Tony to know it's his, until Tracker comes back. Maybe we'll work it like your gift of Violet from Michael, except we want Tracker to live to be with his boy again."

"A puppy is a perfect gift for Tony. He'll get to see him often and watch you work with him. What a wonderful idea you two had. Did Tracker request language training? Which one did he choose?"

Ben smiled. "He chose French because he wants Tony to continue his French language training. Tony lived in France for almost five years. His French is a little rusty but it's coming back. He'll probably teach us a thing or two, I'm sure. Let's go."

I took his hand. "Oh, Ben, I feel so happy and free. Let's run."

We ran until the last block and then slowed to cool down pace.

"Thank you, Ben. I'll see you in a few hours."

When I slipped back into Cade's room, Zach was sitting by his brother's bed waiting for me. He didn't ask for an explanation, but made a whispered comment as he left.

"You smell like you've been dancing with the wind, Sara, and your eyes look like you've swallowed a star."

CHAPTER TWENTY

Tracker and Ben took off for the farm when we got home from Mass. Tony wanted to work on a project for his friend and needed crayons, so we decided to try to catch someone at home over at Doc Pete's. Margot sat with Cade while Tony and I gathered up Violet from her favorite place by the fire and headed out.

Dodie and I settled Tony at the kitchen table with his project and took our late breakfast into the library. She was doing well at her new job and was ready to take it on alone. Perhaps her work would be so well done that Doc Pete would let her continue, and give his wife Laura a permanent break, after all her years of faithful help in the office.

When I asked her about her friend from home, she seemed uneasy as she murmured, "I think he might be coming over from Omaha for the Christmas Eve party at Campbell's. Sara, something's not right between us now. Would you make sure you get a chance to visit with him?

"I don't even like to think it, but I fear he's no longer interested in a relationship since he found out I was penniless."

"How did he find out?"

She wrinkled her brow in puzzlement. "I have no idea. I certainly didn't tell him."

"What does he do for a living, Dodie?"

"That's part of my concern too. I simply don't know. I've asked oblique questions about it but he always seems to change the subject."

"I'll do what I can, including alerting all my kin to the problem. We'll find out what his intentions are. I don't know if Cade will be well enough to go so I may be there for only a short time. May I tell Ben Johnson too? He'll be a good innocent-seeming bodyguard who will look after you, and Tim can keep an eye on things too."

"Oh, thank you. I did so want to go to the party."

We were just finishing up our visit when Tony and Violet came looking for us. He held up a well-wrapped cylinder. "It's finished, Aunt Sara. I hope Tracker likes it. Everything's cleaned up so we can go when you're ready. I'd like to get home soon so I can wrap it in Christmas paper."

"We're on our way. Call us if you need a ride Monday afternoon, Dodie. What are you taking for food?"

"A special casserole dish from Nebraska. I was feeling a bit homesick today and decided to go through my recipe files. This was one of my mother's favorites.

"Thanks for coming, Sara, and you too, young man. I'm so happy for you both. How amazing to have found each other in the nick of time like that."

Tony grinned as he put on his coat and we headed out. "Nice lady. Did you know her before, Aunt Sara?"

"Yes Tony, I did. It's another story for a cold winter night in front of the fire. Come on. Let's give Violet a run."

Zach was pulling into the drive from a house call. He was pleased with his big truck. It handled well in the slushy snow. With the medical practice he and Jamie had taken on, they ended up making a lot of trips into the country.

Cade was wakening from a late morning nap when we went in. Margot had been sitting at his bedside while he slept, and when I went in she had such a worried expression on her face that I took her aside.

"What happened, Margot? Is he all right?"

"Ma'am, I'll tell you as soon as we get him settled by the fire." She whispered, "Perhaps Tony would read to him. Where's Doctor Cameron?"

"He just came in from a house call."

"We need to talk to him as soon as we can."

"All right. I'll tell him."

I found Zach in the kitchen foraging for a snack. His grin was rueful.

"I missed breakfast again. I'll be a shadow of my former self soon. Do you know what's for lunch?"

"Sorry, Tony and I just got back ourselves. We'll need to ask Margot. Listen, just grab something quick and come with me. Margot says she needs to talk to us as soon as possible. I think something happened to Cade while he was napping. She seems pretty upset and Cade doesn't look as well as he did earlier."

We settled Cade in front of the fire with Tony and *The Secret Garden* and then joined Margot in the bedroom. Had some phantom come to torment Cade as he slept? Was his medication unleashing terror in his soul?

Zach remained standing while he motioned to us to sit down.

"Margot, can you tell us what has happened to worry you so?"

She was weeping, as her hands twisted in her lap.

"Sir, I was here, sitting with the Commander as he slept. He began to twist and turn in his bed and then he began to speak. I didn't understand what he was saying at first. It was a language I haven't heard since my childhood in France and I couldn't translate enough to follow the conversation.

"All I know is that he was terrified. He was trembling as he struggled out of bed. Then he said in English, 'I don't hate you; I feel only pity for you. Please forgive me for what I was not able to give you. Be gone now, pitiful wraith.'

"He collapsed on the bed and wept. He never wakened and I didn't touch him for fear he might harm himself or me."

Zach's immediate concern was for Margot, who was still terrified.

"Sara, would you go find Thad in his office and tell him Margot needs a long walk in the snow with him. She needs to get out of the house for a while."

As I left the room, I heard him soothing Margot and telling her she'd done just the right thing, not to waken Cade. Thad came with coats and boots in hand and they took off toward downtown.

Zach asked, "Where's Tracker? Let's see if he can do something with Tony so we can talk to Cade right away."

So I went off again to set up the meeting. Tracker and Ben had just gotten back from Foresters'. I asked them to take Tony to the store on foot for some popcorn to pop in the evening, and to try to stay away for at least an hour if they could manage it. When they took off, we settled down with Cade in front of the fire.

Zach was gentle with his brother.

"You didn't have such a great nap this morning, did you?"

First, Cade looked puzzled, then he looked very frightened.

"I had a bad dream, that's all. I'm afraid to tell you about it. She won't come again, I told her not to."

Zach said quietly, "Why do you think that will make any difference?"

"Because if I don't believe it, I'll be afraid to go to sleep ever again."

"Do you know how long you'll last, brother? You need to tell us about it, right now, before you forget what happened."

We sat waiting. At first he shook his head no, as though he were trying to blot the dream out of his mind. Then, he shut his eyes and began in a whisper.

"It was my wife. Susanna. She was very angry and ugly to me. She said that she hated me and that she had wanted to leave me and go home but she was tainted because she had married a gentile and they wouldn't let her come back. Then she said she had come to claim me, to pay me back for what I had done to her."

Zach and I watched as Cade struggled to continue his story.

"I was determined not to let her destroy me now. I felt heartrending compassion for her plight. Our marriage wasn't perfect, most aren't, but we didn't make the time together to work things out. I felt only pity for her. I asked her to forgive me. The strangest thing happened then, Zach. She began to cry and she faded away."

Cade turned away from us. I hoped his tears were ones of relief because he was able to tell someone he loved what had happened. I stepped to him and took him in my arms.

"It's over now, My Dearest. We will pray for her together; for her peace, and that she won't return to your dreams again."

I made the sign of the cross on his forehead and left the brothers together as I went to take care of the practicalities of lunch. The soup was ready and I put the loaf of whole wheat bread into the oven to bake. The two brothers were in Thad's office talking. Violet and I were enjoying the fire when the happy sounds of Tony and Tracker returning from their errand wakened us from a stolen nap. Tony came to my chair.

"Where's the Commander? Is he all right? We can't let anything happen to him now. I'll stay with him and not leave him, I promise."

I lifted him onto my lap. It was time for Tony to have some "woman loving" and some assurance he had lots of people to help him watch over his Uncle Cade.

I held him as close as I dared. "This morning, your uncle had a very bad dream, one that scared him a lot. We don't know what caused it, maybe his medications or something he ate. He's better now and his brother Dr. Zach is helping him. Do you have any secret ways to get over a bad dream, Tony? Maybe you could share them with him a little later."

Zach came out to us a few minutes later looking preoccupied but relieved.

"Who still needs to wrap presents?"

Tony waved his hand.

"Come on, we'll have a try at it. Anyone who can tie sutures ought to be able to tie Christmas bows."

They went off down the hall, hand in hand. Tears were glistening in Tracker's eyes as he watched them go.

"I hate to have to leave him so soon. What am I going to do, Sara?"

"What we're all going to have to do while you're gone; we'll pray for your mission to be as short as possible and that you'll return to us unharmed. How much longer is your hitch?"

"Until July 1, 2002. I can't tell you where I'm going this time but I'll try to send mail to Tony as often as I can."

"Will he be able to get letters to you?"

"Yes, but the censors will use a heavy hand first."

"Tracker, I'm so frightened for us all. Will there be an end to this in our lifetime?"

"I don't know, Sara, but I fear not."

I went off to stir the soup. A little later Thad called to let us know he and Margot were at Gary's for lunch so we needn't wait for them.

We were a little surprised when Jamie came to the back door about the time we were ready to eat. He spent some time with Cade and then we sat down together. I watched the men take places at the table. They were careful to leave an open place for Tony between Tracker and Cade. I don't know what Zach said to Cade after I left, but he looked a thousand percent better and as if he were in control again.

I figured Jamie was there for a special reason. After lunch he wanted to talk to us all and he didn't waste time with niceties.

"Margot is not handling the extra stress and confusion of all you people well at all. Even though you've helped as you could, it's been an extra burden at a time when she needs light duties and serenity instead. I'm concerned for her baby and I think you need to find another place to live.

"I would like to invite you to use my house until such time as you scatter to other spaces. Sara, would you be willing to take on the role of boarding house matron, especially if I promise you the help of our widow lady? She's been helping with Millie's care and needs to move on now to another post."

I didn't need to consider the offer for very long. I knew Jamie's home. It would be perfect for taking care of the men.

"I accept, Jamie. Thank you. It won't take more than an hour or so to clear us out. I don't know about the others but I have no possessions except a couple of suitcases and a box of books. I've been concerned about Margot for days. I wish we could have done this sooner."

He handed me a set of keys to the house and then continued. "I think that Tracker would like to say something very special to Tony."

Tracker waited a moment and then stood so he could see Tony as he spoke.

"Your mother, Jenny Cameron and I were going to be married last June when she finished her assignment in St. Louis. Instead she died in a terrible accident and I had to go to the Middle East. I came for you as soon as I could, Tony, and I was thankful to find you safe in the arms of your family.

"I was planning to adopt you when Jenny and I were married. Would you allow me to do it now? Would you still be my son and let me love you and let me be your dad?"

Tony looked up at his beloved friend, tears glistening in his little lashes.

"Sir, how did you know? It was the only, only thing I wanted for this Christmas. How did you know that I go to bed each night thinking about how it would be if we were a family? I love you Tracker. My answer is Yes, Yes, Yes."

He whispered, "I made a gift for you for Christmas. Do you think Santa would mind if I gave it to you early?"

He was already up from his place and down the hall at a dead run. He returned with a long cylindrical package. He was dancing with excitement.

"Open it, Tracker."

I glanced at Zach as the drama unfolded. His expression was one of relief and gentle love. He had helped Tony wrap the package and knew what was inside.

They smoothed the large sheet of drawing paper out on the table and Tony began to point out what the picture was about and who each person was. He had drawn his "family" as he envisioned it in his mind's eye and I was close enough to see that he was a gifted, young artist.

Tony was totally immersed in his story. He pointed out the people, identified them, and explained their position in the picture. Standing in the center, he had placed himself and Tracker, hand-in-hand.

In the first half-circle around them, stood his Uncle Cade, Uncle Zach and me. The third grouping contained the Penards, with Margot holding a small babe, Ben Johnson, Tim Campbell, and all the Forester family, including a small baby in Kylie Lou's arms.

Hovering in the space above the widening circles of protection was a drawing of his mother, Jenny, her beautiful red hair streaming behind her in the wind, and her arms wide open, as if to protect him. In fact all of us were included in her reach. She was weeping, and there were flowers springing up where the tears fell to earth.

In the middle distance on a rise of ground, stood a wonderful likeness of my dear friend, Jacques Grayson, who had been one of Jenny's close friends. Back and down in a slough was a shadowy figure dressed in black, with his back to the rest of us. No doubt it was Tony's conception of his unknown father, who had abandoned his mother before he was born.

His understanding about the situation and his positioning of the people was uncanny. I moved to his chair and kissed him. "I'm so happy for you, Tony. Don't hurry your story. I'll start your packing." I kissed him on the cheek as I said, "I love you both very much."

As I left the room, I heard Tracker ask Tony about my likeness.

"What is that soft blue color around her, Tony?"

He answered in a very matter-of-fact tone, "That's her presence. Once since I came, it was so big it filled the whole room, but right now it's very small and weak. She isn't feeling well and is very tired. We should try to do more things to help her."

Where had he learned about auras? Cade also had the skill and was still sitting at the table. It would be interesting to hear what he thought about Tony's comment.

When I realized that because of Jamie's kindness we

would have a place to live while we began to build the house, I couldn't help crying in relief.

I heard the men doing their chores of packing, cleaning and stripping the beds so that I could do a washing and leave clean bedding for Margot.

When everyone left the kitchen, I cleaned up for the last time and sat down to write a note to the Penards. There was no way to repay their kindness and hospitality except to do the same for someone else needing care.

At two o'clock everything was in order. We packed our possessions into the trucks, and made our way across town. I let the men unload as I chose the large downstairs bedroom for Cade and me.

I needed a nap and so did Cade, but first I found the linen closet and took bedding and blankets to each room for the men to make up their beds. Then they were on their own to make their nests the way they wanted them.

Millie's preparations for tomorrow's party were complete and the house was decorated for a large crowd. The Christmas tree was lovely but for show, there were no personal ornaments.

Then I remembered that most of her possessions were destroyed in the fire and perhaps all her family heirloom ornaments with them, unless Lars had realized how valuable they were and had stolen them. I checked in the kitchen and found the refrigerator filled with goodies for the party and many things waiting on the counter tops for tomorrow's preparations.

I passed the order on; everything in the kitchen was off limits until after the party. I made arrangements for the men to take the Penards to Gary's for dinner; and to bring back something for us. Then I made a small sign for our bedroom door.

> *Please do not disturb except for dire need*
> *We plan to sleep until further notice*
> *The Camerons*

I didn't even feel guilty when I looked at the clock and it was after midnight. Cade was hungry so we padded off to the kitchen with Violet close behind, to see if they had left some supper for us. Perched on the edge of the counter was a lovely picnic hamper with a note:

Happy Christmas Eve Picnic
Many thanks and much love.
Z.C., Y.S., B.J., B.T., T.C.T.

Nestled on top of the Christmas-green plaid tablecloth was a bouquet of yellow sweetheart roses. Inside were two dainty chicken sandwiches, a container of fruit salad, individual blueberry tarts and a small bottle of wine.

I carried the basket in by the fireplace and spread the cloth, while Cade stirred the embers and tossed on two logs. When we finished our meal, we curled up together as best we could and slept until the cold of early dawn sent us back to our bed.

We heard Zach take off to spend his usual early day with Yvette before he headed off to work in the clinic. Gary's would close early for the holiday and we'd see them at the party. Ben and Tim left for Foresters' to care for the dogs and wouldn't be back until party time either.

I continued to be amazed at how resilient Cade was. In the few days since he'd been home, he was now able to get around by himself, albeit slowly and carefully. His appetite had come back and he tucked away enough food to feed an army.

Since his confrontation with the wraith of his former wife, Susanna, he and his brother seemed to have an even greater sense of solidarity and understanding. There was even a trace of merriment as he prepared for the holidays.

Tony and Tracker disappeared downtown, probably to enjoy a breakfast of cinnamon buns at Gary's and we did absolutely nothing but snuggle in front of the fire. I hadn't realized how exhausted I was until I had a chance to rest.

CHAPTER TWENTY-ONE

About two o'clock Christmas Eve afternoon, the Campbells and their helpers arrived to begin putting out the Christmas party. Since we were not part of the crew, we stayed out of the way in our own rooms. About three, Cade and I decided to put on our party clothes, bundle up against the cold wind, and make the tiniest trip out to the end of the block. We would arrive at Campbell House like real guests.

There was soft Christmas carol music coming from the living room when we came in the front door. I recognized the arrangement I'd made for Jamie and expected to find him playing with Millie. Imagine my surprise when we entered the room to find not Millie but Brian Tracker, doing very well at his sight-reading. Tony was sitting next to the Christmas tree, listening with rapt attention as the two men played with genuine pleasure. Another side of the interesting Mr. Tracker was emerging.

Tony got up from his place when he saw us come in. He stood watching as the maid helped Cade with his coat and then took the cloak from my shoulders.

Tony's eyes filled with tears. "Ma'am, you're so beautiful. I've never seen you dressed up before. If your hair were red, you'd be almost as beautiful as my mother was."

I opened my arms and he clung tight to me for a moment. I knew we would have some serious grieving time to live through and Tracker wouldn't be there to help.

Then Tony grinned. He looked around to make sure no one but his Uncle Cade could hear. "The blue presence goes great with your green dress, ma'am."

He took off down the hall at a dead run. Tracker played from another book of carols when Jamie left to greet guests. Tony returned to sit on the piano bench, turning pages as Brian sang.

Jamie came to greet us in the hallway. His voice was as always, quiet and gentle.

"Thank you so much for your thoughtful gift, Sara. It must have taken many hours to put it together. I especially like the painting you made for the cover. Have you seen it, Commander?"

Cade reached out to touch his arm.

"Please, call me Cade. It suits my situation and state of mind much better right now. No, it was something she worked on as a surprise. I'd like very much to see it."

As Jamie handed him the folio, Tracker paused from his playing and took me across the room for a cup of punch. He made sure Tony was not with us, before he turned to speak to me.

"Abe dug up the infamous hate letter and let me bring it here. It was on my office stationery so I called my former secretary about it. Even though her initials were on it, she didn't remember typing anything like it. I compared the signature with some of my former wife's handwriting. There's no doubt in my mind; my signature was forged. Probably it was planned as a last insult and cruelty before she left with my law partner.

"Sara, please don't say anything to Tony. He doesn't know I was married to someone else for a time after I came back to the States from France. I'd given up hope that Jenny would marry me and made a terrible mistake.

"As a 'rising star' in the Pittsburgh law community, I thought I needed a trophy wife on my arm. My greed drove me to marry without love.

"At least it's over now. She has totally broken off her relationship with me. First, she ruined me financially, and then sent the divorce papers.

"I've sent the proper papers for finalizing Tony's adoption. Cade has all the information he needs to take care of Tony's financial affairs while I'm gone. When I get back, I plan to open a law office in Campbell's Point and settle down to raise my son. Whatever else happens is up to God Himself."

"Or Herself, as the case may be," I smiled. "We may not have an easy moment to say good-bye tomorrow. I wanted you to know that the Cameron clan and everyone else in Campbell's Point will take care of Tony for you until you return. You will be in our prayers constantly until then."

Tracker bent to my hand and gave me a very accomplished kiss. I wondered where he was educated to have so many continental skills. He returned to the piano and continued playing carols for us.

Dodie entered the front door, her casserole cradled in a beautiful, red and green quilted cover. Ben was right behind her, looking very serious. He switched to party mode as they drifted into the room and Dodie went to the kitchen with her food. Cade and I descended on him at the same time because we knew she'd expected to come with her Nebraska friend.

Ben nodded, "Everything's under control, thanks to your tip-off, Sara. They checked Dodie's friend out on the wire. When Sam and his deputies found out who he was, they watched for him and picked him up at the city limits. They're on the way to Pittsburgh with him. I'll fill you in later, but he has half a dozen aliases and several warrants out for his arrest; white-collar embezzlement, but enough to put him away for a good long while.

"Dodie doesn't know yet why he didn't get here. The great news is she's going to be in for some big money. One of the banks was offering a nice reward for information on him and a big pile of money for his capture.

"Now, it's time to enjoy the afternoon and visit with some of my new friends." He headed over to speak to Gary from the grill, as Dodie returned from the kitchen.

Cade needed to sit down, so I settled him in a chair in front of the fire. It was nice to be just a guest at a party instead of the hostess, as I'd been for so many years during my academic marriage.

Millie looked wan and weary; her eyes seemed to carry the haunted look of complete exhaustion and something else I couldn't put my finger on. I wondered if she were trying to do too much too soon after her recent ordeals. I spoke to her when she was alone for a moment.

"I've been concerned about you, Millie. Please do take care of yourself. I really won't be needing help to look after things here. The men help as they can and do a reasonable job of caring for their own needs. I think you should keep your woman helper for a while longer.

"It was a great kindness for you and Jamie to provide us with a roof over our heads until spring and we appreciate it. I'd like to come to visit after the holiday rush is over. I'll bring my knitting and we'll dream about spring. I have a sack of sunflower seeds for your cardinals and perhaps we can share seed catalogues and send in some orders."

We talked a bit more and then I was on the way to ask

Cade if he wanted something to eat. As I passed the hallway, Abe Forester came in, dusting snow from his coat. He didn't come in far, only enough to get the door closed behind him.

He must have asked for Jamie because the little maid took off running to find him where he was visiting with friends by the Christmas tree. I watched him calm her down as he went to the front door. Zach and Yvette had just arrived and Doc Pete and Laura were there. In minutes the medical team got together and disappeared.

The party guests remained at a discrete distance and didn't learn anything, but Tony was right up beside them and heard it all. He came to me as soon as they left and handed me a note. It was from Kylie Lou. When I finished reading it, I knew what needed to be done.

"Tony, Go find Ben for me, please."

When they came back to the front door, I explained the situation. "We need to help Priscilla bring the Crosswick children inside from Abe's truck and unload their things onto the porch while they wait for their mother.

"You're the one who's been at the Forester house every day, Ben, and you're probably already well-inoculated with flu virus. We have some people here that must be protected from it; Millie, Margot and Thad, Cade, Tony, Tracker and me."

I stepped into the room to make a happy announcement to the group. "There's going to be a Christmas baby in Campbell's Point. Kylie Lou Forester is on her way to Pittsburgh for the birthing. Everything's fine but she asks for your prayers."

Then I found Margot. "You and Thad should probably say your good-byes and slip out before the children come inside. Kylie Lou's note said the Crosswick children came down with the flu this morning, baby Pam and Lane are very sick. We don't want you to pick up something from them.

"Excuse me, I need to caution Millie too and I think I should encourage Cade to say goodnight. May we come over tomorrow after Tracker leaves? Tony is going to need a lot of extra loving in the next few days."

I was surprised when Thad gave me a hug.

"Bless you, Sara, and Merry Christmas to you and the Commander. We'll see you tomorrow afternoon."

Margot clung to me a moment as she whispered, "God be

with you, Sara." Then they hurried out the back door.

I found Tracker, explained about the flu problem and asked him to escort Millie home. I suggested Dodie might like to help too. Then I found Tony again.

"Would you please take Cade to his room and stay with him. Perhaps you could continue *The Secret Garden* reading. I think the book is by my bed in the book crate.

"For now, you must stay away from the Crosswick children so you won't pass the germs on to your Uncle Cade. We'll write a letter to Steven so you can tell him good-bye, as soon as we have an address.

"I don't want you or your dad exposed to the flu right now, or you won't be able to share Christmas with us tomorrow. He'll be back in a few minutes to be with you and I'll be in, as soon as I can. I need to be protected too so I won't give it to Cade.

"Honey, it's not like the plague but for the people who've been hurt or sick recently, it could be just as dangerous. I love you. Now, run along."

I watched as he went to Cade and explained the situation. They disappeared down the hall to our room. Tracker was helping Millie into her coat and Dodie was with them as they left the house. There were still several dozen people in the room; most didn't know about the extra complications.

I was relieved to see Jamie return to the party and after a few moments I told him what I'd arranged. I retrieved Violet from her back porch isolation and went down the hall to our room, just as Ben and Priscilla brought the Crosswick children into the front hall.

The discrete knock on the door a bit later was Tracker, reporting safe delivery of the ladies. Millie had asked to go home with Dodie, saying she needed to protect herself until the flu epidemic was over.

Tracker joined us and we read to each other. The gentle closeness was a special joy to close the swirl of excitement of the Crosswick leave-taking. We heard the noise level lower as the guests said their good-byes, and then heard the sounds of cleaning up.

The next knock at the door of our room was Jamie letting us know the house was ours again. He looked completely exhausted. His workweek had been heavy, even with three of them in the office most of the time.

He said, "I need to get home to Millie and I'm on call until Zach gets back from Pittsburgh. Merry Christmas folks, there's plenty of food left so you won't have to cook tomorrow unless you want to. If I don't see you before you leave, Brian, take care of yourself and come home to us as quickly as you can. We'll keep an eye on Tony until you get back."

We finished the chapter and headed out into the post-party living room. Tony and Tracker took care of the fireplace while I checked Cade into a chair and went to see what was left in the kitchen. We were dishing up late supper when Zach returned just long enough to get his duffle.

"I'll see you guys in a few days. I'm going to Yvette's until I make sure I didn't get the flu. I wouldn't want to be the Typhoid Mary of the group. Tracker, it was good to meet you, have a safe journey. We'll look after Tony so well he'll be wishing you hadn't asked."

He grinned at Tony as he continued. "We'll see you in the summer. Roger will be knee deep in clover and the kid will be into a bigger pair of jeans. Tony and I have a date to write to you each week and we'll even try to sneak some drawings past the censors. Take care, man."

His eyes were glistening as he turned to leave. "Merry Christmas brother, and you too, Sara. I want you both to get some rest; doctor's orders.

"Oh, I almost forgot, it's a boy. Kylie Lou and Abe are delighted and the kid has a voice like a baseball umpire already. They named him Timothy Samuel and he's perfect."

He disappeared down the hallway and out the front door. I knew it was the wisest thing he could have done, but I was heartbroken that he wouldn't be with us tomorrow for Christmas.

We sat down to begin our supper just as Tim whizzed in to get his things. He stood at the door just long enough to explain that he was going out to the mountain to spend Christmas with the Foresters and wouldn't be back until the flu was gone from the family.

"Tracker, you take care now. Do what you have to do but get back as soon as you can. Tony and I'll look after Roger for you and we have some big projects planned in the spring.

"Oh, I almost forgot, Ben sent a note for you all. He's staying out there too to look after things until Abe and Kylie Lou and the new baby get back on Thursday night. I'll leave it on the table by the door. Maybe you can nuke it to get rid of the germs. Merry Christmas everyone, see ya."

The whoosh of cold air came down the hallway as he slammed the door behind him.

I sighed as I looked around our tiny group. "I feel as if everyone we cared about has abandoned us on an ice flow. Tony, would you like to read the Christmas story for us since we didn't get to go to midnight Mass. Then we'll sing some carols and get you tucked into bed so you can dream about sugarplums and wonderful Christmas surprises."

He knew where my bible nestled in the book crate and hurried off to get it. I happened to look up just as a glance passed between Tracker and Cade. It puzzled me. It wasn't a sugar-sweet Christmas grin, but a look such as passed between men before they entered battle together. I felt the hair stand up on the back of my neck and I shivered even though the room was warm.

I was surprised to find my carol folio still on the piano. Jamie must have forgotten it in the confusion of the evening. Tracker reached for another book of carols and began to play. We began with "Silent Night" and then Tony read a portion. After "Hark the Herald Angels Sing", Cade took a turn. We finished the Christmas story with "Joy to the World". Then, Tracker took Tony off to bed while Cade and I remained to enjoy the quiet and peace of the night.

When I was sure Tony was in bed, I decided to bring out the gifts to put under the tree. They were stashed in several hiding places and it took a few minutes to put everything out.

I helped Cade get settled in bed for the night and then whispered to him, "I'll be back in a little while. I'm going to have a few moments of quiet prayer before I come to bed."

The Christmas tree lights were still on and a small lamp on the piano gave a golden glow to the room. I knelt in front of the crèche displayed on a separate table next to the fireplace.

The fire was nearly out and the old house was beginning to creak and groan as it settled in for the night. It was becoming drafty and cold, so I didn't think anything of it when I felt a draft across the back of my neck. I was thinking about returning to the warmth of my bed, when all hell broke loose.

Someone dropped a blanket around me, and took off running. I could hear the sounds of fighting, furniture and glass shattering and crashing to the floor and bone crunching against bone. The grunts of gut punches meant ugly business. The keys of the piano made a tortured, discordant shriek, as someone smashed onto them and I heard a big piece of furniture smash to the floor with a tinkle of shattering glass and strange bonging and ringing sounds.

I had no idea where we were going. I kicked and struggled against my assailant's hold and against the blanket covering my face. He was so strong I finally stopped trying. He whispered into the blanket, "That's better, Sweetheart. It's just Sir Galahad again. Have you forgotten? I told you I saved ladies in distress. You stay put until I come for you."

He opened a door and left me on the floor. He was gone before I could get untangled from the blanket cocoon. I was trembling so hard I couldn't stand. It had been Zach's voice, but he was supposed to be at Yvette's.

It was silent now and I was terrified. There were no tears. Something very bad was happening and I would know soon enough what new tragedy was upon us. I was on my knees trying to pray, when Zach returned to my room. Cade wakened and watched as Zach handed me a glass of brandy.

"I know you don't usually drink but you need this right now."

He sat down in the chair beside me and waited for me to finish it. "Sam and Doc Pete are on the way to Pittsburgh to take him to the hospital. Sara, he's very sick."

I clutched his wrist while I tried to slow down my terrified brain.

"Zach, for God's sake, what are you talking about? Who's sick? What happened?"

Zach took my hands in his.

"Sara, I'm so sorry. I know how much you cared for him and tried to help, but sometimes it just isn't possible. Sometimes the demons that inhabit people simply won't let them go."

My voice dropped to a whisper.

"Who, Zach?"

Deep in my heart I knew, but someone else would have to speak the fateful, damning words. I couldn't bear to hear them from my own lips.

His voice was filled with compassion as he looked into my eyes.

"Jamie Campbell. Thank God Tracker warned us, so we

knew to keep special watch on Jamie tonight. Doc Pete and I have been worried sick about him for days. We didn't know what he might do or when. Maybe when he got home tonight and Millie wasn't there, something snapped."

My hands tightened into fists and I wept. Somehow, I felt guilty because I was relieved it was finally over. I'd watched Jamie for the many weeks since we'd returned to Campbell's Point, as he struggled with his problems and seemed to be sinking deeper and deeper into depression.

Only his frantic work schedule kept him going. What had he planned for this evening? Was he the one fighting in the Campbell living room? Why did he return to the house so late after he'd already said his good-byes?

I had to shut it out. I had to put it into a compartment I couldn't see or hear or feel. The most important thing in my mind now, was to get the living room cleaned up so we wouldn't spoil Tony's Christmas.

When we went out into the living room, I knew it was hopeless. It would take hours just to clean up the broken glass. I went to the kitchen to gather up what boxes I could find and the men started to help me pack all the presents to carry away. Both Tim and Ben were there. Apparently they'd been warned they might be needed. Now they were doing what they could to sweep up the shards of glass.

I made Tim stop long enough for me to patch the nasty, still-bleeding cut over his eye.

"Did Jamie do this to you?"

His eyes filled with tears. He nodded yes, as he whispered, "But he didn't know me."

How devastating for Tim to see his friend in such a state and to know that Jamie had lost everything.

In the middle of the packing I looked up at Tim again. "Is Millie all right?"

"Yes, but only because she begged Tracker to take her to Doc Pete's to stay with Dodie and Laura. Jamie said something to Millie before the party that terrified her. Something about his going out to the farm to sing carols after the party. That, plus the other things she told Tracker, concerned him enough he called Zach to warn him."

I looked across the room at Zach.

"What was Jamie going to do?"

He shrugged his shoulders. "We may never know, but he was within inches of giving you a huge dose of knock-out shot. Ben took the syringe from his hand and the label was on the side. Perhaps he was planning to take you with him to the farm."

My heart was filled with sadness.

"Dear God in heaven, that poor man, that poor tortured soul. May God have mercy on him now."

I glanced up to check the time on the grandfather clock and realized it must have been one of the things I heard smashing to the floor during the fight.

"What time is it, gentlemen?"

"Twelve o'clock."

"What do you suggest we do now to try to salvage Christmas morning for Tony?"

We put our heads together and talked about how we could do it. Tracker hurried down the hall to get the box he'd planned to give Tony in the morning. He packed all his own things, ready for the leave taking at noon. When he finished, Brian turned to Tim.

"Would you take me to the airport at noon? I think it would be better if I said good-bye to Tony here in town with his family around him."

Then he said to the group, "When Thad found out what might happen tonight, he said we must come back to their place; for Christmas and to stay. I think we should take them up on it.

"When Tony first stirs, we'll make it a happy trip, bundle him in a blanket and tell him Santa went to the wrong house. We'll all go to Margot's. We'll whisk him right by this room and he won't need to come back. Do you think it will work?"

"It has to." I whispered.

I was weeping as Cade gathered me up to return to our room. I couldn't bear to think about spending a moment longer in this house, filled as it was with the anguish, grief, and yes, the madness of the Campbell family. I went to find Zach.

"Please call Thad and tell him we're coming now. Tracker can bundle Tony up in a blanket. It won't take more than a few minutes to pack Tony's things. If anything else must be done, someone else will have to do it. I can't come back here again."

In thirty minutes we were packed and ready to go. Thad and Margot were at the door to take Tony to his room. He rubbed his eyes and was asleep again when his head hit the pillow. We carried the boxes and luggage to the hallway and arranged the gifts under the tree. I fell to my knees in utter exhaustion and grief, as Margot took the men to their rooms. Tim went to a corner of the upstairs in a small room.

Zach decided to return to Yvette's. She needed to find out that he was safe and he would need her to carry some of his grief. And, he was on call for the foreseeable future.

Ben had left for the farm since he needed to get back to look after things out there. Tracker decided to sleep in Tony's room in a chair, in case Tony wakened and was afraid.

Cade and I prepared our own nest. Our clothing fell into a heap of shard-laced dishevelment as we undressed and collapsed into exhausted sleep.

CHAPTER TWENTY-TWO

It was seven o'clock. I was putting on my robe when a soft knock came at the door.

"Aunt Sara? Please wake up. I just can't wait any longer."

I opened the door and took Tony's wriggling body in my arms. "Merry Christmas, Sweetheart. Give us five minutes and we'll meet you by the tree. Have you been down yet?"

"Yes." He whispered, "I've been sitting by the tree for hours. I didn't want to wake anybody up. I was so good, but now, I can hardly wait. Please hurry."

I smiled up at Tracker. "We'll hurry, Tony. Have you wakened Tim yet?"

"Oh, is he here?" He whispered, "Which room is he in?"

I pointed to the end of the hall and he went flying down. "Merry Christmas, Tim. Wake up! Wake up! Wake up!"

Thad came up the stairs fully dressed and ready to corral Tony. He swept him into his arms and hugged him. "All right, munchkin. Give Tim time to get dressed. Let's take Tracker downstairs. We'll start the fire and check on what Margot's doing."

They left as I helped Cade get cleaned up and into his favorite Cameron shirt. He still had to leave one sleeve folded and his arm tucked inside, but otherwise he looked amazingly well after the night just past. I found my old favorite wool slacks and sweater and slipped into them. As I put on Jacques's moccasins, I thought about how upset Jacques would be over Jamie's plight, since they'd been in medical school together and were friends.

I took Cade's hands in mine. "It's time to go spend a happy day with a very special boy. This won't be an easy morning but we have no choice. We want Tracker to believe Tony is safe and with family now."

I sighed as our gentle kiss promised solidarity in our task. I longed for the peace and rest of the next few days and hoped it could begin now.

Margot stopped her stirring at the stove and took me in her arms.

"Sara, I was so frightened. I didn't say I wanted you to leave our home and I certainly didn't want to leave you at Campbell House. It was how I knew something was very, very wrong and I was terrified for you.

"I knew something bad was going to happen. Jamie must have been plotting to get control of you alone. We were so fortunate the men were there to save you from what he planned to do."

I looked into her eyes. "Do you know what he planned?" Then I turned away. "No, I don't want to know right now. We'll wait for another time to talk about it, perhaps the men will tell Cade, if they figure it out themselves. I wonder where they took Jamie."

Margot turned away to continue starting breakfast.

"Didn't Thad tell you? Jamie's gone."

My voice was barely a whisper. "No."

"He died on the way into Pittsburgh to the hospital. Sam and Doc Pete stopped by a couple of hours ago to tell us. They said the kindest thing we should believe is that Jamie died of a broken heart."

We clung to each other, and then, she turned to the stove to continue the mundane job of fixing breakfast. I could smell the bacon beginning to cook in the pan and Margot was making tiny dollar pancakes on the griddle.

Our lives would go on and our grieving would not be over soon. Now we must think about the living.

"Do you think Tony can bear to wait while we eat breakfast?"

Margot smiled. "At our house it was a tradition to make the children wait just a little longer for their presents. We didn't have many and they were very special.

"I think Tracker has some special things to give Tony. He asked Ben to go up to 'Jenny's House' with Roger and go to a secret room. I guess he and Jenny designed the room for storage and protection from fire and theft. Ben was to bring down a box packed from her worktable. He brought the box into town last night before the party. I'm not sure it's a good idea for Tracker to be going through her things so soon, but he wanted to."

Tony took the breakfast delay with good humor. We carried our hot chocolate into the living room by the tree.

Tracker had brought Tony's large drawing back downstairs and placed it with the other gifts. As the youngest and only child present, Tony knew he would be asked to play the role of Santa's helper. This included deciding the order of gifting.

When we finished, everyone felt a comforting glow of gentle love as our gifts were given and received with joy. Ben had delivered a small package for Tony and Brian from Priscilla Forester, and they saved her gifts until last.

Thad was pleased with his fairy tale book and promised to read to Tony when he and his dad got back from their trek on the new snowshoes. The snow had been steady since before midnight and there was plenty for a maiden run. My gifts included very special books for each person and I'd managed to finish Cade's warm socks. My most precious gift was from Cade, who had asked his brother to find a set of four silver combs for my hair.

Pricilla's gift of the camouflage pillowcase was greeted with a big grin from Tony. We watched with some curiosity as Tracker opened his small envelope. Inside was an exquisite sketch of Tracker and Tony with a background of the woods in winter.

Ben came in just as we were finishing and brought a present for the Penards.

Then, Tracker got Jenny's crate and came to stand beside Tony.

"What I'm going to give you now is not a Christmas present but a remembrance of your mother. The tools came from your mother's drafting table or from the special box where she kept her colored pencils and paints."

They went to the table and Tracker lifted the box and put it in front of his son.

"First though, I have two folders for you to give to your Uncle Cade for safe keeping while I'm gone."

The first folder was blue and had a photo on the front. It was the unmistakable likeness of Roger as a fine, young gelding; with a wonderful, happy man mounted and ready to ride.

Tracker explained, "That's Roger, and my father who loved him very much. One time when I was visiting at home, I promised him that I would take care of Roger and love him as he had. Roger is pretty old in horse years now and if something happens to him while I'm gone, I'd like for you to read his story and look at all his pictures when he's buried."

Tony was nodding that he understood, but his small hands were reaching for the second folder. It held a small photograph album. When he opened it, there were many carefully labeled pictures. It began with old folks, perhaps grandparents or even great-grandparents. As Tony turned the pages, he whispered the names.

"These are my mother's Cameron family pictures. Look, there's one with some little boys. It's labeled Cade, Mike and Zachary. Who's Mike?"

Tracker answered, "He was your mother Jenny's favorite and beloved Uncle Mike. He died last summer."

Cade put his arm around me as he said, "Tony, we all loved your Uncle Mike very much. He was a fine man and an honorable sailor. He belonged to the Navy SEALs for all his working life, even though he was a doctor too."

The next few pages were Tracker's family pictures, his grandparents, then his mother and father. There were pictures of his parents with a passel of kids, sitting in woodsy settings. Tony asked his dad, "Who are all those kids? Are you here?"

Tracker grinned. "Those are all the Tracker children, my brothers and sisters, Tony. Can you figure out which one is the rascal they just called Tracker?"

Tony got it right on the first try.

"Dad? Are all those kids my family too? Where are they now?"

"They're all your family now, all seven of us. Can you imagine five real uncles and two aunts and twenty-one cousins at last count? They live in the United States and some live in Europe. When I get back, we'll make a grand trip and go visiting."

They continued to look through the book. All of his dad's school pictures were there. On the last mounted page there was a lovely picture of his mother Jenny and his new dad, Brian Tracker, in tourist mode. They were standing in Monet's garden in summer with a glorious background of roses.

Tony got real quiet and turned to look at Tracker.

"Am I supposed to take this book with me and look at the pictures if you die, Dad? What will I do if you don't come back?"

Tracker reached for his son and held him close. He was winking back tears.

"Tony, you must believe me. I'll do everything in my

power to come back to you. But you must believe too, that I loved you so much that I was willing to die for you."

He hugged his son and turned to the table again.

"Let's look in the box and see what you might like to have for drawing the pictures to go with the letters you promised to send me."

The rest of the group drifted away, so Brian and Tony could have a few more minutes alone, before Tracker had to leave. I headed for the back door and went out to the porch. It was Ben who joined me, handkerchief in hand. "God Almighty, Sara! This is why war is hell."

Cade's eyes were glistening too when he came out. "I'd sure like to take a bit of a walk. It's still a couple of hours until Tim has to take Tracker to the airport. I don't think Margot is planning to eat until after he goes."

We heard the phone ringing and watched through the glass door as Thad came into the kitchen to answer it. He listened, shook his head and then hung up. He poked his head out the door and told us the news.

"That was the hospital in Bethesda where Tracker was to have his surgery tomorrow. He's off the hook for at least a week. The surgeon honcho fell while he was skiing in Aspen and broke both ankles. He's out of commission and they rescheduled Tracker with someone else on the third of January. Guess I'll go let everybody else know the good news."

He turned and went back inside. I gave both Ben and Cade a big hug. "What a wonderful reprieve. I'm ready for that walk now, My Love. Maybe Ben would like to come along."

Ben was grinning now. "Sure, I'll come at least part way. I have a good Western started. I'm not sure I like the kind of book my librarian friend wants me to read, too mushy. In fact, when she wormed out of me what I really did for a living, she turned real cool. She doesn't like dogs or the country. I think I might be off the hook and on the prowl again."

We laughed as we went in to gather boots and jackets.

Everyone inside was literally dancing with joy. Tim encouraged Tony and Tracker to get going on those snowshoes so he could be next to try them. Margot promised dinner much later and to grab a snack meanwhile. We filled our pockets with Christmas cookies and headed out down the street toward town.

Gary's Grill seemed forlorn, even with the decorations in the windows and wreaths on the doors, or maybe because of them. No lights were on and there weren't any cars and trucks wheeling in to park. No one was going in for a meal or to visit with friends. Well, everything would be back on schedule tomorrow. Not back to normal though, because the news would be out about Jamie's death. The community would be in grief mode once again. Ben turned around to go sit in front of the fire with his book for a while before he returned to Foresters'.

I checked to see how Cade was doing. Then, I took his hand. "Let's go over to Yvette's and tell them the good news about Tracker. Zach will be glad, I'm sure."

We continued on down the middle of the deserted main street. Our footprints were the first on Christmas morning to announce that humans lived in Campbell's Point and that they were abroad in the land.

Yvette lived in a garage apartment on the side street behind the hardware store. I made a big snowball and tossed it at her door. It wasn't long before she poked her head out and motioned for us to come up. When she opened the door, she was dressed in a marvelous red silk jumpsuit with a woven golden belt cinched around her tiny waist. Her gorgeous honey-golden hair was loose around her shoulders. Zach looked like the cat that stole the cream. He shook his brother's hand and welcomed us in.

"Thad just called with the news. We heard both pieces and choose to be in celebration mode for Tony and Tracker. Grief for Jamie Campbell won't be easy to bear and I just can't do it today. Come on in, we're glad to see you."

It was the first time I'd been in Yvette's place and I was enchanted. It brought back memories of my years in Paris. There were delicate lace curtains with patterns of flowers and the lighted candles scented the room with gentle odors of baked apples and pine trees. The casual disarray of their last meal's dishes could be seen stacked in the sink. This was good living for Zach after a hectic and sometimes tragic day at the office. There was a small but well-tended fire in her tiny fireplace and two long-handled forks leaned against the wall, ready to plunge their prongs into the soft whiteness of the marshmallows-in-waiting.

I sighed with contentment. "Yvette, I love it. How simple, pleasant and loving a place you've made for yourself, and now for Zach too. How long have you been here?"

"Almost six years. I had no idea what I was waiting for or hoping for, but it has happened to me now. Zach is the most wonderful thing that's come to me in my whole life. I love him so much I can hardly bear it. Sometimes we just hold each other and cry in disbelief and joy. Come on, I'll show you the rest of the rooms."

She took my hand as we went into the small sleeping area. I was surprised when she closed the door.

Her voice was soft and she held me gently in her arms.

"I'm so very sorry about Jamie. I know how much you cared for him and hoped that you could help him and make it better for him.

"His was a precious soul, Sara, but filled with such anguish and despair that none of us could reach him. Zach feels that he should have been able to save him; he feels so guilty right now.

"But, if it hadn't been last night, it would have come sometime later. At least you weren't physically hurt. Bearing your grief will be difficult, but come to me and we'll talk whenever you need to."

We hugged and continued the trip back to the living area. There was no storage, only room for the absolute essentials of living. The kitchen was tiny but efficient.

I laughed. "I'll bet after a day hanging over those huge pots, you just want to open a can of soup; the kind you don't even have to add water to."

"Gary's been good to me. He always made sure I took good food home from work. Most times it was pretty nice fare. With Zach here, we've made different arrangements.

"Now we're working on different living arrangements. It's sort of a secret yet, but we've decided to buy this duplex and move downstairs where there's more space for Zach's books. She paused with a thought brewing.

"Hey, would you guys like to rent the upstairs until you get your house built?" She reached for Zach's hand and got his nod of OK.

"We'd love to have you and it would be great fun."

I glanced over at Cade and was heartened by his look of genuine interest and pleasure. I joined him as he looked out the back window into the jumble of brush and small understory trees that led down the ravine to the small creek.

It was blanketed in swirls and mounds of snow but in some places you could see the shards of ice around the edges of the water. I saw cardinals flitting in the trees, making brilliant red sparkles as they moved from branch to branch. Two does stepped from the shadows to make their trip down the slope to drink.

He whispered, "What do you think, Sara?"

I'd already made up my mind, but decided we needed to know a little more before I said yes. I had one important question for Yvette.

"Would you take one dear, small boy and a dog named Violet too?"

Cade was grinning at his brother now, as Yvette flew into my arms and planted a kiss on my cheek.

"Yes, of course. That will make it even better. Oh, how exciting; I can hardly wait."

She stopped to take a deep breath. "But we'll have to wait just a little because the kids downstairs won't be out until January first. Tim has promised to help with the remodeling when they leave. With everyone helping it shouldn't take long."

I was looking at Cade now. "The timing is perfect. I don't want Margot to feel abandoned after all the gracious hospitality they've given us. It will give us some peaceful time together while we wait. If you and Zach will have us, we'd like to accept."

She hugged me again and took me off into the kitchen area where we made mugs of hot chocolate to celebrate.

The men were already making remodeling plans and everyone was talking at once. I had an overwhelming feeling of love and peace but also of great expectations. What an amazing Christmas this had been.

I got up to retrieve my cloak with the Christmas gifts for them. I handed one wonderful lumpy package to Zach and smiled.

"These are for your mud-slogging boots and other special adventures. You must have your turn on the new snowshoes. Tony is looking forward to it."

The bulky gray socks with bright red toes, heels and cuffs shouted winter fun.

I had found Yvette's gift at the foreign bookstore in Pittsburgh. I handed her the package wrapped in glimmering golden paper. It contained an illustrated book about the famous herb gardens of France. She looked up from her place on the couch.

"I've always dreamed about going to see these places.

Perhaps when I take Zach home to meet my family, we can visit some of them. Thank you, Sara."

Zach looked at me with a gentle smile. "I asked Cade what he thought you might treasure as a gift, Sara, and when he told me what it was, I hesitated at first to do it. Then as he told me more of your story, I realized how much it would mean to you. My Dear, he said you dreamed of having your American identity back, that you wanted your birth name Rebecca Jane Campbell restored to you. Is that true?"

I looked at my beloved Cade, stunned by his thoughtfulness and understanding.

Then I whispered, "Yes, it's true."

Zach smiled as he handed me a folder. "I've gathered all the proper forms and instructions for you. The paper work can be in process as soon as you wish. You know how slow governments can be, but they promised it could be finished in the next few weeks. Perhaps very soon, we will speak of you as your favorite Forester child My Lady Susan told me she does already. We'll welcome you back to us as 'Becca Jane. Merry Christmas, Sara."

I rose from my place, whispered my thanks, and went to my husband's side.

Yvette said, "We're on our way to Doc Pete's for dinner. If you'll wait a few minutes while we get ready, we'll walk back with you."

It had begun to snow again, with intense purpose and reckless abandon. I felt much the same, though I wondered if snow could feel such joy. I took my lover's hand.

"Take me home, Cade."

He asked me, with a gentle smile of recollection, "And where's home?"

My kiss was gentle and filled with love. "Home is an adventure, it's in the doing, and it's in our hearts."

CPSIA information can be obtained at www.ICGtesting.com
Printed in the USA
BVOW03s1126210813

329019BV00007B/157/A

9 780741 440853